THE
ACCIDENTAL
APPRENTICE

1

WILDERLORE

THE ACCIDENTAL APPRENTICE

AMANDA FOODY

Margaret K. McElderry Books

New York London Toronto Sydney New Delhi

MARGARET K. McELDERRY BOOKS

An imprint of Simon & Schuster Children's Publishing Division

1230 Avenue of the Americas, New York, New York 10020

MARGARET K. McELDERRY BOOKS is a trademark of Simon & Schuster, Inc.

For information about special discounts for bulk purchases, please contact Simon & Schuster Special Sales at 1-866-506-1949 or business@simonandschuster.com.

The Simon & Schuster Speakers Bureau can bring authors to your live event. For more information or to book an event, contact the Simon & Schuster Speakers Bureau at 1-866-248-3049 or visit our website at www.simonspeakers.com.

Interior design by Karyn Lee

The text for this book was set in Georgia.

Manufactured in the United States of America

0221 FFG

10 9 8 7 6 5 4 3 2

Library of Congress Cataloging-in-Publication Data

Names: Foody, Amanda, author.

Title: The accidental apprentice / Amanda Foody.

Description: New York : Margaret K. McElderry Books, [2021] | Series: Wilderlore ; book 1 | Audience: Ages 8–12. | Audience: Grades 4–6. | Summary: Eleven-year-old Barclay Thorne yearns for the quiet life of a mushroom farmer, but after unwittingly bonding with a beast in the forbidden Woods, he must seek Lore Keepers to break the bond and return home.

Identifiers: LCCN 2020031159 (print) | ISBN 9781534477568 (hardcover) | ISBN 9781534477582 (eBook)

Subjects: CYAC: Fantasy. | Adventure and adventurers—Fiction. | Apprentices—Fiction. | Monsters—Fiction. | Orphans—Fiction.

Classification: LCC PZ7.1.F657 Abm 2021 (print) | DDC [Fic]—dc23

LC record available at https://lccn.loc.gov/2020031159

TO JELLY BEAN, MY FEROCIOUS BEAST OF
NAPS, BELLY RUBS, AND ZOOMIES

ONE

Barclay Thorne knew almost all there was to know about mushrooms, and there was a *lot* to know.

He knew the poisonous ones never grew on trees. He knew the red ones with white spots made warts bubble up between toes, but the white ones with red spots cured warts, welts, and pustules of all kinds. He knew which ones made you drowsy or loopy, or could even knock you right dead, if you weren't careful.

"You're supposed to be taking notes," Barclay hissed at Selby. Both boys were apprentices to their town's highly esteemed mushroom farmer, but because Barclay was older and smarter, he was the one in charge. And he took his position very seriously.

"I c-can't write and walk at the same time," Selby blubbered, clutching his quill with his whole fist. Selby was a very pink boy. He had a pink nose and pink cheeks, like a plucked chicken, a resemblance made all the worse by his buzzed blond hair and stocky frame.

In nearly all ways, Barclay was the opposite. Though three years older, he was so short and skinny that Selby would likely outgrow him before next Spring. His dark eyes looked like ink smudges on his papery white skin, and his shoulder-length black hair was combed harshly to both sides, slick with oil to make it lie flat.

He didn't see what was so hard about writing and walking. He doubted it was harder than reading and walking, and Barclay rarely walked anywhere without an open book in his hand.

The two apprentices had been assigned an extremely important mission to find a rare mushroom called the Mourningtide Morel, and for this, they had ventured to the edge of the Woods.

The Woods was no average wood. It was so large that no map could fit all of it, so dangerous that no adventurer dared explore it. It loomed to the west of their town like a great shadow.

The trees along the edge were gray and spooky, their trunks twisted like they'd been wrung out, and their branches reached up like claws toward the overcast sky. It was quiet except for the rustle of decayed leaves and the snaps and cracks of brittle twigs beneath boots. This was the only time to find the Mourningtide Morel: that bleak in-between part of the year after the leaves had all fallen but before the first snow.

Selby stumbled over a tree root and bumped into Barclay's back.

"It would be easier to write and walk if you weren't always looking over your shoulder," Barclay grumbled.

"But we're so close! You know what Master Pilzmann says about—"

"We haven't gone *in*. And the town is right there." Barclay pointed behind them to Dullshire. Their small town crouched on a knobby hill, encircled by a stone wall covered in spears, like a giant thorn bush. The people were about as friendly as thorn bushes as well. They didn't like laziness—naps were expressly forbidden. They hated visitors—visitors could mean tax collectors, circus performers, or *worse*, Lore Keepers.

The only things the people of Dullshire loved were rules. But they only had one rule about the Woods.

Never ever, *ever* stray inside.

Because the Woods would trick you if you let it, leading you too deep within to find your way out.

And deeper in the Woods lurked the Beasts.

But Barclay, being a dutiful apprentice, would never dream of breaking Dullshire's most important rule—especially because of how often he got in trouble for accidentally breaking so many little ones. He would do exactly what he'd come here to do, and that was to find the Mourningtide Morel. With or without Selby's help.

Barclay didn't understand why Master Pilzmann had insisted Selby come along, or why he'd even taken on a second apprentice in the first place. Dullshire didn't need *two* mushroom farmers. And when Master Pilzmann retired, it would be Barclay—not Selby—who took over for him.

After all, Barclay made sure he was the perfect apprentice. He took detailed notes in neat cursive handwriting. He had memorized every mushroom species in *The Filosopher's Field Guide to Finding Fungi* volumes one through nine. Even Master Pilzmann himself had claimed that Barclay was the hardest-working boy Dullshire had ever seen.

Which was why Barclay refused to leave the mission empty-handed. He needed to prove to Master Pilzmann that he only needed one apprentice.

"I'm not leaving. Not yet," Barclay declared, and he continued marching along the tree line.

Selby followed but whimpered as they walked.

As the older apprentice, it was Barclay's responsibility to comfort Selby—not just to teach him. Selby had never been near the Woods before, and even Barclay, as experienced as he was, still thought the twisted trees looked a bit frightening.

But Barclay found it very hard to be nice to Selby. At home, Selby had many brothers and sisters who cared about him. Parents who looked after him. A room of his own. Barclay had none of those things. He'd had the last one, at least, until Master Pilzmann had let Selby move in.

There was no orphanage in Dullshire. If you wanted supper and a bed for the night, then you had to work for it. So Barclay had grown up working many jobs. He'd stacked books in the library, recorded new rules for the lawmakers, and delivered more spears to the sentries. But even though Barclay had tried to be exceptional at everything, when it came time to choose his apprenticeship, no one in Dullshire had offered him a spot. They were too worried about the futures of their own children to care about a scrappy rule-breaking orphan too.

And so Barclay had knocked on old Master Pilzmann's door and begged for this apprenticeship, a job no one else wanted. Master Pilzmann had refused, and refused, and refused. But Barclay kept trying until he agreed.

And it had been fine for two years, all until the day that Selby showed up. He still cried and fled back home every chance he got, but Master Pilzmann hadn't refused *him*. Not once.

"It'll be dark soon," Selby whined to Barclay.

"Not for hours," Barclay told him.

"It's freezing."

"It's Winter. What did you expect?"

"I'm *hungry*."

"Didn't you eat lunch?"

"I fed it to Gustav."

Gustav was Master Pilzmann's pet pig, who sniffed out valuable truffles hidden in the ground. Normally, Gustav would join the boys on quests such as these, but Gustav had mysteriously gained weight this past year, so much weight that waddling exhausted him. He spent all day napping by the fire.

"*You've* been feeding Gustav?" Barclay buried his face in his hands. The mystery of the pig fattening was solved, and once again all of Barclay's problems proved to be Selby's fault.

"I don't like mushrooms!" Selby complained. "They're slimy, and they taste like dirt!"

Barclay could hardly believe what he was hearing. "Then why are you here?" he shouted. It was the very question that had bothered him for ages. He also felt personally offended—he liked mushrooms very much.

Selby's pink face flushed several shades pinker, and he burst into tears. "My mom said it was a good future for me."

This seemed to be a lot of pressure to put on an eight-year-old, and for a moment, Barclay did feel rather bad.

But Barclay couldn't get distracted. If he wanted to keep his apprenticeship, he didn't have time to feel sorry for anyone but himself. This job was the only thing that ensured Barclay really fit into Dullshire, and Dullshire, however small and rural and rule-obsessed, was Barclay's home. He would *never* leave it.

When Barclay had been very small, before his parents had died, he used to dream of adventure. He spent hours imagining the world that existed beyond Dullshire's prickly walls, other towns and cities and kingdoms in far-flung realms beyond the Woods.

But his parents had loved Dullshire—they wouldn't want such a life of uncertainty and danger for their only child. And so Barclay refused to disrespect their wishes. He tried to forget about the call of adventure, concentrating instead on how to *stay*. To belong.

Barclay focused back on the mission, and for the next several minutes, the only sounds were Selby's teeth chattering, his nose sniffling, or his stomach rumbling.

As Barclay knelt to examine a promising fungus, Selby tapped him on the shoulder. "Look. Look."

Barclay swatted him away and pulled out his forager's notebook, to compare the sketch to the subject before him. He frowned. He needed a scarlet dome, but this one was *clearly* crimson. Mushroom foraging was a very precise science.

He dug it out anyway and added it to his basket.

I've done it again, Barclay scolded himself, inspecting the dirt underneath his fingernails. Master Pilzmann hated how dirty Barclay got himself, and how his hair looked wild only hours after combing it. *Repeat after me,* Master Pilzmann would always say when he quoted Dullshire's lawbook. *Filth is prohibited—no dirt, no odor, no potty mouths. Cleanliness is orderliness.*

"Barclay!" Selby squeaked, and Barclay finally stood up and turned around.

The grass between them and Dullshire was *alive*, with

dozens—no, hundreds—of tiny, glowing white eyes peering at them between the weeds.

The piles of leaves beneath the boys' boots shuddered and shook as small figures dashed within them. Selby hopped back and forth as though he stood barefoot on hot coals.

"Barclayyyyyyyy," he wailed.

But Barclay was frozen, his gaze fixed on a single creature perched on a rock. It looked like a mouse, except without a tail and with six curled spikes protruding from its back.

Barclay had seen Beasts before. Sometimes, on breezy Autumn days, strong gusts of wind carried glimmering insects from the Woods to his town, whose stingers turned your skin swollen and green. He'd spotted Beasts flying in V shapes across the sky, seeking out warmer places for the Winter, and leaving trails of glittery smoke behind them. Occasionally, more vicious Beasts snuck out from the Woods to break into chicken coops and goat pens for night-time feasts.

When Barclay was four years old, the Legendary Beast who lurked in the Woods, named Gravaldor, had destroyed Dullshire on Midsummer's Day. Though Barclay had never glimpsed Gravaldor's face, he remembered how the town walls had crumbled from the force of his roar. Gravaldor had torn roofs off homes with his jaws, sinking fangs into stones as though they were butter. His magic had caused the earth to rupture, making whatever remained of their once flat town now stand on a tilt.

It was thanks to Gravaldor that Barclay was an orphan.

Knowledge of Beasts had since been forbidden in Dullshire. Travelers who spoke of them were turned away from inns, in case they could be Lore Keepers, wretched people who bonded with Beasts and shared their magic. Children who played too close to the Woods were punished. Even the Beast-related books in the library were burned, making the entire subject a mystery.

"I thought the B-beasts stayed in the Woods," Selby moaned.

"They usually do."

Barclay had foraged along the edge of the Woods before without ever spotting a Beast.

But Midwinter was only a few weeks away, and like Midsummer, the holiday was known to make Beasts behave strangely.

Barclay took a careful step away from the mouselike creature. He considered reaching into his pocket for the charm he kept to ward off Beasts. But it was already too late for that.

"Don't panic," he told Selby. "They're blocking our way back to town. But if we just think of . . ."

Except Selby didn't listen. Dropping his notebook and quill behind him, he turned around and shot off.

Into the *Woods*.

The hundreds of eyes in the grass seemed to blink all at once. Barclay glanced at Dullshire in the distance, his whole body trembling. Selby was gone. Into the Woods. If Barclay could get around the terrible creatures, he could alert the sentries, who protected Dullshire from the Beasts. Selby had parents and a family, after all. The townspeople would grab their pitchforks and go after him.

But before Barclay could take off, one of the mice leaped out of the leaves and landed on Barclay's boot.

It squeaked.

Barclay screamed.

He shook it off and sprinted after Selby. As soon as Barclay crossed into the trees, the daylight dimmed, swallowed by the knotted branches overhead. The already cold weather went colder, a fine, icy mist prickling against his skin.

Barclay was small for an eleven-year-old, which made him an easy target for older kids looking for trouble. They tore pages out of his library books or stole the coins he saved for apple pastries.

If they could catch him.

Because when Barclay ran, even the sheepdogs struggled to keep up. And so he barreled down the forest hills and soon caught up to Selby, who ducked between the gray trees.

The wind blew, and leaves tumbled farther into the Woods, as if dragged by a riptide. The trees bent low, as though pointing Selby deeper, deeper.

"Selby!" Barclay screamed.

His long hair whipped across his face as he ran, quickly

growing wild and tangled. The wind seemed to push him forward, like it was trying to carry him off as well.

"Selby, stop!"

Behind him, Barclay had lost sight of the edge. There were only trees and mist in every direction.

We've broken the rules, and now we're going to die, Barclay thought with panic. Even if they escaped the Woods without being eaten by a Beast, what would they tell everyone? Selby and Barclay were both terrible liars.

Then Selby suddenly stopped running. Barclay skidded to a halt and slammed into him, knocking both boys down a thorn-covered hill. They rolled in a tangle of leaves and legs and branches, mushrooms spilling out of their baskets and bouncing down after them. They each screamed until they collided with the base of a fallen tree.

"What were you *thinking*?" Barclay shouted, shoving Selby off him. "We could've broken our necks! And—"

Selby let out a strangled sound and scampered back up the hill.

"What . . . ?" Barclay turned around to see what had scared Selby off, and froze.

On the fallen trunk of a massive tree, there stood a girl.

And on her shoulder, there sat a dragon.

TWO

Dullshire might have burned every last book about Beasts, but even Barclay knew stories about dragons. They dropped their screaming victims into the mouths of volcanoes. Or buried you alive in their hoards of gold. Or set you afire and fed your charred remains to their hatchlings.

Barclay didn't want to be swallowed up by lava, treasures, or baby Beasts, so he did what any clever apprentice would do when confronted with danger—he grabbed a fallen mushroom beside him and threw it at the girl's head.

It missed—Barclay was a pitiable thrower. Worse, the girl caught it in her hand and crushed it in her fist.

He swallowed.

"*Hmph.* I was going to ask if you were *all right*," she snapped, "but now I won't bother."

She looked about Barclay's age, with light brown skin, shrewd dark eyes, and very curly brown hair styled in two buns, one on either side of her head. Though most peoples near the Woods were pale, not everyone in Dullshire shared the same complexion. But Barclay had never seen anyone who wore quite so much *gold*. Her coat was so covered in brooches, buttons, and pins that they entirely hid the fabric beneath. Her dragon poked a claw at the shiny buckle of her satchel.

On closer inspection, Barclay wasn't sure the creature on her shoulder really *was* a dragon. It was barely larger than a raven, with silver scales and a sparsely feathered tail. And he'd never heard of any dragons within the Woods.

But, dragon or not, it was still a Beast. It would probably swoop down and bite off his hand if he wasn't careful.

Barclay crawled backward through the leaves. He pulled his Beast-warding charm out of his pocket and waved it around. It was a rope braided with special bits of herbs and twigs, and it smelled putrid, like a skunk.

"Get away from me, dragon!"

"Dragon!" The girl let out a delighted laugh and scratched the Beast below its chin. "Mitzi is hardly that ferocious yet. She's still only a whelp—a baby dragon—but we're very flattered."

Barclay let out a disgusted sound. The Beast had a *name*? It was a vicious killer, not some pet!

Then he realized what she and her Beast were.

"You're a Lore Keeper," he spat, shakily getting to his feet. "You use Beasts for *magic*. You become *friends* with them."

Each word left a foul taste on his tongue. After all, tales of dragons weren't the only ones whispered by the townsfolk. Lore Keepers might believe they kept their Beasts under control, but Beasts couldn't be tamed—wildness was their very nature. In half the gossip Barclay heard, Lore Keepers died from their own Beasts betraying them, and with their so-called friends gone, there was nothing to stop the Beasts from unleashing their destructive magic on the innocent people around them.

So went the story of the Great Fire of Drearyfeld, which had claimed seven unfortunate lives. Or when the poor mayor of Dimfurt had been turned to stone. Or the time the place formerly known as Dismaldorf had been quite literally blown off the map.

The girl rolled her eyes. "You townsfolk are all like trout cursing a Wintertime avalanche."

"That doesn't even make sense," Barclay said flatly.

"Oh, well, it does in my first language." This surprised Barclay, as the girl had a perfect accent. "It means you're all ungrateful. Who do you think protects your kingdoms from the Beasts? What Lore do you think keeps them in the Woods?"

Barclay didn't trust Lore, and he was certain all of Dullshire would be horrified to learn of such magic just outside their walls.

The girl huffed and turned away from him, bending over a collection of glass jars she'd laid out over the fallen tree. Inside were strange items: holly sprigs with berries like crystal, feathers with metallic-tipped edges, dead bugs as large as Barclay's fist, a speckled egg encased in amber, and a greenish goo that boiled even in the Winter cold.

The last jar was empty. She stood over it and rifled around inside her satchel.

Barclay wanted no business with magic, so he whipped around and climbed back up the hill. Selby awaited him at the top, huddled behind the closest tree.

"She has a *dragon*," Selby said with a mixture of fear and awe.

"That dragon will probably eat her one day," Barclay growled.

"Mitzi would *never* eat me!" the girl shouted. "She's a vegetarian!"

Barclay seriously doubted that. He took Selby by the wrist and dragged him away, but when he peeked over his shoulder, he noticed something. The girl had taken a mushroom out of her bag and was lowering it into the last glass jar. It was stout and curved, with a red dome.

A Mourningtide Morel.

A Lore Keeper like her probably didn't even know the value of that mushroom. She didn't deserve it. With his fears quickly replaced by determination, Barclay stormed back down the hill.

"Do you know what that is?" Barclay demanded.

The girl paused and looked up.

"It's a Mourningtide Morel," she answered with a hint of pride.

"Yes. We've been looking for one all day. If you give it to me, then I won't tell everyone in Dullshire that there's a Lore Keeper skulking about in the Woods." Barclay held out his hand, his face burning red. He flushed when he lied. Whether he got the mushroom or not, of course he would tell the townspeople about her. And they would grab their pitchforks, and they would drive her and her Beast someplace else.

"As if they'd dare to come into the Woods and find me," the girl countered.

Barclay moved to grab the glass jar, but she snatched it out of his reach.

"Give it to me."

"Absolutely not. I found it!"

"You're not even using it!"

"Yes I am! I'm making a trap."

Barclay scoffed. All she had was a line of jars. What was she trying to trap? Lightning bugs? "A trap for what?" he asked.

"A trap for Gravaldor."

Barclay's stomach filled with dread even colder than the icy mist. If she somehow summoned Gravaldor, then the tragedy from seven years ago in Dullshire could happen all over again. Barclay had already lost too much to Gravaldor to let him destroy his home a second time.

He climbed atop the fallen trunk. Even side by side, she was still taller than him, but so was almost everyone. When he took a step closer, her dragon—or Mitzi, as she called it—bared its fangs at Barclay and gave a snakelike hiss.

"You can't do this," he told the girl.

"Yes I can. I'm going to bond with Gravaldor, just like I bonded with Mitzi." She rolled up her sleeve to reveal a strange tattoo on her forearm in shiny golden ink. It looked just like her dragon. "Gravaldor is the Legendary Beast of the Woods. And when I bond with him, I'll—"

"You want to bond with him?" Barclay echoed, his voice high and fearful. Just the thought of Gravaldor made him picture his parents—the gentle way his mother treated the books that she read to her students as a schoolteacher, the apple treats his father would bake for Barclay when he learned to follow a new rule. If it hadn't been for Gravaldor, they'd still be alive. If it hadn't been for Gravaldor, they'd still be a family.

All Barclay had ever done was follow in his parents' footsteps. Because he believed, down to his very core, that if he worked hard and tried to follow the rules, he could almost get them back. He could earn the life in Dullshire that he should have had.

He didn't even care about the danger anymore. Or the Mourningtide Morel. Or the dirt under his fingernails.

He had to stop her.

"You'll kill everyone," Barclay seethed. "Gravaldor isn't like your dragon—"

"I told you, she's a whelp—"

"He's huge! He's bigger than trees, with fangs as long as you and me. He's more powerful than any Beast in the Woods, and you'd be eaten before you'd even be able to feel sorry."

She narrowed her eyes. "How would you know? You're just a farmer of . . ." She deflated, trying to think. "What's the word for it in your language? They're squishy. It's a . . . a . . ."

"Mushroom?" he impatiently finished for her.

"Yes! You're just a mushroom farmer."

"I know because Gravaldor once destroyed our entire town." He didn't add anything about his parents because he didn't share stuff like that with strangers. Everyone in Dullshire was right. Lore Keepers were selfish, and they only brought doom.

The girl's face softened, but she didn't back down. She took a few steps closer to Barclay and jabbed her finger into his chest. He wobbled but didn't fall over.

"I need to do this, and you can't stop me." Mitzi squawked in agreement. The girl kept walking and poking him until he'd backed up to the edge of the trunk. "These are the most difficult items to find in the Woods, and I collected them all." She waved the jar with the Mourningtide Morel in front of his face. "These will summon and trap Gravaldor. It's perfect."

Barclay's eyes widened as he examined the mushroom in that jar. Up close, he realized its scarlet dome was actually crimson.

"Wait!" he said. But the girl gave him one more jab, and he toppled off the trunk. He landed painfully in the center of the clearing, a pine cone squashed underneath him.

"Wait!" he sputtered again. "That's not a—"

But the girl had already set the jar down, completing the perfect line.

Suddenly, deep in the Woods behind him, there came a howl.

Barclay scrambled to his feet. To his right, the trees shuddered. Then, to his left, footsteps scurried through the shade. A figure rushed by so fast, it was merely a blur.

"Barclayyyyyyyy," Selby moaned from the top of the hill.

Barclay waved at him to hush. Behind him, Barclay heard the sound of something breathing. There was a low, guttural growl.

His heart pounded, and he desperately clutched his Beast-warding charm. It usually calmed him in dangerous situations, even ones without Beasts. It helped him clear his head enough to think his way out of trouble.

But then a pair of glowing eyes appeared through the trees.

He couldn't think his way out of this.

The girl jumped down beside him. "Once Gravaldor walks closer to the jars," she whispered, "the Lore will trap him here. Then I can bond—"

"I don't think that's—" Barclay started.

There was another growl, and she hushed him. But Barclay knew he was right. Gravaldor was massive and impossible to hide. And the mushroom she'd used wasn't a Mourningtide Morel.

But it didn't matter. Even if this wasn't Gravaldor, she'd summoned something, and now they were all going to die.

The girl held her arms out, as though whatever Beast stalked around them could be tamed like a puppy. "Mitzi, help me."

The baby dragon gave a low huff.

"Mitzi, we've talked about this!" the girl hissed. "If I'm going to be Grand Keeper one day, you can't be my only Beast." When Mitzi still did not comply, she added, "But you'll still be my favorite!"

At this, Mitzi seemed to relax. She crouched low on the girl's shoulder, prepared to attack whatever monster circled them. The girl glanced down at Barclay. "Now, don't make any sounds. No sudden movements. We don't want to alarm—"

"Barclayyyyyyy," Selby cried again.

Everything next seemed to happen at once.

Something tore out from the trees, claws raised straight at them.

A light burst out of Mitzi's mouth, so bright that Barclay had to close his eyes.

But even without his sight, he knew the growl he'd heard before. It was low-pitched and dangerous, the sort of sound a bully might make if they had backed Barclay into a dead-end alley. It was the sound of victory. It meant the predator had found its prey.

A breath blew hot against Barclay's neck.

He ran. He ran as fast as he could.

He knew better than to flee. Many wild animals only attacked once the chase began. Barclay was basically asking the Beast to eat him. But as smart as Barclay might have been, he was too terrified to stop himself.

He heard the sound of footsteps pounding after him. He ignored them and quickened his pace. He was running faster than he ever had in his life. The gray trees blurred past him like a smear in the corner of his eyes, and the air that usually whipped at his face and knotted his hair had gone eerily still. It seemed impossible, but he swore he was going faster than the wind.

And the pair of eyes, he realized, weren't behind him. They were beside him.

The Beast wasn't running after him. It was running *with* him.

The thought startled him so much, he tripped and fell facedown. When he groaned and rolled over, the last thing he saw was a mouthful of black teeth.

THREE

Barclay woke up covered in leaves, Selby and the girl panting over him.

"He's dead!" Selby wailed.

It took Barclay a moment to remember how he'd ended up here, on the ground, aching all over, with only Selby and a stranger. But as he squinted at the gnarled branches overhead, he remembered where he was—the one place he was forbidden to go. The Woods.

Barclay sat up and whipped around. Then a terrible pain shot through his shoulder, and he looked down to find his sleeve had been shredded and an ugly red gash stretched down his arm. Beneath it were hints of glimmering gold.

"Where is it? Where's the Beast?" Barclay asked, panicked. He looked around, but doing so made the world tilt like he was tumbling down another hill.

The girl's nostrils flared. "The Beast is there." She poked at his wound.

"Ow! What was that for?"

"You have a Mark. Like mine."

She rolled up her sleeve again to reveal her golden Mitzi-like tattoo. Only this time the Mark moved. It padded across her skin, then curled up and yawned, as though preparing to go to sleep.

Barclay realized Mitzi was no longer perched on the girl's shoulder. The dragon was in the tattoo. The magic of it all made Barclay want to rub his eyes, to make sure what he was seeing was real.

"It was supposed to be my Mark," the girl continued. "Even if I messed up the trap, if you hadn't been there, then I would've bonded with the Lufthund—"

"Bonded? Bonded like a Lore Keeper?" Barclay winced as he smeared away some of the blood on his arm and stared at his Mark in horror. He'd barely gotten a glimpse of the Beast that had chased him, but the tattoo resembled a wolf. It moved, prowling menacingly over the top of his shoulder, its fangs bared.

"Yes. Exactly like a Lore Keeper," she huffed. "A Mark is where a Beast dwells when it isn't out in the world."

As she spoke, the Mark on Barclay's shoulder thrashed, and the Beast snapped its jaw.

Selby stared at it openmouthed. "Does this make Barclay a Lore Keeper?"

"No," Barclay hissed. He would never become a Lore Keeper. Beasts weren't companions—they were monsters. He might've broken Dullshire's most important rule, but it hadn't been his fault. He hadn't chosen this.

Suddenly he felt sick. He staggered to his feet, only to immediately throw up on the forest floor.

When he'd finished, he held out his arm, which pulsed painfully where the Beast had slashed him. "Get it off me," Barclay told the girl.

"Why should I help you?" she snapped. "You threatened to have your town run me away! You tried to steal the mushroom from my trap. And now you've bonded with the Beast that I should have bonded with."

"I didn't bond with it! It bonded with me!"

"But that's not how it works. Did you touch it? You would've felt a spark—maybe a pinch? You must've—"

"I didn't," he insisted. All he remembered before passing out was the teeth.

"Is it Gravaldor?" Selby squeaked.

"No, Gravaldor looks like a bear," the girl answered, rolling her eyes. "His Beast is—"

"I don't want to know what it is," Barclay snapped. "Just get the Mark off me!"

The girl crossed her arms. "I don't know how to remove a Mark. Most people don't want to! Most people want—"

Barclay didn't think he could hear more of this, or he might be sick again. He grabbed Selby's shoulder. "Come on. We're going back."

Selby cringed as Barclay touched him, and Barclay swallowed and dropped his hand.

"What if the Beast gets out?" Selby murmured.

"I . . ." Barclay's mouth went dry. Then he, Barclay Thorne, Dullshire's hardest-working but most troublesome apprentice, would become another cautionary tale. Another Lore Keeper who brought destruction with him.

The girl shook her head. "Beasts can't come out of their Marks unless you summon them. Or unless they break their bonds. But that's very rare! If it was going to happen, you'd know. The Mark would start to turn black."

If Barclay could see the tattoo's color changing, that would give him time to escape Dullshire if he needed to. He could run into the Woods and let the trees swallow him whole. Then, far, far away, Dullshire would be safe.

But he would be gone, alone in the Woods with a deranged Beast.

Barclay didn't mind having responsibilities. In fact, every year of his apprenticeship, he looked forward to Master Pilzmann assigning him new ones. It had begun with chores—Barclay learned to chop firewood, to feed Gustav, and to fetch water from the well. As he grew older, Barclay began interacting with customers and tending to the mushroom cellar. Now he led foraging trips all on his own.

Each time, Barclay had known that he was ready for the new responsibility. Even when it was hard or he was tired, he liked how much Master Pilzmann relied on him. Whenever his teacher called him exceptional, Barclay felt a flutter of pride in his chest. No one else in town thought of orphans like that.

But this responsibility was far greater than anything else asked of him. If a Beast lived in Barclay's skin, then it was Barclay's responsibility to make sure it stayed there. It was his responsibility to keep Dullshire safe . . . no matter what.

"We're going back," Barclay said. Though his words were firm, his voice shook.

"They'll let you go back?" the girl asked. "You said they'd chase me away for being a Lore Keeper. So what will they do to you?"

Barclay's heart filled with dread. Dullshire didn't make exceptions. At least, not for Barclay, who didn't have family to fight for one.

"They won't know," he murmured, as determined as he was terrified.

Then he grabbed Selby's hand and led them through the maze of gray trees. It might have been Barclay's imagination playing tricks, but as the wind blew and the branches prickled, it seemed as though every tree now leaned away from him to clear his path. As though the wilds recognized one of their own.

It wasn't until the boys arrived at Master Pilzmann's house that Barclay remembered he was returning from his trip empty-handed. They'd failed to find the Mourningtide Morel, and judging from the ominous clouds darkening the sky, the first snow was coming. Now Master Pilzmann would have to wait until next year.

The house was strange-looking on the outside. When Gravaldor had attacked seven years ago, his foot had smashed the back of the house, so Master Pilzmann had needed to rebuild those walls. Several years later he'd added a second story for Barclay's bedroom and for storage. Each addition had been built of something different, making the home like a quilt of brick, stone, and wood. And like all houses in Dullshire, Beast-warding charms dangled from each of the windows, ropes and beads and chimes that reeked and rang and warned stay away, stay away.

Barclay and Selby entered around back, where a flyer had been pinned to the door.

❧ ATTENTION RESIDENTS OF DULLSHIRE ❧

As of today, the twentieth of Winter, four new rules have been issued by the mayor's office:

Rule #1192: sneezing is hereby prohibited in the town square.

Rule #1193: all pets must be examined by sentry officials for any Beast magic, especially ducks.

Rule #1194: Rule #827 has been revoked.
Carrot cake is reinstated as a birthday cake
option.

Rule #1195: no babies are to be named
Kuthbert with a *C*—only with a *K*.

The boys took down the flyer and pushed open the door to the pantry. Inside was crowded with baskets and crates, each filled with different types of mushrooms. The whole place smelled like mushrooms, and mushrooms—for the most part—smelled like dirt. This was the only room in the house not up to Dullshire's typical standards of cleanliness, and it was also Barclay's favorite. He liked the smell, and he didn't mind the filth.

The boys crept through the door to the living room. They found Gustav curled up on the rug and asleep in front of the fire.

Master Pilzmann made a noise of greeting from the kitchen, where he was wearing a burlap apron and washing mushrooms in a bucket of water. He was exceptionally tall—the tallest man in town. He constantly needed to hunch below doorframes, and his drooping gray mustache reached down to his chest. For special occasions Master Pilzmann wore a strange round hat that even made him look like a giant mushroom.

"You're back late," he told the boys, so absorbed in his

washing that he didn't look up from the sink. "I was getting worried."

Barclay carefully adjusted the straps of his bag so that it covered his wound, then attempted—and failed—to smooth down his messy hair. "We're sorry. We didn't mean to take so long. It's just that . . ." He swallowed. He hated lying. "We couldn't find the Mourningtide Morel."

It's not a lie, he told himself. *We're just not telling him the* whole *truth.* The thought didn't make him feel good, but it did help him keep his voice steady.

"Is that so? That's not like you, Barclay," said Master Pilzmann. He didn't sound angry, but Barclay still felt a twinge of guilt. He hated letting Master Pilzmann down.

"I'm sorry," he managed. "It won't happen again."

"I don't doubt that," he said. "Well, remember to take off your shoes—I just mopped. And supper's on the table. Mushroom soup. It's probably cold by now, but it's still good."

Selby made a disgusted face.

"Mrs. Havener at the library stopped by today to let me know that they've purchased several more books. She said something about adventure and history, and she seemed very excited for me to tell you, Barclay."

Normally, the thought of new books at the library would thrill Barclay, as there wasn't a subject he didn't like to study. And though he'd buried his dreams of travel in the past, he still loved reading about adventure. But tonight he had other things on his mind.

Setting the freshly washed mushrooms aside, Master Pilzmann finally looked up at Barclay, and his jaw dropped on seeing the dirt and flecks of leaves covering Barclay's clothes.

"My *boy*. What happened to you?"

Barclay's face reddened, as it always did when he lied. "I—I fell."

"Running again? You can't keep breaking so many rules—the mayor will sentence you to community service for the ninth time. And you're filthy. Is that . . . blood?! Where could you have—"

"I'll go bathe," Barclay squeaked, then he left his basket on the table and hurried out the door toward the well.

Master Pilzmann's house was at the southern edge of Dullshire, against the town wall, so there was no one to see Barclay as he hauled a full bucket of water to the outhouse. He stood, naked and shivering, as he wet a cloth and wiped the grime away.

Within minutes, someone knocked. "I brought you fresh clothes," Selby told him. "And medicine."

Barclay cracked the door and grabbed them, not in the mood to say thank you.

"Has the Mark gone black yet?" Selby whispered.

Yet? Barclay's heart clenched as he examined the tattoo, still a brilliant gold that gleamed brighter than a coin. Clearly, Selby believed it was only a matter of time before the Beast escaped.

The Mark squirmed on Barclay's shoulder, as though trying to pry itself off his skin.

Maybe Selby was right. The girl had said the Lore Keeper forms the bond, not the other way around. What had happened didn't make sense. It was an accident, a mistake. Maybe the Beast felt the same way. And if it broke free, there was no telling what it would do.

"It's fine, just go," Barclay grunted, and he heard Selby scamper off.

He applied the ointment, cringing as it stung, then put on the clean clothes. He left the outhouse and threw his old sweater in the garbage. It was a shame to lose it—he only owned four—but if he took it to the tailor, then she would ask questions about how he'd gotten such a large tear.

It really was a matter of "yet," he realized. Because if the Beast didn't break the bond and eat him, then his lie would unravel—and this mistake would cost him way more than community service. Either way, his life was over.

He blinked back tears and headed inside.

A second after he'd taken a seat at the table, Master Pilzmann cleared his throat. "Did you wash your hands? Your fingernails?"

"I . . ." Barclay looked down, his cheeks hot. Dirt still crusted under his nails. No matter what he did, he never managed to fit in.

His chair made a loud screech as he stood up and hurried to the sink. He dunked his hands into the pail and scrubbed until his skin pruned and his knuckles reddened. He didn't usually mind the dirt, just like he preferred his hair long. But now he couldn't look at his hands without all the events of the day rushing back to him.

As he scoured the dirt from under each fingernail, he thought about all the years spent trying to convince Dullshire to accept him, all to be ruined by something that wasn't his fault. And he couldn't help thinking how Dullshire had bullied him about things outside of his control his entire life. None of it was fair.

Neither he nor Selby ate much at supper—Barclay because he was far too nervous to stomach any food, Selby because he didn't like mushrooms.

"And here I thought carrots had been totally banned for years," Master Pilzmann prattled. "Turns out, I'd been confusing them with turnips this whole time! I'm very glad to be straightened out—I've been so put off with Mrs. Kraus. Hard to trust your neighbors when they could be running an illicit produce stand . . ."

Barclay, normally interested in town gossip, paid no attention.

At some point the topic of conversation must have changed, because Master Pilzmann leaned over and touched Barclay's damp hair and Barclay flinched. Master Pilzmann's hand was dangerously close to the Mark.

"I'll cut this tonight. It's much too long. . . . I know that's how you like it. But I do agree with Mr. Jager—it's starting to look rather *wild*. And—"

"I do like it long," Barclay said sharply, leaning away from him.

"But it's . . ." Master Pilzmann sighed, and the sound of it made Barclay's heart clench.

"Am I a good apprentice?" Barclay asked quietly.

"What? Of course you are." The man's face softened. "What's brought this sullen mood about? It's only bad luck you didn't find the Mourningtide Morel! Tricky little grubbers—"

"Then why does it matter if I like my hair long?"

Barclay's voice was louder than he'd meant it to be, but he was angry. Dullshire's many rules were meant to keep the citizens safe—especially from the Woods—but so many of them were nonsense. Barclay was smart and dependable, and he tried so hard. So why didn't all that matter more than a few silly broken rules? Why did it feel so impossibly hard to belong?

Master Pilzmann paled. Barclay never raised his voice at him.

"It's just that . . . you stick out quite a bit, my boy. Always dashing about like you're in a hurry. Filthy as a sheepdog that ran off in the Woods. And the reading so much about adventure . . . You must know how people talk. . . ."

When Barclay didn't respond, Master Pilzmann said, gently, "Never mind about the hair, then."

Barclay wanted to groan. It wasn't about the hair. It was about how Master Pilzmann was so obviously waiting for Barclay to mess up. How all of Dullshire was just waiting to get rid of him.

"If I'm a good apprentice, then why is *he* here?" Barclay asked, glaring at Selby, whose eyes filled with tears. "I'm a better apprentice than he has ever been."

Master Pilzmann's mouth hung open, aghast.

"Go to your room, I suppose," he said, as if entirely unsure how to punish Barclay, who had never needed punishing from him before.

Barclay considered ignoring him. If there was ever a time he'd like to run, it was now. Running—like his Beast-warding charm—cleared his head. But he was also bone-tired and couldn't afford to break more rules, so he said nothing and slugged up the rickety steps to the attic, where the two boys slept.

That night Barclay lay in bed staring at the flickering candle on the nightstand between him and Selby. Outside the charms dangling from the windows chimed. The tinging used to soothe Barclay, but now it only sounded haunted. As if the monsters the charms warded away should include *him.*

"What if it escapes while you sleep?" Selby whispered.

Barclay hadn't realized the other apprentice was still awake. He rolled over so his back faced him. "It won't. I'll wake up every hour to check it."

"Will it eat everyone?"

"No," Barclay hissed. "Go to sleep."

"Does this mean you can do magic now?"

"Selby," he groaned. He didn't want to talk about this.

He didn't want to think about this. He just wanted to wake up in the morning and learn that this day had never happened and that his very boring life had once again returned to normal.

"Promise me," Barclay pleaded. "Promise me you won't tell anyone."

"I promise," Selby said.

Barclay sighed. "Good. I'm sorry I was mean to you." And he relaxed enough to fall asleep with his charm clutched between his fingers, hoping that he didn't dream of an adventure.

FOUR

Dullshire was a town of slights. Everything, from the buildings to the lampposts, leaned on a slight tilt—a remnant of Gravaldor's earth-breaking magic from seven years ago. The roads were slightly cobbled, with stones loose enough to kick and trip over. The clocktower in the main square was slightly behind. The town wall was slightly crumbled.

The people were slightly paranoid.

Charms dangled on the ledge of every window. Pitchforks and torches rested on each porch, always at the ready.

Barclay glanced at these pitchforks warily as he walked down the street. He resisted the urge to yet again examine the Mark on his shoulder. It'd continued to thrash and prowl across his skin when he'd checked this morning, and though the bright gold hadn't darkened, his thoughts were still in nervous tangles. Not even walking into the library helped calm him.

Mrs. Havener, the librarian, peered at him from behind the desk. Though very slender, she always wore a heavy Winter coat and three pairs of mittens layered over one another, making her look like a stuffed scarecrow. Barclay had never known if this was because Mrs. Havener was perpetuatlly cold or because she was very proud of her wife's prolific knitting.

"Are you feeling all right, dear?" she asked. "Your cheeks are all flushed!"

Barclay raised a hand to his face, and it was hot to the touch. "I feel fine," he lied, making his face flush even deeper.

Mrs. Havener reached for a stack of books behind her and slid them to Barclay.

"We have new books from the city! This one is *The Extensive History of the One Hundred Kingdoms. . . .*" Indeed, the tome was large enough to be mistaken for a leather-bound trunk. "*The Encyclopedia of Foraging Finds* . . . Ordered that one for Mr. Pilzmann . . . Oh! And this one I ordered especially for you, Barclay."

She handed him a copy of an adventure story titled *Myths of Monstrosity*. Its cover featured a dragon's head staked on a sword.

Normally, Barclay would thrill at such a story of danger and heroism. But now he cringed, thinking of Mitzi and the girl and everything that had happened in the Woods.

"I—I think I'll take the history one for now." He groaned as he picked up the gigantic book.

Mrs. Havener's face fell in disappointment. "I thought you loved adventure stories."

"I'm not really the adventure type," he barely managed to squeak out.

Then he thanked Mrs. Havener and left, hoisting the massive book into his arms. He headed in the direction of the town hall, and the closer he walked, the more decorations he passed.

There was a festival in Dullshire tonight, celebrating events from not just one kingdom but *two*. Because Dullshire was so rural and insignificant, none of the neighboring kingdoms that surrounded the Woods had bothered to lay proper claim to it. Occasionally a tax collector came from one duchy or a trader visited from some far-off realm, but the people of Dullshire were quite confused by it all. So, always preferring to be safe than sorry, the town celebrated the holidays of all of its nearby kingdoms. Today marked both the coronation of Konig Gebherd of Humdrum and the birthday of Princess Katrin of Diddlystadt.

Though Master Pilzmann had given Barclay and Selby the day off to celebrate, Barclay wasn't so sure he wanted to join the festivities. As much as he'd like to sample the food, he knew he shouldn't be calling attention to himself in case someone discovered the Mark.

But even if it was for the best, it was hard not to stop as he passed the town square.

There was dancing—couples skipping to double-timed beats with arms linked, fiddlers and drummers playing along from the balcony of the town hall. Food stalls lined the edges of the courtyard, beckoning Barclay closer with smells of apple dumplings and potato pancakes. The decorations were dizzyingly colorful: the blue and gold streamers of the Humdrummish flag clashing with Diddlystadt's vibrant orange, black, and green. There were no balloons, of course—balloons had been banned since that disastrous jousting match between Mr. Bielke and his goat last year—and the lawmakers had recently forbidden all tournaments of beanbags or hopscotch. But even in a town full of rules, there were still plenty of ways to have fun.

Without even meaning to, Barclay had wandered into the center of the square, still carrying *The Extensive History* in his arms.

"Barclay?" someone said behind him, making him turn.

Selby motioned to him from a nearby table, which he was squeezed into with his many siblings. He clutched a half-eaten bratwurst on a stick in one hand, and even though it wasn't a mushroom, he suddenly looked unhappy to be eating it.

"W-what are you doing here?" Selby asked uneasily.

Barclay glanced longingly at one of the stands, wishing he had some money. "I was just passing by."

Beside Selby, his siblings cheered. Barclay looked to the center of the square, where a very blond, very pink man was being wheeled in circles in a cart.

"What's going on?" Barclay asked.

"B-because of the konig's birthday—"

"You mean the konig's coronation," Barclay corrected. "And the princess's birthday."

"R-right. They're giving a prize to the man in Dullshire with the m-most children, and my dad won."

Barclay wasn't surprised, as Selby had more siblings than he could likely count. In the center of the square, a Dullshire lawmaker awarded Selby's father with, in lieu of a trophy, an especially large ham.

"Why are you stuttering so much?" Barclay asked him. Selby only stuttered when he was nervous.

"I . . ." He flushed extra pink. "I'm nervous about apple smashing and hammer throwing later." This made sense to Barclay, who was also made easily anxious when it came to sports. "The families with the most wins gets a real trophy."

Barclay's shoulders sagged. He'd been to enough of Dull-shire's festivals to know how these games worked—without a family to compete with, Barclay would be excluded.

"And b-because Master Pilzmann's looking for you," Selby blurted.

"He is?" Barclay asked fretfully. "Did he say why?"

"No."

"Did he look angry?"

"No."

"Did I do something wrong?"

At that, Selby took an especially large bite of his bratwurst, and promptly choked on it. After several moments of coughing—with both Barclay and one of Selby's sister taking turns whacking his back—Selby swallowed his mouthful and managed, "I'm going to get a drink." And then he fled.

Barclay, now alone amid such a large crowd, felt twice as terrible as he had that morning. No doubt Master Pilzmann wanted to scold him for his behavior last night. Maybe Barclay would even be fired as an apprentice, and then what would he do?

Not ready to face his fate, Barclay headed somewhere else: the gloomy graveyard tucked behind a hill outside of town. Barclay tensed as he reached the gate in the wall that surrounded Dullshire. A large banner hung over it.

WELCOME TO DULLSHIRE
NO BEASTS
NO MAGIC
NO RIFFRAFF

The gray trees of the Woods loomed to the west. Barclay walked down a path in the opposite direction, and he swore he could sense someone—or some*thing*—watching him. The frosty wind made his skin prickle.

The graves of Franz and Alice Thorne rested side by side

beneath the shade of an elm tree. Barclay visited them frequently, often with a book. But this time he hadn't come to read.

He sat on *The Extensive History* and leaned back onto his father's tombstone.

"I made a mistake," he murmured. "I broke the most important rule, and I'm scared."

Barclay told his parents the entire story of what had happened in the Woods. If he was going to spend his life lying to everyone he knew, then this was his only time to be honest.

But saying the words didn't relieve the weight on his chest. If anything, it made him feel worse. His parents had been killed by Gravaldor, and now their son had bonded with another Beast from the Woods. It would have been better if the Beast had eaten him.

"I'm so sorry. I wish I could take it back. I wish . . ."

He wished they were here so that they could help him. So he'd have people who cared for him no matter how troublesome he was. So he, like Selby, could have a home to run back to when he got scared.

He missed them. So much.

Barclay didn't have friends to ask for help either, other than Master Pilzmann and Mrs. Havener—and he'd disappointed both of them in the last twenty-four hours. Would they be able to fix this? Barclay doubted that they knew anything more about Lore Keepers and Beasts than he did.

"Why can't I belong here?" Barclay asked his parents.

Nothing answered except the wailing of the wind.

When he'd returned to town, he intended to go straight to Master Pilzmann's and beg his forgiveness. He avoided the festival and its cheerful passersby, and he clutched the charm in his pocket, feeling deeply alone.

"What are you carrying?" a voice asked him sharply.

Barclay jumped, dropping the massive copy of *The Extensive History* on the ground. He scrambled to pick it up—he hated to ruin such a new book.

Once he'd lifted it, he looked at his companion. Only, there were not one but three boys, all a few years older than him. Poldi, Marco, and Falk. Falk was the leader—the biggest, meanest of the bunch—and he wore thick gloves good for punching and leather boots good for kicking.

Barclay glanced down the street, but it was empty except for them. Empty was not a good sign. Normally, he would run. But he couldn't while carrying *The Extensive History*, and he couldn't lose it. He'd already hurt Mrs. Havener's feelings once today.

"I asked you what you're carrying," Falk grunted.

"It's a book," Barclay answered stiffly. He considered adding, *Not that you'd know, would you?* But he thought better of insulting him, considering Barclay couldn't flee afterward like he usually would.

"Look at the size of it! I'm surprised a twig like you can carry it." Falk took a menacing step forward, as did his two backups. "Think you're better than all of us, reading books like that? You think you're so smart, but if you were smart, you wouldn't be a lousy mushroom farmer, would you?"

Barclay was used to these insults, and he knew—no matter what he carried—Falk and his gang would find any excuse to torment him if they saw him walking past.

So he took a careful step back and said, "I'm just going home. I don't want to fight you."

"I bet you don't. You hate that I'm better than you at it."

Barclay was good at a lot of things, but only because he had to be. Dullshire would hardly tolerate a rule-breaking orphan if he weren't. But that was also why Falk hated him, since Falk's strength was his one and only skill. A fact which Barclay, admittedly, often reminded him of.

"That's n-not true!" Barclay stammered, then he prepared to do something to Falk that he'd never done before: compliment him. "You're better at loads of things than me, and I don't mind. Like, well, eating things that I can't." He'd once switched Falk's lunch with Gustav's pig food, and Falk had eaten it all. He hadn't even gotten a stomachache. "It's a bit remarkable, actually."

Falk narrowed his eyes, and Barclay immediately caught his mistake. "Remarkable" was a big word to Falk, and Barclay usually used those to tease him.

Falk nodded, and Poldi lunged forward, blocking Barclay's path to escape. Behind him, Marco shoved him in the back. Barclay dropped *The Extensive History* with a thud.

"Bet that thing weighs more than you, huh?" Falk shot him a toothy, threatening smile.

Barclay swallowed and reached down to pick it up, but before he could, Marco grabbed a fistful of his coat. Soon Barclay was trapped, with both arms locked behind his back.

"Get off!" He jerked in Marco's grip, but it didn't do any good. It never did.

Falk reached down and picked up *The Extensive History*.

"Give it back," Barclay snapped.

"You want it back? Well . . ."

As he spoke, Marco pushed Barclay down to the ground, his cheek pressed against dirt and stone. Poldi pinned him there.

Falk held *The Extensive History* over him.

"I wonder what would happen if I dropped this on your face? I'll drop it, and you can have it back."

Barclay considered yelling for help, but doing so had only earned him extra kicks and punches in the past. Besides, Falk never got punished because Barclay had no parents to demand it. Master Pilzmann was too oblivious for such squabbles.

All Barclay could do was squeeze his eyes shut and brace himself for a broken nose, his heart hammering in terror.

But when Falk did drop the book, a sudden wind tore across the street, so strong that all the shutters around them swung and smacked against their frames and walls.

Barclay heard a loud thump, then a groan. And when Marco let him go so that he could sit up, he saw Falk lying flat on his back, clutching his face. A bit of blood dribbled down his cheek.

"What happened?" Marco asked.

"The wind blew it at him!" Poldi answered.

"I don't believe—"

"I saw it—"

"Arghhhhh," Falk groaned.

While the others were distracted, Barclay scrambled to his feet. He regretfully abandoned *The Extensive History* and took off into a run, shouts of "No you don't!" and "Where do you think you're going?" echoing behind him.

And last, just as Barclay plunged into the crowd of the festival, he heard Falk holler *"Barclay Thorne just did magic!"*

FIVE

As Barclay ducked behind a fried food stall to hide, he tripped over a loose cobblestone and barreled into a sack of potatoes. The freshly dug-up vegetables tumbled out over Barclay's clothes, covering his hands and clothes in dirt.

But Barclay had more important worries on his mind than Dullshire's rule about cleanliness.

Once he had checked to make sure he was safely out of sight of the festivalgoers, he wrenched down his collar to look at his shoulder, where the Mark writhed, as golden as ever.

Sudden winds didn't just pick up history books and throw them at bullies.

Barclay's stomach turned, thinking of what Falk had shouted. *Barclay Thorne just did magic!* Falk wasn't bright, but he had quickly guessed the truth—and made even quicker work of spreading it. Already, anyone who was listening was probably horrified. *Magic? In Dullshire?*

Barclay struggled to his feet, stumbling over more potatoes. He needed to think fast if he was going to fix this.

But what if he didn't deserve to? He hadn't just accidentally used magic—he'd accidentally used magic to hurt someone. It didn't matter if Falk was due a broken nose. Barclay had been so worried about the Beast escaping its Mark that he hadn't considered that *he* was just as dangerous.

Maybe he should leave. He could run into the Woods and never come back, but that meant leaving everything behind. Barclay's everything wasn't much—it was no friends, one apprenticeship, and two graves.

But it was still his home.

Barclay took a deep breath and emerged from behind the fried food stall, only to come face-to-face with Poldi.

"Here he is!" Poldi shouted, and Barclay froze like a startled deer. Then Poldi lunged for him, and Barclay darted away. Maybe he was imagining it, but he swore he was running as fast as he had in the Woods. His feet barely even seemed to scrape the ground, and he had no control over his balance. He raced through the festival, tripping over fallen streamers, slamming into dancers, knocking over barrels of beer and apple juice.

"Oi! B-boy!" stammered Mrs. Kraus as onions and carrots toppled from her produce stand.

"There's no running in town!" blustered Mr. Jager, a lawmaker who had been awarding another father the second-place ham.

"Barclay Thorne!" called out the baker.

But Barclay was too busy fleeing Poldi to pay any of them attention. Until Barclay skidded around a game of hammer throwing—ducking so as not to be clocked in the head—and collided with Marco. The two of them crashed into a bale of hay.

Barclay recovered first. He stood and held his hands up to Marco in front of him and Poldi behind him. "I can explain," he choked out.

"You can't trick us," Marco snarled. "We saw it!"

As the two of them took menacing steps forward, two more winds tore across the square. Marco and Poldi were swept off their feet and thrown back ten feet through the air.

Suddenly the music of the festival screeched to a raucous halt. Many of those around them gasped. Mrs. Kraus even screamed, her hands flying up to cover her mouth.

"Did you see that?" someone whispered in the crowds.

"He didn't touch them," Mrs. Kraus moaned, now fanning herself.

"It looked like magic," a person behind her called.

Soon every pair of eyes in Dullshire turned to Barclay in a communal, suspicious glare.

Barclay's face flushed as he desperately tried to come

up with a lie. But he couldn't. His throat seized up, and he backed away, scared of his secret, scared worse of these powers he couldn't control.

"I didn't . . . ," he managed hoarsely. "I didn't mean . . ."

The winds from earlier picked up again, gusting alongside the fearful swooping of his stomach, making the fallen streamers and stalks of hay swirl around Barclay's feet.

"No," Barclay whispered, trying to make it stop. But the magic was wild, and it didn't listen to him.

The baker, a burly man with dark brown skin and a flour-coated apron, stepped forward and tightly grasped Barclay's shoulder. Barclay sprung backward from the pain of his wound—and the fear of revealing his Mark.

The winds reacted, growing stronger until they formed a vortex, and Barclay stood scarecrow-still at the center. Many around him screamed. Some even raced away. The banners with the flags of Humdrum and Diddlystadt were torn down. Loose potatoes and fallen apple chips soared in the air. Mr. Jager shrieked as his impressive, curly wig was ripped from his head and launched into the sky like a tawny owl.

If that had not all been terrible enough, there was a loud, mechanical groan. Barclay whipped around, squinting through the dusty, high-speed winds, and watched in horror as the already crooked face of Dullshire's clock toppled off the tower and fell to the ground with a sickening *crack*! The wooden disk splintered in two.

Only then did the winds die down, exposing the ruins

of the town's festival square and Barclay at its center. He crouched, his arms braced over his head, and he trembled all over.

Marco was the first to move. He launched himself forward, grabbed a fistful of Barclay's coat, and yanked the smaller boy to his feet. "I caught him!" Marco announced proudly.

"Don't touch him!" Falk called, appearing behind them. He looked a mess—blood smeared all over his nose and chin. "He's dangerous!"

Falk and his cronies had barely regarded Barclay as more than an ant before, but now Marco let go of Barclay as though he'd been burned.

"Boys, what is going on?" Mr. Jager asked, aghast, his bald head gleaming in the afternoon sun. His gaze roamed over Falk's broken nose, over the baker's now tattered apron, then to Barclay, whose hair was tangled, his skin smattered with dirt, his clothes covered in hay. Lastly, he looked to the clocktower, even more broken than when Gravaldor had attacked.

"Barclay is a Lore Keeper, sir!" Falk announced.

"What do you have to say for yourself, Barclay?" Mr. Jager asked him.

Barclay had gone red all the way to his ears. "I . . ." He searched the crowds for a friendly face, but Selby and his family were gone.

Then Mrs. Havener stepped forward, looking disheveled

and missing a few mittens from the winds. "There must be some kind of mistake. Barclay is just a boy."

"But look at him," Mrs. Kraus said uneasily, her hand clutched to her heart. "Doesn't he look a bit . . . *wild*?"

An uproar ensued over whether he was innocent or guilty, and as much as Barclay wanted to lie and claim it had all been a misunderstanding, he couldn't. They were all right to be afraid of him. He was dangerous and wild and out of control.

"We should throw him in the river!" someone suggested. "Lore Keepers don't float!"

"If the boy had any parents . . . ," Mrs. Kraus mumbled.

"You can't honestly believe this is true," Mrs. Havener growled.

"It *is* true!" a voice bellowed, and everyone turned to see the mayor arrive, Selby and his parents close behind him. The mayor, a serious-looking man barely taller than Barclay, marched to the center of the crowd, dragging Selby by the wrist. "This boy told me everything! Barclay has bonded with a Beast from the Woods!"

Selby let out a high-pitched wail.

Selby told his parents, Barclay realized. It was no wonder Selby had looked so nervous this morning. He'd broken his promise.

Barclay wasn't angry, though. Even if Selby hadn't spilled Barclay's secret, Barclay had already managed to ruin his life entirely on his own.

"By the power vested in me, and by the tenants of Dull-shire's principle rule," the mayor declared, "I pronounce you, Barclay Thorne, guilty of—"

But Barclay didn't stay to hear his punishment. It was too much—the destruction, the stares, the horror. Breaking yet another rule, he sprinted away, too fast for anyone to catch him. And he didn't stop until he had thrown open the door to Master Pilzmann's house.

"I need your help," Barclay rasped, nearly in tears. "I ran after Selby into the Woods, and something happened, and now I'm a Lore Keeper, and . . ."

His voice vanished when he saw Master Pilzmann standing beside Gustav with a grave expression on his face. He held a traveler's bag. It looked full.

"I already know, my boy. The mayor and Selby's family were just here." He thrust the bag into Barclay's arms. "You need to leave, and you can never come back."

SIX

L-leave?" Barclay sputtered. The traveler's bag dropped from his hands, sending clothes and canisters spilling across the floor. "It was an accident! Isn't there . . . There must be a way to reverse the magic!"

"I don't know how to reverse it, and we don't allow magic here. That is a *rule*, and there are no exceptions."

Although Master Pilzmann's voice wasn't unkind, Barclay wasn't prepared for such harsh words from him. Dullshire was his *home*, and Master Pilzmann was the closest thing to a parent he'd had in a long time.

But Barclay didn't have parents. No exceptions.

"Don't make me leave," Barclay pleaded as Master Pilzmann picked up Barclay's possessions and shoved them back into the bag. "I didn't mean to hurt Falk. And the clocktower, it can be fixed, can't it?"

"What happened to the clocktower?" asked Master Pilzmann sharply.

With a fresh wave of shame, Barclay explained the events of the festival.

Master Pilzmann shook his head. "If Selby had come straight to me, I could have . . ." A shadow swept over his face. "Well, I don't know what I could have done, but I certainly can't do anything now. After Selby's parents reported you, the mayor came straight here. And if his mind wasn't made up before, I'm quite sure it is now. The laws about magic . . . They're very strict, I'm afraid."

Then Barclay realized that Master Pilzmann wasn't trying to evict him.

He was trying to save him.

"This is not your fault," Master Pilzmann told him gently.

"Then why do they want me to leave?" Barclay's voice rose to a shout. He would normally never shout at Master Pilzmann, and now he had done it twice in two days. Hopelessness seeped into him as the reality of his situation set in.

"I'm supposed to stay here," Barclay whispered. "And when *I* have children, they'll live here too. Just like my parents and my grandparents and my—"

"You were never supposed to stay here, Barclay." Master Pilzmann closed the drawstrings of his bag and slipped its straps over Barclay's trembling shoulders. "Do you want to know the real reason I kept turning you away when you asked to be my apprentice?"

"Because I'm an orphan who's always breaking the rules?"

Master Pilzmann's face softened. "I turned you away because you aren't meant for this. You think staying in Dullshire is the life you were supposed to have if your parents had never died. There are other ways to honor their memories than following the same path they did. They're proud of you, I'm sure, but they'd rather you find a path of your own."

As if in response, a breeze wafted through the window, and it smelled like earth and pine—like the Woods. It made the hair on the back of Barclay's neck stand on end.

"What happens if they catch me?" he asked, turning to the window that faced back toward the center of town.

Master Pilzmann paled. "You mustn't think about that."

"But I don't even know where to go." The next town down the road was no different from Dullshire, nor was the next or the next or the next. That only left one place for him.

The Woods.

"If you let them, your feet will put you on the right path." Master Pilzmann ushered him toward the door. "Now it's time to leave. You *must* leave, or—"

He was cut off when Barclay threw his arms around him and squeezed tightly. "I'll miss you," he choked out.

"As will I, my boy," Master Pilzmann said with a quaver.

After Barclay reluctantly let go, he opened the front door. To his shock, a mob of men and women was already marching down the street toward their home. They were faces he recognized—the mayor, Mr. Jager, the other farmers.

The torches they carried left a trail of black smoke.

"Run," Master Pilzmann urged him.

Barclay didn't have time for one last look goodbye. He took off.

Even with a wounded shoulder, even carrying a heavy bag, Barclay ran as fast as he could through the town. The wind picked up behind him, pushing him along like it had in the Woods. He ran down the main street, across the bridge over the creek, and through the fields of cabbage and sheep. In a matter of minutes, he was merely a small figure in the distance, Dullshire a smudge of black across the gray, Wintery landscape behind him.

This time, when he ran into the Woods, the trees bent low to embrace him. Their branches uncurled and thickened like a shroud, allowing Barclay to disappear completely.

Within moments, he lost sight of the edge.

And only then, when he was surrounded by dark, twisted trunks and that same eerie mist, did he slump against a tree and put his head in his hands.

His entire life was gone.

He sat there for a long while. He ate a few of the mushrooms and nuts that Master Pilzmann had packed for him. He cried a little—something he hadn't done in a long time, not since he was younger than Selby. Then he reached into his bag for his notebook and drew a map of what little he knew of the world. It had Dullshire, a few dots for other towns in Diddlystadt, an *X* at the bottom to represent the capital of Humdrum, and black covering almost everything else—the Woods.

A whole world of places, but none for him.

"Are you back foraging for mushrooms?" a voice asked, and Barclay looked up to find the girl from yesterday standing in front of him, Mitzi once again perched on her shoulder.

"Does it *look* like I'm foraging for mushrooms? Go away. I don't want to talk to you. All of this is your fault."

She examined his traveler's bag with sympathy. "What happened?"

"What do you think happened?" He clenched his fists, causing the map to crinkle. "The Beast made me do magic, and it went out of control! Because I . . ." He swallowed. "Because I'm dangerous."

"It's normal to experience a burst of power like that, when your bond is so new. But don't worry—it shouldn't happen again. Though it seems like the damage is already done." She sighed. "This wouldn't have happened if you hadn't tried to stop me."

"If I hadn't, you could've set Gravaldor loose on the town."

"The same town that forced you to leave. Very grateful, aren't they?" She crouched down in front of him, all of her golden buttons and jewelry flickering in the hazy daylight. "So where are you going to go?"

"That's none of your business."

"I'm only trying to help you. You don't need to be so rude."

"I don't want a Lore Keeper's help. Especially not *yours*."

She smirked. "I'm pretty sure your Mark makes you a Lore Keeper too."

"It doesn't. Because I'm going to find a way to remove it, and I'm going to come back."

As soon as he said the words, he knew that they were the right ones. It didn't matter what Master Pilzmann had said. *This* was his path. Maybe he would go on a journey to a city or across the world. But he *would* come back home, and everything would return to the way it was supposed to be.

She stole the map that he'd drawn out of his hands and gave him a pitying look. "Where are you going to learn how to fix it? Here?" She pointed at the Humdrum capital. "No one there can help you. No one will *want* to. If you need answers, you're only going to find them in a Lore town. There's one only four days from here, deeper in the Woods."

"I'm not going to a town *full of Lore Keepers*," Barclay hissed.

"If Lore is your problem, then you need Lore to fix it. Besides, I'm going back there myself. I still need to trap Gravaldor, but I used up the last of my ingredients. You can come with me."

"I'm not—"

"Or you can get run out of every place you visit. That's

what's ahead of you. Pitchforks and locked doors. Not answers." She handed him his map back. "The choice is yours."

Barclay hesitated. He didn't know if what she said was true, but the prospect of more pitchforks frightened him . . . almost as much as being entirely on his own.

"Fine," he agreed bitterly. "I'll go with you."

"Good, because it's dangerous to travel these Woods alone, even with a Beast." She held out her hand to help him to his feet, but he refused it and stood up on his own. "My name is Viola Dumont. You already know Mitzi."

Mitzi squawked.

"Assuming we don't get eaten along the way," Viola continued, "we're going to make it to the closest Lore town, and you can get back to your miserable mushrooms before Spring comes."

SEVEN

The deeper the pair journeyed into the Woods, the more fearsome the Woods became.

The twisted gray trees gave way to new kinds: trees with thorns like daggers growing up their trunks, trees with knots in their bark that looked like faces. The first snow was falling, and the gnarled roots that snaked across the white ground reminded Barclay of decayed hands reaching out of a grave. Crows cawed overhead, as though urging him to turn back, to run.

As they set up camp for the night, he shivered and clutched his charm while Viola collected sticks for a fire.

When she finished, Barclay expected her to rub the twigs together to ignite them. Instead, she stared intently at the wood, her fingers white-knuckled around it. Then a red light appeared from her hands. Several sparks burst out, followed by flames, catching like a torch.

Barclay grimaced.

"The fire isn't burning you," he commented, more in disgust than awe.

"It's *my* fire," Viola replied, as though that was reason enough to defy nature.

"And this is *my* knife." Barclay brandished the small blade he used to slice particularly stubborn mushrooms. "But I could still cut myself with it."

"You'd cut yourself with your own knife? That doesn't seem smart."

"*No*, I'm just saying—"

"It's Lore. Or magic, as you probably call it. But since we're going to Sycomore, a *town full of Lore*, you should start calling it Lore and start talking like a Lore Keeper. Not some Elsie townsboy."

"But I *am* a townsboy," Barclay said, and he was proud of it. And he didn't know what Elsie meant.

"And the towns aren't very nice to Lore Keepers, are they?" Viola gave him a pointed look. "You hate Lore. You hate Lore Keepers. With that attitude, what Lore Keeper is going to want to help you? Not everyone is as kindhearted as me, you know."

"Kindhearted? It's your fault that this happened to me!"

She ignored his comment and began tying the food they had gathered—mushrooms, thanks to Barclay, and a rabbit, thanks to Viola—around a spit.

"I just think it would be a good idea for you to learn more about Lore Keepers before you go marching into Sycomore and making demands."

Barclay didn't *make demands*. At least, he didn't to anyone other than Selby, since Selby was supposed to listen to him.

"I'm going to get more water," he grumbled, snatching both of their canteens and storming downhill toward a stream.

Mitzi followed him, crouching behind bushes and watching him menacingly. He fought down his panic. Viola didn't like him much, but she wouldn't let her Beast kill him, would she?

Then Mitzi shook her butt and pounced on a pine cone. She tumbled onto her back, gnawing it. Barclay didn't know whether or not to feel silly for being scared. After all, Mitzi *was* a dragon.

While he filled the canteens, a wind blew and shook the trees overhead, sending a cloud of violet leaves fluttering down. On one side they looked like ordinary leaves—albeit purple ones. On the other there were beady black eyes and hundreds of spindly legs. Each stem was actually a long mouth, like a leech.

Barclay shrieked and swatted them away as they tumbled around him. Mitzi, startled by his noise, took off flying toward her Keeper.

"What's wrong?" Viola called from atop the hill. "You scared Mitzi."

Barclay sprinted up and cowered at Viola's side. "Those leaves are actually Beasts."

"Yes, they're called Kafersafts, and they're totally harmless."

"No Beasts are harmless."

"Some are." Viola pried Barclay's hand off her shoulder and sat him down. "This is exactly why you need a lesson. You're clueless. Now you're going to think every leaf, twig, and blade of grass is out to kill you."

"No I won't," he shot back, eyeing the crinkled brown leaves around them suspiciously.

Viola rolled her eyes. Then she pulled off a mushroom roasting on the spit and offered it to Mitzi. Mitzi nibbled it out of her palm while Viola scratched her head, like she really was some pet.

"There are five classes of Beasts," Viola told him. "The class tells you how powerful a Beast is and how hard it is to find. A Kafersaft is in the bottom class, the Trite class. They have a little power but aren't even strong enough to bond with. They do have uses, though. The sap from a Kafersaft tree is a common ingredient in all sort of elixirs, like Chamelion Lotion and Hornpecker Serum."

Harmless or not, Barclay was still spooked by their hundreds of buggy legs.

"Here," Viola offered, handing him a mushroom. "You can feed her, if you like."

Barclay absolutely would *not* like. But Mitzi, sighting

the food, had already scampered to Barclay's feet. And he'd much rather feed her the treat than his finger.

He held his breath as she gobbled it down off his hand, then he hurriedly checked his skin to make sure it hadn't turned scaly or infected.

"See, she likes you," Viola said as Mitzi brushed Barclay's leg with her feathered tail. "You're not special, though. Mitzi likes everyone."

Barclay almost—*almost*—came close to reaching down and petting Mitzi on the head, but then Mitzi made a belching sound and vomited the chewed-up mushroom all over his boots.

"You have to eat that now," Viola told him seriously.

"I . . . I do?" Barclay asked, horrified.

Viola looked him dead in the eyes. "Do you want her to eat *you*?"

As he fearfully bent down to scoop it up, Viola let out a howl of laughter.

"I'm sorry, I just . . . I didn't expect you to actually do it," Viola said, wiping tears out of her eyes. "I don't know how many times I have to explain to you that Mitzi isn't going to eat you."

"She's a *dragon*," Barclay grumbled, kicking the sick off his shoes. "What am I supposed to think?"

Mitzi climbed back onto Viola's shoulder and pecked at her golden pins, very undragonlike. Viola smirked at him while she scratched Mitzi's chin.

Barclay frowned. He wasn't used to being the one who didn't know anything, and he didn't like it.

"So what class is Mitzi?" he asked.

"You're skipping ahead. There's still the second class, the Familiar class. They're the most common Beasts to bond with. They have a small amount of power and are very easy to control. A lot of Guild apprentices have them." Viola began counting off on her fingers, which Mitzi bent down to try to nibble. "Mitzi is in the third class, the Prime class. She was *not* very easy to find, but when she gets bigger, she'll be very powerful."

"What do you mean by 'apprentice'?" Barclay asked.

"Having a Beast makes you a Lore Keeper, but the most prestigious Keepers work for the Guild. And they start out as apprentices. Masters can take on up to three of them. You usually start when you're between ten and twelve."

Barclay furrowed his eyebrows. "How old are you?"

Viola looked away and cleared her throat. "*Anyway.* The fourth class is called the Mythic class. They're incredibly rare and hard to find. Guild Masters sometimes have them. They're very, very powerful. Closer to monsters, as you might call them." She met his eyes seriously. "Your Beast, a Lufthund, is Mythic class."

"*What?*" said Barclay. That seemed all the more reason to get rid of it. Powerful and monstrous was a combination he wanted nothing to do with.

Viola turned the spit over the fire, not looking at him.

"So you can imagine how *I* feel. Those ingredients for the trap were hard to find. I've been searching since Summer! This was my one chance other than Midwinter. And even if I made a mistake and summoned the wrong Beast, I still could have bonded with it. But *you* got in the way."

"I told you, *I* didn't bond with it! The Beast bonded with *me*."

"And like I said, that doesn't make sense. The Beast doesn't forge the bond—the Lore Keeper does. You use summoning ingredients to lure the Beast. And once they're in the trap, you touch them, and it just . . . snaps. You feel this spark. And then the bond is formed."

That was most definitely not what happened to him. Maybe Viola didn't know as much about Beasts as she thought she did.

"What if the Beast doesn't want to bond with you?" he asked.

"They don't have a choice."

"Well, no wonder Beasts try to break their bonds all the time. It doesn't sound very fair."

Viola's mouth dropped open. "That . . . That almost never happens! You don't know what you're talking about. Beasts are companions! Their Lore is *made* for bonding. It makes them stronger, just like it does the Keeper, which is why Lore Keepers have been doing it for hundreds of years. And once you have your Beast's trust—"

Suddenly Mitzi sneezed, and a bright light burst from

her mouth. The force of it sent her tumbling backward into the snow. She seemed unfazed, though—she immediately rolled over and began gnawing on her tail.

"I don't know why I'm arguing with you," said Viola, sighing. "Any Master in the Woods would be *thrilled* to have you as an apprentice, and you don't even want your Mythic class Beast."

Barclay's stomach gave an unexpected clench. *Thrilled* to have him as an apprentice? *Him?* "W-well," he stammered, caught off guard. "I don't want to be an apprentice either."

"Is that supposed to make me feel better?" She glared at him.

Even if Barclay did believe that his entire predicament was her fault, he couldn't help but feel a little sorry. He knew what it was like to work hard and still not feel as though you'd achieved anything. It was frustrating, and it hurt.

So, rather than pushing the subject, he said, "You mentioned there are five classes. So what is the fifth class?"

"The Legendary class, the most powerful, ferocious Beasts in the world. There are only six. You already know of one of them."

"Gravaldor," Barclay murmured, shuddering. "Can people actually bond with them?"

"They have in stories. But not for a long time, maybe centuries."

"But you were trying to trap Gravaldor. What makes you think *you* can?"

"It's not that I think I can. It's that I need to."

"But that sounds—"

"You know, I'm just trying to help you, and you're being very rude," she snapped. Then she crinkled her nose. "*And* smelly."

Barclay was so surprised by her outburst that he felt more annoyed than sorry. *Touchy, touchy,* Master Pilzmann would say about her. Besides—he sniffed his armpits—he smelled just fine.

He stalked off and sat on the base of a giant tree. It was freezing cold. They still had three more days until they reached Sycomore. And his only companion was the very person who had gotten him into this mess. This was not the adventure that Master Pilzmann had promised him—this was a nightmare.

Something groaned loudly above him, and Barclay stood and whirled around. He saw nothing.

Suddenly his shoulder stung. "Ow," he said, pulling the fabric of his coat and sweater down to see if his cut had opened up again. The wound looked fine, but the Lufthund in the Mark had stopped its usual prowling across his skin and stilled, as though on alert.

Then Barclay heard the sound again. It reminded him of Master Pilzmann's snores—deafening and guttural.

"What is that?" Viola asked from several yards away.

"I can't tell," Barclay said, his dread rising, his Mark stinging all the worse. They had been walking for so long that it'd been easy to forget he was in the Woods . . . and the Woods was deadly.

Suddenly the ground beneath him shook, and roots ruptured the earth. The tree that Barclay had been sitting on bent down low, and he realized the sound he'd heard was its trunk contorting. It twisted and coiled, and the more Barclay stared at it, the more the bark began to look like scales.

The roots withdrew, slithering, and something tremendous burst from the ground, sending a cloud of dirt billowing into the air. Barclay and Viola coughed and stepped back as the roots whipped around and hissed, like a giant tongue.

As the dirt dispersed, two bright amber eyes narrowed at them.

The tree was not a tree at all.

It was a Beast.

EIGHT

In the books Barclay had read from the library, the heroes emerged in times of greatest peril. No villain was too villainous. No monster, too monstrous. For a hero's heart was ironclad and full of courage.

Barclay screamed at a pitch so high, the crows nestled in the surrounding trees cawed and fled to the sky. He dashed toward Viola and clung to her arm as the Beast came into full view.

It looked like a giant snake, with bark instead of scales and eyes the color of tree sap. Its head, which had been buried in the earth, was caked in dirt and crawling with worms and beetles. It slinked closer to the pair of them.

"We should run," said Barclay frantically. Running had always been his best and only strategy.

"It's a Styerwurm, a Prime class. That means it's—"

The snake stretched open its mouth, so wide that it actually turned its jaw inside out. Barclay stared in fright at its endless expanse of stomach—dark and pink.

"Yep, yep," Viola squeaked. "We run."

They took off. The Styerwurm slithered after them, tearing through the trees. Barclay, being smaller and faster, quickly outpaced Viola, and he was far too terrified to turn around to see if she was still behind him. The Beast was every bit as ferocious as the sort in stories he'd heard, and now they were about to be eaten.

Viola screamed, and Barclay finally looked over his shoulder to see her on the ground. She'd tripped and fallen, and the snake was catching up at an alarming speed. Its rootlike tongue stretched through the leaves and snow toward her.

"Help me!" she called.

Barclay, who was a pitiful, cowardly excuse for a hero, who didn't particularly even like Viola, ran back to help her. He grabbed her arm and hoisted her up. A long cut stretched down her shin where she'd scraped it, and she hobbled a bit when she put weight on that leg.

"Thanks," she breathed.

"Never mind that, let's just *go—*"

Barclay's words quickly turned to shrieks when the tongue wrapped around his ankle and yanked him back. He flew through the air, hanging upside down. Belongings from his bag toppled out onto the forest floor, and the world spun around him as the tongue whipped him this way and that.

"Viola!" he screamed.

"Just be calm!" she called. "The Styerwurm has a very weak stomach, so it shakes its victims to death before it eats them."

"How can I be calm when you tell me that?!"

Indeed, the tongue switched from swinging Barclay around to shaking him like a piggy bank. Barclay attempted to kick and pull at it, but its grip would not budge. Spots of black bloomed in his vision.

"Just . . . just hold on! Mitzi, help!" Mitzi emerged from her Mark and appeared on Viola's shoulder with a determined squawk.

A blinding light burst from Mitzi's mouth, the same attack that she had used the day before to ward off the Lufthund. Barclay switched from prying at the tongue to covering his eyes, but the snake, if affected, didn't stop thrashing him. Barclay's breakfast from this morning threatened to return for an explosive encore.

"Is it working?" he shouted. "Because it doesn't feel like it is!"

"I'll try something else!"

The light faded, and Barclay opened his eyes in time to see Viola raise her hands, palms out. A faint beam of red light shot out of them directly at the Styerwurm's forehead, and there was the sound of something sizzling. The snake wrenched back, dropping Barclay into a heap on the snow.

Barclay jumped to his feet and staggered, dizzy, to

Viola's side. He pulled his charm out of his pocket and waved it around, making the air reek of skunks.

"What are you *doing*?" hissed Viola.

"It's a charm! It wards away Beasts."

"That's ridiculous. There's not Lore in it!"

Of course it worked—he'd bought it from Mrs. Esser, Dullshire's most respected charm-maker. But he agreed they needed a better plan.

"Can't you trap it or something?" he asked.

"No. I don't have the right ingredients for a Styerwurm."

"What about bonding with it?"

"You think I want a Beast like this? It's huge! And its brain is the size of a pine cone."

Stupid or not, the Styerwurm only grew angrier at Viola's attack, and it narrowed its eyes at them and slithered forward, paying no mind to Barclay's charm. It opened its jaw wide, wide, wide, and even though Viola stood her ground, Barclay tore off in the opposite direction.

He turned around in enough time to watch Viola get swallowed whole.

"Viola!" he screamed, but he was too late. The Beast's mouth had closed, and Viola and Mitzi were gone.

She's been eaten, he thought wildly, *and I'm next.*

He wished that he could undo all the events of the past few days. That he had never chased after Selby in the Woods. That he had never demanded Viola stop her dangerous trap. That they'd never broken any rules.

But he couldn't take any of that back. And now he was going to die.

"Barclay!" he heard something shout. It sounded an awful lot like Viola, and Barclay realized with extreme panic that it must have been her ghost. "Barclay!"

He looked around for a glimmer of her spirit form but saw nothing. His gaze fearfully fell back on the Beast, who was writhing uncomfortably after eating something it had not had the chance to shake to death first.

"Barclay!"

It was then that he realized that Viola's voice was coming not from the life beyond but from the Beast's stomach. Something jutted out and punched at its abdomen, and it was not indigestion. Viola was *alive*. And she was trapped inside.

With the Beast distracted by its queasiness, Barclay raced to its side, where he'd seen her move. "Viola! I'm here! You need to get out!"

"Of course I need to get out! Do something!" Her voice was muffled by the low groan of the Beast's unhappy stomach.

"What am I supposed to do?"

"Anything!"

Barclay reached into his pocket and grabbed his dull mushroom knife. He plunged it into the Beast's side, but it was too small. It didn't even go past the barky scales.

"I can't!" he screamed.

"Use your Beast! It's a higher class!"

Barclay could think of many reasons why that was a terrible plan. First off, he didn't even know how to summon his Beast. And even if he did, they were already dealing with *one* vicious monster. They certainly didn't need to deal with *two*.

As he hesitated, the Styerwurm whipped around, whacking Barclay on the stomach and sending him flying down a hill. He tumbled to the bottom and landed painfully at the edge of the creek.

A red light burst out of the Beast's stomach and beamed into the sky. As Barclay climbed his way up the hill, he watched in horror as its flesh broke apart and a bloodied hand appeared out of it, reaching for freedom. The slice grew bigger and bigger until it was human-sized. First Mitzi fell out, then Viola after her. Barclay caught them both before they took the same tumble down the slope.

The Beast, in a considerable amount of pain, let out a moan and turned around. It slithered away, and far in the distance, Barclay saw it once again bury its head in the earth.

"Yuck," Barclay said. Viola and Mitzi were covered, every inch of them, in stomach juice. He held one hand to his mouth and used the other to wipe the filth off his clothes.

Viola's curly buns were soaked, and the wispy hairs around her temples were plastered to her face. She wiped the pink gunk off her forehead, only for Mitzi—perched on her shoulder—to shake herself off and fling bile everywhere.

Viola glared at Barclay. "This is your fault!"

"My fault?" he echoed angrily. "You're the one who got yourself eaten."

"Because *you* leaned on that tree that wasn't a tree!"

"Because *you* were being so touchy!"

Viola's nostrils flared, and she jabbed her finger into Barclay's chest.

"You're lucky I thought of something, or I'd be *dead*, no thanks to you. I don't care if you're getting your Mark removed. You're a Lore Keeper, and you could have saved me. Just like I saved you."

Barclay swallowed. She *had* saved him. Even though Barclay didn't want to be a hero on an adventure, if this *were* an epic story, she would be the hero, and he would be the world's absolute worst sidekick.

NINE

After three more days of traveling, the pair had only gotten grumpier. Barclay was exhausted from lying awake every night, terrified they would encounter another humongous, hungry Beast. Viola was irritated from eating almost nothing other than the mushrooms Barclay foraged. And Mitzi was worn out from using her light Lore so much to keep them warm. They'd rarely spoken except to complain about the cold or their sore feet, and so Barclay jolted in surprise when Viola suddenly announced, "We're here!"

At first, Barclay didn't know what she meant. There was no wall, no road, no point where the forest ended and civilization began. But then he saw that the grass and weeds below them grew from the cracks between cobblestones. Trees sprouted up in the middle of streets, lanterns dangling off their branches with fireflies glowing within the glass. The stumpy, ramshackle cottages clustered together like toadstools, decorative wreaths of moss and thorns hanging on their doors. Ivy crept along each building as if the earth was trying to swallow the town whole.

If Sycomore was a bit strange, the people were *outra-geous*. Even Viola, covered head-to-toe in gold pins, didn't stand out much. They wore long cloaks of fur or tweed. Feathered hats, pointy hats, flat hats. Shoes ranging from thigh-high boots to delicate glass slippers. Their features, too, varied widely, with skin in a range of shades different from Barclay's ruddy pale or Viola's light brown. Though most were bundled up for Winter, golden tattoos still peeked out from people's skin, writhing and moving much like Barclay's own.

And *everywhere*—on people's shoulders, poking at windows, playing on chimneys, climbing trees, flying overhead—were Beasts.

A scurry of chipmunks, with tails of thorns and bramble, darted in circles around Barclay's feet. Beehives crystallized in ice bobbed on a few of the trees and tolled like bells as the wind rocked them back and forth. Up ahead, a Beast like a giant moose with golden antlers had fallen asleep in the center of the road, forcing pedestrians to walk around it. Barclay even passed a man carrying a shovel and a bucket whose sole job seemed to be cleaning up droppings along the streets.

Barclay and Viola had not been very friendly since the incident with the Styerwurm, but nevertheless, Barclay still shrunk behind her as they walked, clutching his Beast-warding charm, which—as per usual—seemed to do nothing to keep the Beasts away.

"This is Sycomore," Viola explained. "It's the largest Lore town within the Woods, and it has everything you need. There are apothecaries, Beast kennels, trinket shops, Lore doctors, and one of the six locations of the Guild."

"Where do I need to go to remove my Mark?" Barclay asked. "To a doctor?"

"To the Guild. But I should probably come with you—it can be confusing here."

"Great. Then let's go." The sooner they found someone to help him, the sooner his problem would be fixed and he could go home.

"I have errands to run first," Viola told him.

"For what? More ingredients for your trap for Gravaldor?"

He hoped that wasn't the case and that Viola had changed her mind. If Viola had accidentally gotten herself swallowed by a Prime class Beast, then how would she best a Legendary one?

"No," she sighed. "I'd need the Mourningtide Morel, but it's impossible to find after the first snow. My only other chance is Midwinter, which isn't for a few weeks. And if I'm going to stay in Sycomore for a while, I'll need supplies."

If she was going to stay in Sycomore for a while, she had

time—Barclay didn't. But she was already marching into one of the closest stores. Its windows glittered with gold, and its sign was written in a script Barclay didn't recognize. The symbols were jagged and hooked like the curls of a claw. After a moment examining it, Barclay realized with a start that he could read it. *The Draconis Emporium.*

The bells over the door chimed as Barclay followed Viola inside, resolving to ask her about the mysterious script.

But no sooner had he entered than he came face-to-face with a mouthful of vicious teeth, directly at eye level. He yelped and jumped back, and the shop filled with the chuckles and titters of other customers. A giant skeleton of a dragon, nearly fifty feet long, hung from the shop's ceiling. Its skull and open jaws dangled right in front of the door.

Barclay stooped low to avoid it and wove through the maze of flame repellents, shiny objects, and enchanted dragon scales until he found Viola. She peered into a pot of reptile treats.

"Why can I read the language outside?" His gaze wandered down to the sign beside the treat container, written in the same craggy symbols. It read *Vegetarian*, and he was not the least bit surprised that most of the other pots beside it read *Carnivore*. Clearly, some dragons were just as ferocious as he'd heard.

"It's Lore-speak. Everyone who's bonded with a Beast can read it, just like all Lore Keepers can understand each other, even if we're from all over the world." Viola shoveled a few treats into a burlap pouch. "Haven't you wondered why you haven't heard me make any more mistakes? It's because I haven't been talking in Woods-speak anymore. Admittedly, I *am* pretty good with languages—I've been taught all my life. But even I'm not perfect."

Despite Viola's oh-so-humble proficiency, Barclay still felt silly for not noticing. Even when they'd passed such a diverse array of people on Sycomore's streets, he hadn't considered why he'd never overheard any words he couldn't understand.

Finished with the treats, Viola began rifling through a bowl of gold pins.

"How could you possibly need more pins?" Barclay demanded. Her coat was already covered in them.

"Mitzi likes them. They keep her from nipping at my ears."

The shop owner rushed over and, to Barclay's surprise, gave the two of them a deep bow. Barclay had only ever seen someone bow when they asked a partner to dance. Given that the shop owner was very old and bald, except for a few white hairs that sprouted from behind his ears like onion weeds, Barclay hoped he wasn't asking Viola to dance. For her sake.

"M-miss Dumont!" he sputtered. "I didn't know you'd be paying a visit. Anything! Anything you could want! No charge!"

"Don't be silly, Mr. Buchholz," she answered calmly while Barclay gaped. "I couldn't."

"But of course you can! Tell your father that I absolutely insisted, and—"

Viola pulled a coin purse from her bag and thrust a gold piece into the man's hands. "I'd rather tell him that *I* insisted."

After finishing with her, the man turned to Barclay. Except instead of saying anything, he crinkled his nose and hurried back to his counter.

"What was *that* about?" asked Barclay.

"That? Oh . . . He's just very polite," Viola answered.

"To you, maybe," he muttered.

That was how it went in nearly every shop. Viola purchased new treats for Mitzi. ("The Buzzerbeetle juice and apricot flavors are her favorite," she told him.) And the owners tried to gift her bundles of additional items she didn't need. She also bought herself a new scarf because she claimed her old one still smelled like worm belly, but she walked out with a free pair of mittens as well. Meanwhile, all Barclay got was a few disgusted looks and an uneasy half smile.

Next she and Barclay roamed the shelves of a cramped bookshop.

"It's not just politeness. Why does everyone treat you like you're a princess or something?" Barclay asked. "And why do they treat me like I have mold growing on my teeth?"

"They treat you like that because you smell bad." When Barclay huffed with offense, Viola added, "It's that charm you carry around. It reeks like skunks."

Barclay didn't realize it smelled even when it was in his pocket. He must be used to it. After all, Dullshire had such charms everywhere. The whole town must smell like a herd of skunks, and he'd never realized it.

"And I'm not a princess," Viola continued. "My father is just . . . important." As the bookshop owner passed, she ducked down behind him to avoid notice. "It's a bit annoying, actually. I don't want my father to hear I . . . never mind."

She went back to perusing the book titles, each written in the Lore script. Though Barclay still didn't want anything to do with Lore Keepers, he couldn't help but look through the stacks too. Reading was his favorite pastime, after all, and he was curious what sort of collection a Lore Keeper might keep. There was a yellowed, weathered copy of *An Almost Complete Cartography Collection: Six Half-Done Maps of the Wilderlands*. A glossy paperback of *Ghostly Beasts That Go Bump in the Night*. And a leather-bound edition of *A Traveler's Log of Dangerous Beasts*.

Viola pulled out the last one and flipped through its pages. The writing wasn't printed—it was scribbled and messy, like the notes of a madman.

"I've been wanting to read this! The author, Conley Murdock, is famous. He traveled all across the world studying deadly Beasts. I heard he was writing a sequel, but I guess we'll never read it now. . . ."

"Why? What happened to him?" asked Barclay.

"There was some kind of accident. He was eaten by the Legendary Beast of the Sea. It was front-page news in the *Keeper's Khronicle*. I heard his partner barely made it out—"

"The Sea?" he echoed.

Viola laughed. "The world is a *lot* bigger than just the Woods. There are six major regions to find Beasts, which we call the Wilderlands. There's the Woods, the Desert, the Sea, the Jungle, the Tundra, and the Mountains. Six Wilderlands, six Legendary Beasts."

Truthfully, Barclay had only heard rumors about such places in books. They must have been very far away indeed. The Woods had always seemed endless to him—an entire world to its own.

"Have you ever been to any of them?"

"I've been to the Desert, the Woods, the Jungle, and I live in the Mountains. Mitzi is a Mountain Beast as well. All dragons are."

"What about places that aren't the Wilderlands? Do they have a name?" Barclay asked.

"The Elsewheres," Viola answered, shrugging.

Well, that certainly sounded insignificant. Barclay felt a bit snubbed on Dullshire's behalf.

Then Viola snapped *A Traveler's Log* closed. "You know, I think I'll buy this. I'm sure there's loads I could learn about Gravaldor in here."

She counted the number of coins left in her purse. Then

she reached into her bag and pulled out *another* purse, also full.

Barclay swallowed down the urge to ask how rich she was, deciding that was rather rude. Instead, he examined one of the heavy gold coins—one side engraved with a dragon, the other triangular peaks of what he guessed were the Mountains, though a few of them had trees instead. He frowned. "What kind of money is that?"

"It's Lore money—kritters, we call it. You probably just have Elsewheres money, don't you?"

A sick feeling filled Barclay's stomach. He hadn't even considered that Sycomore would use different money than Dullshire.

"Don't worry," Viola told him. "I'll pay for removing your Mark."

"No, definitely not," said Barclay quickly. He was used to working for what he needed. No work meant no food—no charity, no exceptions.

She gave him a pointed look. "It's no trouble. And it will be hard to find a Lore Keeper willing to help you for free."

"Then I'll find one who will take *my* money."

"No one will. Just let me—"

Barclay groaned as she jingled her purse. He might have been an orphan, but he still had his pride. He left her to her errands and stormed out of the shop.

Even though he didn't know his way around Sycomore, it wasn't hard to find the Guild. It was the largest building in town, with a massive, snowy tree jutting right out of its center. To Barclay's surprise, several tiles on its roof were missing, its windows caked with dirt, and its wooden frame termite-eaten. A fraying banner hung from the awning.

WOODS APPRENTICE EXHIBITION
60+ LORE MASTERS IN ATTENDANCE
ALL LORE KEEPERS AGES 9–14
WELCOME TO REGISTER

Several kids his age crowded beneath it. They were dressed as outrageously as the rest of Sycomore: tip-dyed pelts, clothes embroidered with golden thread, swords slung over their shoulders—all so different from the plain styles of Dullshire. Several had young Beasts growling at their feet or cradled in their arms.

"I heard the Horn of Dawn and the Fang of Dusk will be there," one girl said excitedly.

"That's why you're here, right, Tadg?" another asked.

"The Horn of Dawn and the Fang of Dusk nearly killed each other in a duel to the death. You think they'd both be anywhere at the same time?"

The boy who answered—Tadg, Barclay assumed—had an unmistakable sneer in his voice. That didn't seem to stop the other kids from watching him with wide, awestruck expressions. Tadg looked about Barclay's age, with fair skin and light brown curls that shadowed his cold, bored expression. His sleeves were rolled up, revealing a golden Beast Mark that coiled and snaked across his hand and reappeared above his collar—so large it covered his entire arm.

Barclay didn't know this boy, but he reminded him of Falk. Kids who only got to be leaders by acting smug and better than everyone else.

Barclay ignored the group as he strode toward bulletin boards covered in hundreds of pieces of parchment. They said things like LICENSED SURVEYORS NEEDED TO EXCAVATE VALUABLE LOST BEAST ARTIFACTS and KEEPERS TO HELP SAVE THE FELSNIPS FROM EXTINCTION and GUARDIANS NEEDED TO PROTECT TOWN FROM PACK OF MISKREATS.

Each of them offered a reward.

Barclay could put up a flyer of his own. With so many Lore Keepers in town for the Exhibition, surely someone would know how to help him. But he had one problem: he had no reward to give.

It was hard to concentrate on this problem, however, because the kids behind him had begun to chatter louder.

"The Fang of Dusk is the one who's here," said the last kid. "It's why my parents let me travel to the Woods and enter a year early, even though next year's Exhibition will be at home in the Jungle."

"But the Fang of Dusk has never accepted apprentices

before!" the first girl squeaked, and nearly dropped the fox-like Beast asleep in her arms.

"Maybe no one's good enough for her," Tadg said, shrugging.

The boy next to him looked shocked. "But you have a Mythic Beast! If anyone has a chance, it's—"

Barclay, unable to help himself, let out a loud snort. After all, *he* had a Mythic Beast. He hadn't even been trying to bond with it, so how hard could it have been?

His outburst earned him a number of suspicious and annoyed looks from the group. He quickly cleared his throat and turned back to the bulletin board.

"You have something to add, do you?" Tadg demanded.

Barclay was so used to running from Falk that he peeked down the street for an exit. "No," he replied nervously. "I didn't say anything."

Tadg squinted at him. "You have a reason to be skulking outside of the Guild?"

Barclay didn't like the idea of talking to Tadg or his band of admirers, but if they were entering the Exhibition, then they *were* Lore Keepers. Maybe they could help him—or find someone who could.

"I'm looking for help." He spoke with his best grown-up-pleasing voice, which he used in Dullshire whenever he'd been spotted breaking a rule. But it didn't work here. In fact, it made several of their expressions sour. "Maybe you know someone who could help me?"

"Help with what?" asked Tadg, his arms crossed.

"I'm looking to remove my Beast tattoo. I mean, my Mark."

All at once, the group burst out in laughter.

"I knew it! Listen to him talk! He's an Elsie!"

"He's smells like a skunk!"

"It's probably just a Dizzisnuff that he thinks will kill him."

"How did he even make it here without being eaten?"

Barclay's face heated at their words, and he was about to storm away when Tadg stepped into his path. His usual sneer was even meaner.

"If you're worried that your Beast will escape, even an Elsie like *you* could control a Familiar class bond."

"It's not Familiar class," Barclay said darkly.

Tadg raised his eyebrows. "You're probably confused. Summon it, then. We'll set you straight." His voice choked, as though he was trying to stop himself from laughing again.

Barclay didn't know how to summon the Lufthund. Nor did summoning a Beast so dangerous in a crowded square sound like a good idea. Even if Viola assured him it wouldn't happen again, this reminded him too much of what had happened at Dullshire's festival, when Barclay's powers had gone out of control.

Just then, a woman appeared behind Barclay and put her hand on his shoulder. She had wild, dark hair that hung to her waist and a collection of different weapons slung in her belt. They were each far larger than his mushroom knife.

"I know someone who might be able to help you," she told Barclay.

In her presence, the others stopped their laughter and shot one another nervous looks.

"You do? I'd be really grateful if you could recommend me," Barclay said. He used his grown-up-pleasing voice again, and this time it earned him an approving look from the woman. Even if her grip on his shoulder was a little too tight.

She pointed down the street. "Go to the Bog's Inn and ask for Soren Reiker."

Barclay muttered a thank-you and began to walk away. However, for the second time, Tadg blocked his path, eyeing the woman warily.

"Do you have another joke to add?" Barclay asked sharply.

Tadg opened his mouth to speak, but then he seemed to think better of it. He shook his head and stepped back, letting Barclay pass.

Barclay stalked off down the street wishing that Sycomore could be—if only a little bit—more like home.

TEN

The farther Barclay walked in the direction the woman had pointed, the bleaker his surroundings turned. The trees, once sparse, now covered most of the street, forcing Barclay to climb and weave his way down the path. Branches and thorns snagged at his clothes. Four-eyed Beasts lurked in the treetops, watching him ominously as though tracking their supper.

The Bog's Inn looked as dismal as its neighborhood. The sign creaked and swung even though no wind blew. Most of its windows were boarded up.

Barclay warily pushed open the door and entered a lounge. The innkeeper peered at him shrewdly from behind the reception desk. She wore an eyepatch with a brass button sewn in the center, like the eye of a doll.

"What brings you here?" she crooned.

"I'm looking for a man named Soren Reiker."

She nodded and leaned behind her desk, looking at something Barclay couldn't see. "Go fetch the man on the top floor."

Barclay expected a small child, or maybe even a dog, but to his horror, a giant ratlike Beast scurried from behind the desk. Its tail was made of metal plates, and they screeched loudly against the wood floor as it scampered up the stairs.

The old woman gave Barclay a smile. Most of her teeth were missing. "Would you like some tea?"

Barclay would actually love a cup of chaga mushroom tea after so many days spent wandering in the cold, but he didn't want any here. He rubbed his arms, but his hair wouldn't stop standing on end. He was considering giving up on the creepy Bog's Inn and finding Viola when a man appeared at the foot of the stairs.

"What can I do for you?" he asked in a chipper voice. He was clean-shaven and wore expensive clothes, and his teeth—unlike the innkeeper's—were all accounted for and very straight. He was even sort of handsome, like a hero from an adventure story. "My name is Soren Reiker."

Barclay shook Soren's hand. "My name is Barclay, Barclay Thorne. I'm looking for someone who might be able to help me remove a Beast Mark."

Soren gave him a sympathetic smile. "Took on a bit more than you could handle, did you?"

"It was all an accident," Barclay explained.

"I'm sure it was," said Soren kindly. "But it's a tough job, removing a Mark. There are some questions I need to ask, as I'm sure you understand." He placed his hand on Barclay's shoulder, making him wince from his healing wound where the Lufthund had slashed him. "I charge fifty thousand kritters for all Familiar class Marks."

That seemed a good deal higher than the posts Barclay had seen at the Guild, but Soren quickly soothed his nerves.

"It's expensive, I realize. But like I said, it's a tough job. And not many people can do it, you know."

Barclay withered. "I only have Elsewheres money."

Soren's grip on his shoulder tightened a bit.

"That's too bad. It's not worth very much if the people of the Elsewheres don't let us spend it. But don't look so down. A boy your age with a Familiar class bond can get a good job in this town. Tell me, what sort of Beast is it? A Dizzisnuff? A Ziggopatch? They're well suited to apothecary shops—"

"It's a Lufthund."

Soren's eyes widened.

"That can't be right. Lufthunds are exceedingly rare and difficult for even an experienced Lore Keeper to bring down. There are few Beasts like them in the whole Woods!"

Barclay hesitated. Viola had sounded quite sure, but it had all happened so quickly. She could easily have been mistaken. Barclay had always been more inclined to believe grown-ups.

"I'm not sure," Barclay admitted. "But I think that's what the Mark looks like."

Soren paused for a moment, then he smiled wider. "Well, let's figure that out for you. I'll do it free of charge. After all, it's important to know what Beast you've bonded with."

He steered Barclay in the direction of the stairs, and the two climbed up to Soren's rooms. They were clean and polished, unlike the rest of the inn. He had a number of papers strewn about his desk, along with several jars. Barclay recognized a few from the items Viola once had, like the bubbling green goo and lump of dead bugs.

"Let's start with examining the Mark," Soren said. "Can I take a look at it?"

Barclay shrugged off his heavy overcoat and showed Soren his shoulder. The angry gashes across it had stopped swelling, but they still burned a vicious red. The gold Mark of the wolflike Beast was visible below it.

Soren sat down on a stool and put on a pair of horn-rimmed spectacles. "Looks like he took a chunk out of you." He gingerly pressed on the Mark, and Barclay winced. "What do you know about Lufthunds, Barclay?"

"Not much. I know they're Mythic class. And I remember how it looked. Like a wolf."

"Yes. Lufthunds appear rather canine. At full maturity, they can grow to be four feet tall and six feet long. They're clever hunters, but not pack animals, like traditional wolves. Their loyalty is hard to earn, but once achieved, nearly unbreakable. Apart from flying Beasts, they are the fastest species in the world. They've been known to dissolve completely into wind. Their howls can conjure storms. Their

Keepers are also given tremendous speed, and several other wind abilities as well. The powers of a Keeper complement the Beast, you know."

There was something strange in Soren's voice, but Barclay couldn't put his finger on it.

Then a stinging pain shot through his Mark, just like in the Woods before the Styerwurm had attacked. Like a warning, Barclay realized.

Soren reached over to his desk and grabbed a number of instruments: some gauze, an elixir, and a scalpel.

"You were right, Barclay. I think we do have a Lufthund on our hands," he said breathlessly.

"What are all those tools for?"

"I'm going to remove it, like you asked. Don't worry—it will be free of charge."

Soren pressed the edge of the scalpel against Barclay's shoulder, and Barclay jolted back.

"You're going to cut it off?" he asked, horrified.

"I need to see how deep it goes. It's a shame it's so large— some even touches your chest. Removing your arm? That would be easy. Clean. The chest? That gets messier."

Barclay tried to scramble to his feet, but even though Soren was no longer touching him, Barclay suddenly felt a firm hand pushing him down.

Wisps of white swirled about the room. And then Barclay *saw* the hand clutching him. It was pale and skeletal, its bones held together with nothing but air. A figure began to come together beside him, and it was tall and gaunt and looked like it was made of smoke. It stood on two legs with hunched shoulders—almost like a human—but its long, narrow face reminded him more of a stag. Antlers grew out of its head in all directions. Its eyes sockets, empty and large, glowed crimson.

Barclay screamed but didn't make a sound. The noise flew from his lips in white curls of smoke, and the Beast opened its mouth and swallowed them.

"This is an Ischray," Soren told Barclay, his voice still calm as Barclay began to panic and squirm in his seat. "He's truly remarkable. He can silence any noise. Ischrays are rare enough to be Mythic class, but they unfortunately aren't powerful enough to pass the Prime class. But I'm still rather fond of him. I'm a collector, if you will."

Soren pressed the knife into Barclay's skin.

"And now your Lufthund will be mine too."

Barclay should've heeded the sinister signs of the Bog's Inn. Should've run as soon as he felt the warning pain in his Mark. He'd been so desperate for help that he'd left Viola and wandered right into a trap, and Viola wasn't here to save him now.

Come out! Come out! he thought frantically. He didn't know how to summon his Beast, but Tadg and the others had made it seem so simple. *Come out!*

A gust of wind tore across the room, making tears run from Barclay's eyes and sending Soren's papers fluttering to the floor. For a brief moment, the Ischray thrashed, its body of wisps and smoke blowing apart. Then the air stilled, and it came back together.

The Lufthund stood in the corner of the room. It had black fur, matching its black claws and black teeth. Though not nearly as large as Soren had described, it was the size of an average wolf—probably not fully grown yet. Its fur was thickest along its face and around its neck, thinning all the way down its back to where the vertebrae protruded out and Barclay could see its bones.

It lowered its head and growled.

"What a beauty," Soren breathed, and he stood up, leaving Barclay pinned down by his terrifying Ischray.

Attack him! Help me! Barclay thought, but the Lufthund didn't seem to listen. It only growled once more as Soren approached it with an outstretched hand.

"Shhh, boy," Soren tried to calm it.

Don't listen to him! Do something!

The Lufthund glanced over and met Barclay's eyes briefly. They were dark, just like his.

Then it snapped its head away, ignoring him and his distress.

Soren had talked about Lufthunds like they were undefeatable. Where were those gusts of wind now? The howls that brought storms?

But then Barclay remembered: he had powers as well, even if he didn't know how to control them. That meant even without the Lufthund's help, Barclay wasn't defenseless.

A wind! A breeze! Something!

Barclay fanned at the air, tried to whistle, snapped his fingers . . . nothing. The Ischray watched him curiously, and its head bent lower. Barclay turned his face away as the chilling wisps of the Ischray's body grazed his cheek.

What had happened in Dullshire was chance—he hadn't even understood what he was doing. It was foolish to think Barclay could use his powers on command without practice, without knowing anything about his Beast.

But he needed to think of something. He needed to be clever.

When Barclay had told Soren that the only things he knew about the Lufthund were its name, its class, and what it looked like, he'd been wrong. He remembered what had happened in the Woods when they'd bonded. He remembered running faster than he ever had in his life. He remembered the Lufthund keeping pace beside him. He remembered what that felt like, to be faster than the wind.

He reached his hand up toward the Beast's face, and he thought about that feeling.

Wind!

A torrent of air rushed out of Barclay's palm toward the Ischray. Its wispy body burst apart like a fractured cloud, and Barclay jumped to his feet before it could put itself back together.

"Stop!" Soren growled at him, but the Lufthund growled louder. It pounced on Soren as Barclay threw open the door and raced downstairs. He barreled through the lounge and into the woodsy street outside. A breeze blew past his neck as he ran, and Barclay turned to see the Lufthund beside him.

They met eyes once again. *Thank you,* Barclay told it. And he meant it, even if he didn't want to feel grateful to the Beast that had ruined his life.

The Lufthund nodded like it'd understood. Then its black form faded, as though blown away in the wind. Barclay felt his skin prickle as his Mark came alive once more.

Soren shouted after him, but he was already in the distance. Because when Barclay ran, it was very hard to catch him.

ELEVEN

Barclay found Viola standing outside the crumbling Guild House, her hands on her hips, Mitzi hissing on her shoulder. He was so relieved he could have kissed Mitzi on her little whelp snout.

"You just ran off!" Viola hissed. "I looked everywhere, and I've been waiting for ages."

"You have?"

After Barclay had stormed out of the bookshop, he'd doubted she wanted to see him. Especially when he seemed to be the only person in this town not showering her with praise and gifts.

"Of course I have," she huffed. "Sycomore isn't like Dullshire. You could get into trouble on your own."

Barclay nervously glanced over his shoulder, but Soren was far, far behind him, on the other side of town. Barclay had learned his lesson; he wouldn't leave Viola's side again.

"Speaking of trouble . . ."

Barclay told her about what had happened while they'd been separated, including every detail of his frightening encounter with Soren.

"I don't understand," Barclay sputtered. "He must have been breaking the law. He tried to steal my Beast! He tried to kill me!"

Viola hesitated, then gently said, "Of course he was breaking the law. But around here, I'm not sure the law is very important."

"What do you mean?"

"The Woods has a reputation for being . . . how do I put this nicely . . . rustic?"

"Rustic?" Barclay repeated, confused.

"Backward? Bumpkin? Middle of nowhere? Sycomore isn't just the largest town in the Woods; it's the *only* town in the Woods. The other Wilderlands have cities and monuments and universities, and the Woods has . . . trees. That's why the Guild House looks so rundown—the chapter here doesn't receive much funding. And I've heard that the man who runs Sycomore doesn't care much about rules or lawbreakers."

Barclay had never heard something so ridiculous. He didn't care about *rules*? Dullshire had too many rules, certainly, but not all of them were silly. No wonder Sycomore was chaos.

"Then how do you stop people from doing bad things?" he asked fretfully.

She put a comforting hand on Barclay's shoulder.

"I don't know, and I don't like the way things are done here, same as you. Because you're not a Lore Keeper and you've bonded with a really powerful Beast, people will try to take advantage of you. And we can't let them."

Viola had said "we." He still didn't want her money, and she might have been the person who got him bonded with a Beast in the first place, but he was grateful for her help. It was nice to know that he wasn't alone.

"So come on," Viola said. "Let's go find someone who can really help you remove your Mark."

When Viola turned to enter the Guild House, she glanced up and frowned at the tattered Exhibition banner.

"I didn't realize this was happening so early," she said. "No wonder it's so crowded with travelers here. I wonder if . . ." She shook her head, suddenly fidgety. "No. He wouldn't be."

"Is there a problem?" Barclay asked.

She plastered on a smile that looked quite fake and straightened several of her pins and brooches that had gone crooked.

"No, this is good. Removing Marks isn't common knowledge, so it's lucky for us that a number of accomplished Lore Masters are in Sycomore right now."

Then she pushed open the doors and motioned for him to follow her inside.

Based on Viola's descriptions of the Guild, Barclay had imagined it to look more like an office. Instead, it looked like a pub. The inside, much like the outside, was falling apart. Wobbly barstools were missing legs. The uneven wooden floor was sloshed with beer. The green paint was peeling off the walls like skin after a sunburn.

It was cozy, at least. A brown coat of arms hung over the fireplace mantel, and the walls around it were decorated with plaques of stuffed Beast heads and maps of places Barclay had never heard of before. The thick tree that sprouted up and grew from the room's center was covered from top to bottom with nailed flyers. Beasts of all sorts perched in the rafters or crawled across the floor, growling and hooting and munching on fallen scraps.

"Like I said before," Viola told him, "there are six Guild locations around the world, one in each Wilderland. The headquarters is in the Mountains, where the Grand Keeper is. Everywhere else just has a High Keeper who runs the place. The High Keeper here is Kasimir Erhart."

She pointed to a man on a couch by the fireplace. He had a long, matted gray beard that covered most of his embellished tunic. His head hung back, his mouth open. He was fast asleep. It was no wonder he didn't care about rules if he'd rather nap all day than do his job.

The young woman beside him didn't seem to mind that he slept. She wore a long braid of dull blond hair tucked beneath a slouchy oversized coat that reminded him of a

Dullshire sentry uniform, very soldierlike, with lots of chainmail. Barclay couldn't see her face, but from here, it looked as though she was staring intently into the flames.

Viola searched around the room, and she pointed at a group of people sitting at a high-top table. "I recognize them! They've done work for my father."

She strutted over to them, leaving Barclay no choice but to follow.

There were three people at the table. The first was a man with brown skin and copper glasses shaped like hexagons. The second, a woman, had red hair knotted with twigs and leaves, and fair skin covered in dirt, as though she'd been unearthed only minutes before, like a fresh mushroom. Last was another woman, also light-skinned, but much smaller and older—so small and old, in fact, that Barclay was shocked to see the five empty mugs of beer in front of her.

"Viola Dumont," the man said with surprise. "What are you doing in the Woods? I thought you were apprenticed to Cyril Harlow."

Viola flushed. "I am. I've just been traveling alone, for the time being."

The man said nothing, only raised his eyebrows and swept his gaze over the two of them.

"This is my friend, Barclay Thorne." She shoved Barclay forward. "Barclay, this is Mandeep." She nodded at the man. "And this is Floriane. And Athna." She pointed at the dirt-covered woman and the elderly one. "Barclay needs some advice, if you don't mind us asking."

"Not at all." Floriane gestured to the two open stools. "Please, sit. What is it that you need?"

"I'm trying to remove my Beast Mark," Barclay explained, taking a seat. "It bonded with me by accident, and I don't want it."

"You're not the first Elsie to want your Mark removed," Floriane said gently.

"But it's not possible," Mandeep cut in.

Floriane shot Mandeep an annoyed look. "I know this might be hard for you to believe, but just because *you* don't know how to do something doesn't mean it's impossible."

Mandeep pursed his lips and leaned forward. "Do you know the different types of Lore Keepers, Barclay?"

In Dullshire, there was only one type of Lore Keeper: the unwanted kind. After meeting Tadg and then Soren, the only Lore Keeper who had proven a better sort was Viola.

Rather than saying that, Barclay politely shook his head.

"There are Lore Keepers who gather Beasts to brew potions, enchantments, and the like. Apothecaries, we call them. Like Floriane." Floriane smiled brightly. "There are Surveyors, Lore Keepers who save Beasts from extinction or who search for new Beasts, never seen before. Like Athna." The older woman gave no indication of hearing her name and only finished her stein of beer. "There are Lore Keepers who study the magic of Lore itself, like me. A Scholar."

He straightened proudly.

"And as a Scholar, I can tell you, there is no way to remove a Beast Mark that wouldn't kill you."

Barclay felt all his dreams wither into dust. He managed to nod like he understood, even though he did not. He didn't understand how something so unlucky could happen to him. He didn't understand how the people he grew up with had so easily cast him out. He didn't understand why the world had to be unfair.

"But I *need* to go home," he said, quickly molding his hopelessness into determination. "I traveled all the way here. I ran from a giant worm. A man even attacked me to try to steal my Beast. There has to be a way!"

Mandeep's eyes widened. "Who attacked you?"

"Soren Reiker."

The three of them exchanged dark looks.

"I'm sorry, but I'm afraid there isn't much we can do about it," Mandeep told him. "Soren is very popular here, and he's close friends with the High Keeper. He could strip us of our Guild licenses if we tried to stop him. It's not fair, but that's how it is here."

Viola had already told Barclay as much, but he still couldn't help but feel a mixture of shock and disappointment.

Floriane cleared her throat. "Don't listen to Mandeep about your Mark. He just likes knowing things, whether or not he's right."

"Then who would *you* suggest to the boy, who would

know better than me how to remove it?" Mandeep asked with annoyance.

"Runa Rasgar," Athna said. Her voice was surprisingly steady for all her beers, though she did let out a loud belch.

"Who is that?" Barclay asked hopefully.

"The Fang of Dusk," Floriane explained. "She's a Guardian, a Lore Keeper who specializes in protecting the people of both the Wilderlands and the Elsewheres. Using enchantments to keep Beasts within the places where they should be, like the Woods."

Barclay didn't realize any Lore Keepers did things like that. Then he recognized the nickname. Tadg and the other would-be apprentices had mentioned her earlier that day. The Fang of Dusk was famous. And important.

"How do I talk to her?" Barclay asked.

"She's right over there." Floriane nodded toward the fireplace, to the woman sitting silently beside the High Keeper.

"But she's with the High Keeper," Barclay said uncertainly. She could be as bad as Soren.

"Oh, I wouldn't worry about that," Mandeep told him. "I don't think I've ever seen someone so unhappy to be a guest of honor. Erhart hasn't left her side all day, trying to show her off to all the visitors and giving her a grand tour. I bet his nap is the first peace she's had since she got here."

"Well, we can't just go over and talk to her," Viola hissed.

"Why not?" asked Barclay. "I thought your father was important. You can talk to anyone."

Mandeep gave him a faint smile. "I'm afraid *we* are anyone. Runa Rasgar is not."

"She's frightening," Floriane said.

"She's respected," Mandeep countered.

"Then what are we?"

"Tolerated," Athna muttered into her empty stein.

Though Barclay was grateful for their help, he wasn't much fazed by their warning. He was used to convincing people to help him. It had taken him dozens of tries to convince Master Pilzmann to make him his apprentice, after all. Barclay would *not* give up. Not yet.

He gave them a polite thank-you, and—despite Viola's protests—marched over to Runa and the snoring High Keeper.

Barclay cleared his throat. "Um, excuse me, Miss Rasgar?"

Runa turned around, and Barclay saw that the right side of her face was marred with a gruesome scar, where sharp claws had raked across her pale skin nearly all the way to her ear.

"I suppose that name belongs to me," she said, "though I'm not used to being called 'Miss.'"

Her cool gray eyes swept over the two of them and settled on Viola, who looked more uncomfortable than Barclay had ever seen her.

"Viola Dumont . . . How is Cyril?"

"H-he's well," Viola managed. She fretfully fiddled with

her pins again, even ones that didn't need straightening.

"How unfortunate," Runa responded. "Whatever you've come to ask, do keep it brief. I don't want Erhart to wake up. He keeps asking for money . . . desperate to fix this place . . ."

"Please, Miss Rasgar." Once again Barclay used his grown-up-pleasing voice. Runa gave him no smile, but Barclay wasn't certain she was the sort of person who smiled, anyway. "I'm looking for a way to remove my Beast Mark. Is it possible?"

Her gaze returned to him. He swallowed.

"It's possible, but dangerous. More so depending on the Beast."

"It's a Lufthund," he told her.

Runa was the first person who didn't looked shocked by this statement. "And you want to be rid of it? Do you realize how many others your age would give anything for such a powerful Beast?" She snorted, glancing around the room. "How half of these Masters would do the same?"

Barclay was already well aware of how far other Lore Keepers were willing to go.

"I just want to go home," he said firmly.

"Where is home?"

"Dullshire."

"The town that was destroyed by Gravaldor seven years ago, yes?" Her face—ever so slightly—softened. "How long have you been in Sycomore?"

"Since this morning."

"Tell me, what do you think of Sycomore? Of Lore Keepers?"

"It's . . ." Barclay's face reddened from lying. "Different."

"You can be honest."

He looked at his boots. The room was loud with Lore Keepers laughing, with Beasts cawing and howling, the fire crackling. Dullshire was never this loud, this unfamiliar. Dullshire had no men willing to saw off arms to steal Beasts. Nobody laughed at him for being an "Elsie." In Dullshire, even if the laws sometimes annoyed Barclay, there were *real* rules, good and bad, right and wrong.

"I hate it," he said softly. Beside him, an expression of hurt crossed Viola's face.

"A fair assessment," said Runa, "for someone who has only been here since this morning."

Barclay opened his mouth to tell her that his opinion wouldn't change no matter how long he stayed, except Runa continued.

"I'm going to help you, but only on one condition. The Exhibition is beginning—it's why I'm in Sycomore. The Exhibition is a series of exams for potential students to showcase their skills and their Beasts so that they can be taken on as apprentices with the Guild. It's very difficult— even dangerous."

Of course it's dangerous, Barclay thought. *Everything here is.*

"And if you place first in the Exhibition," Runa continued, "I will tell you how to remove your Mark."

Barclay gaped. "*First?* But I . . . I don't know anything about Lore!"

"I'm not trying to play with you or humiliate you. If you're not strong enough to place first, then you won't survive removing your Mark. I will not kill you. So prove to me that, if I help you, I won't."

TWELVE

O utside it had begun to snow, and Barclay shivered as he stomped to the town square, Viola tripping over herself to keep up.

"The Exhibition starts tomorrow," Viola told him.

Barclay's already terrible mood soured further.

"There are three events, one each week for three weeks."

Three weeks stuck in Sycomore.

"Runa was right to call the Exhibition dangerous. Apprentices have been known to get injured—even die—"

"Just *stop*, Viola!" Barclay shouted, whipping around. "You're not helping. How am I supposed to compete? I don't know anything about magic—"

"About *Lore*—"

"I'll get myself killed! Or make a fool of myself! Either way, I won't win, and I won't be able to go home."

Barclay's imagination was already conjuring up terrible futures for himself. He could stay in Sycomore forever, cleaning up Beast droppings along the streets until a Beast accidentally ate him. He could run off to some faraway village, change his name, grow a beard, and speak to no one until the day he died.

"You won't be hopeless! You'll probably be the only apprentice in the Exhibition with a Mythic class Beast."

"I don't think so," Barclay said, thinking of Tadg. "Besides, that won't matter if I'm the first apprentice in Sycomore to be eaten by my own Beast."

Viola rolled her eyes. "Are you going to enter or not?"

Barclay sighed, his anger already settling into something sharper, harder—like stone forged into steel.

Viola didn't know him very well. She only knew him as an Elsie, but Barclay was more than that. He was the boy who'd had to work for his every meal. Who'd memorized everything he could about mushrooms before he even started his apprenticeship so he could prove to Master Pilzmann that he was worthy of the job. Who'd never had anyone looking out for him.

"Of course I'll enter," he said determinedly. "I could die. I could make a fool of myself. But I'm still going to try to win."

At that, Viola took him by the shoulder and marched him around to the back of the Guild House, where kids lined up in front of a registration table. Barclay recognized a few of the faces from earlier, including Tadg. He was, once again, surrounded by a crowd of admirers. He kept his sleeves rolled up to show off his massive snakelike Beast Mark, even though it was bitterly cold.

Viola untucked her scarf from her coat and wrapped it around her head like a makeshift hood, then yanked it down so that it nearly covered her eyes. It looked a bit funny, though, as her hair buns made it all lumpy.

"What are you doing?" asked Barclay.

"I don't want to be recognized."

"Afraid people will dote on you?"

"No," she snapped. "I'm afraid people will think *I'm* entering. There will be gossip."

Her words reminded him of what the three Lore Masters had said earlier, that Viola was the apprentice to a man named Cyril Harlow.

"You're already a Guild apprentice, aren't you?" he asked.

"Yes," she squeaked, ducking behind his shoulder. She clearly cared a lot about what people thought about her.

"Do apprentices often travel without their Masters?"

"Um, yes. All the time."

He narrowed his eyes. Every person in Sycomore had been surprised to see her here.

Before he could question her further, he was interrupted by commotion ahead of them.

"What did you say to me?" a voice sneered.

Barclay recognized that voice, and he turned to see it

belonged to Tadg. He was leering at two kids who appeared to be brother and sister—twins. They were the same height, with the same scruffy brown hair, beige skin, and patchy coats. They each had a dark birthmark on their cheek. For the boy, it was on his left. For the girl, it was on her right. Like mirrors of each other.

"I didn't say anything," the boy grunted. He fumbled with a strange deck of cards, each black and shaped like a hexagon.

"Yes you did," Tadg growled. "I dare you to say it again."

The girl stepped in between them. "Abel was only wishing you luck. As a fellow competitor." She held out her hand for Tadg to shake.

He did, but once their hands touched, the girl let out a startled cry and wrenched hers back. It happened too quickly for Barclay to see what Tadg had done. Some sort of sneaky magic, he suspected.

"Get away from her!" Abel shouted, pushing Tadg away. Abel's deck of cards spilled to the snow.

Barclay was shocked to see the adults at the registration desk do nothing to break up the fight. He was even more shocked when Tadg, stumbling back, caught eyes with *him*.

"You! Elsie!" he called.

"Just ignore him," Viola muttered, and Barclay nodded and turned away. For the next few minutes in line, Barclay felt Tadg's stares hot on his back.

The man at the registration desk unrolled a new sheet of parchment. He wore square spectacles and a dark green fur coat. "Name, age, and hometown?" he asked Barclay.

"Barclay Thorne. Eleven. Dullshire."

The man glanced up at him with furrowed eyebrows but didn't comment. "How many Beasts do you have?"

"One."

"What is its species?"

"It's a Lufthund."

The man dropped his quill in surprise, splattering ink on Barclay's application. "A-and its name?"

"Its name?" Barclay had never thought to give his Beast a name.

"Yes. What do you call it?"

"Um . . ."

"I like Alpha! That's sort of wolflike," Viola suggested. "Or Loup! I know a Keeper with a wolf sort of Beast with that name. . . ."

"Why would I name it?" Barclay mumbled. "It's not a pet! It's the root of all my problems, that's what it is."

The man nodded and wrote down *Root*. Then he slid the parchment around.

"You need to sign here. It acknowledges that you understand the risks involved with the Exhibition, which could result in the injury or fatality of you and/or your Beast."

Barclay's hand didn't shake as he signed. He was ready for this—whatever it took.

Then he muttered a goodbye and turned around, bumping directly into Tadg's chest. His arms were crossed.

"What happened to removing your Mark?" Tadg asked. "Careful. In the Exhibition, you might be in over your head."

"I don't need you looking out for me," Barclay grunted.

"I'm surprised they let you enter, being an Elsie. I can't wait for the practical round. We can all take bets on how fast you'll be eaten."

"Or how fast you'll be eating your words," Viola countered.

Tadg's gaze turned to her. She still wore her scarf down over her face. He squinted at her. "You look familiar."

She snapped her mouth shut, as though she hadn't meant to speak. Then she yanked the scarf down lower. "Doubt it."

"You're the Dumont girl! The daughter of the Grand Keeper."

The others around them stopped chattering to stare.

The Grand Keeper? Barclay thought. No wonder everyone treated Viola like a princess. Her father wasn't just "important"—he was the head of the Lore Keeper world!

"No, no," she said quickly, her voice weaker than Barclay had ever heard it. "You're mistaking me for—"

"I thought you were apprenticed to the Horn of Dawn?" Tadg asked.

Viola seemed to give up trying to lie, but she still stared at her boots. "I was—I mean, I am. I'm not competing. I'm here to support my friend."

Tadg peered at Barclay more curiously, then he scoffed, "An Elsie isn't worth your support."

Barclay pulled Viola away, then he spotted the twins waving at them from the edge of the snowy courtyard and headed toward them.

"We saw Tadg giving you trouble," said Abel. He dried the snow off his strange cards with his threadbare sweater. Up close, Barclay saw that all the cards had people drawn on them—the top one was of Runa Rasgar, the scar on her face just as gruesome as it had looked in person.

"Seems like there's a club," his sister mumbled. Around her shoulders, she carried a backpack near to bursting with notebooks and Beast-like figurines. It looked too heavy to carry, but the girl seemed unfazed by its weight.

"What did you say to him earlier that made him so angry?" Barclay asked.

Abel shrugged. "You know . . . He looks for reasons to be angry. He doesn't like anyone who doesn't fawn all over him just because he has a Mythic class Beast."

Barclay seemed to remember it was Abel who had started the argument, but knowing Tadg, Barclay didn't blame him.

"It *is* kind of impressive," the girl said, sighing wistfully. "I'd love to see it, just once. I could sketch it or take some notes. I've never—"

"Traitor," Abel muttered.

His sister shrugged, then she stuck out her hand for Barclay to shake. "I'm Ethel Zader. This is Abel, my brother."

"I'm Viola, and this is Barclay," Viola told them.

"Is it true that you're the daughter of the Grand Keeper? And you're from the towns beyond the Woods?"

Viola and Barclay both nodded hesitantly.

Ethel and Abel smiled, a matching starry look in their brown eyes. "That's neat," they said together.

Barclay had been prepared for more snickering, so their eagerness was a surprise. Bullies like Tadg and Falk he was used to. Friends . . . not so much.

"We're from the Woods," Abel said blandly. "Just like nearly all the Lore Masters and students. It'll be really competitive this year for apprenticeships. The good ones, anyway." He had a look on his face like he liked the challenge.

"Competitive" wasn't what Barclay wanted to hear.

"What makes an apprenticeship good?" asked Barclay.

"The fame of the Master!" Abel answered. "The places you'll travel, Beasts you'll encounter. The farther and more powerful, the better!"

Barclay smiled weakly. "If you say so."

"We're going back to the inn to eat and study for the written exam tomorrow," Ethel said. "Do you want to join us?"

"It's a written exam tomorrow?" Barclay choked. He'd never failed a test, but his competitors had been around Lore their entire lives. Barclay barely even knew the basics.

"Don't you know?" Ethel said, frowning. "The first exam is always a written one. I heard High Keeper Erhart even wrote this exam himself!"

Barclay's panic rose. "This is going to be a disaster."

"Cheer up!" Abel said, slapping his back. "You can't fail out of the Exhibition unless you die! And we can study together over cider."

Barclay and Viola's stomachs both rumbled.

Several minutes later the four of them had wandered into a tavern called the Ironwood Inn. It had a cozy atmosphere, fluffy carpets and blankets all over the floors and chairs—even if they did look like they were made from squirrel and raccoon fur. On the bottom level was a tiny restaurant famous for hot mugs of spiced pear cider. Even with the threat of impending doom, Barclay felt much better with his belly warm from the drink.

Ethel returned from the twins' rooms with her arms full of more books. Barclay didn't think he'd ever met someone with so much *stuff*.

"What is all this?" Barclay asked, nodding at her pile and her bag.

"Oh, just some collectibles." She reached into her bag and pulled out a stack of notebooks. She opened one and showed Barclay the sketches of different species of Beasts, writing scribbled into every free inch of the page. "I've got all sorts. The figurines are my favorite. But I've also got maps. And posters. And . . ."

She spilled out a drawstring pouch of tiny items, like feathers and baubles. Barclay admitted most of the collectibles were interesting, like a tooth made out of what looked like solid silver, and a bone shaped like a star. He didn't touch the brown clump on the end, though. He suspected it was scat.

"This is my favorite," Ethel said excitedly, holding a flat, grooved white stone in her hand. "It's the shell of an Oystix. I think it drifted into the river from the Sea!"

"That's just a rock," Abel said flatly.

Ethel stuck her tongue out at him.

Mitzi, who had been sleeping on Viola's lap as she flipped through the opening chapter of *A Traveler's Log*, looked up at the spread of treasure. She climbed onto the table and pecked at each of the trinkets.

"I love your whelp!" Ethel cooed. She reached out to pet Mitzi, who stole a shiny piece and ducked away.

"Sorry," Viola said, prying the piece out of Mitzi's mouth. "You know how dragons are with shiny things. Such a little thief."

"I wish I could have a dragon," Abel moaned. "If I ever get to go to the Mountains, I'll have *ten* of them. I'll be invincible."

Barclay had never imagined anyone could love Beasts, let alone love Beasts this much. Lore Keepers were not what he expected at all. He didn't know whether it fascinated him or disturbed him.

"Ten dragons? How many Beasts can a Lore Keeper bond with?" Barclay asked.

"There's not actually a limit," Viola answered. "But the stronger they are and the more you have, the harder it will be for you to control them and their Lore."

"Well, I'm plenty strong," Abel said, puffing out his chest. "I'll collect twenty Beasts. No—fifty! One hundred!"

Ethel rolled her eyes. "Says the boy who once tried to bond with a regular rat."

"It had an abnormally long tail!" Abel shot back. "It looked like a Rattle!"

"How many Beasts do you have now?" Barclay asked.

"We just have one each, but don't ask what they are," said Abel. "We're keeping it secret. We'll need the element of surprise to pull ahead in the Exhibition."

At this, several of Ethel's figurines were inexplicably swept off the table and to the floor. Ethel hurriedly bent down to pick them up, casting an irritated look, not to Abel but behind him. Except there was nothing here.

Barclay glanced at Viola, who knitted her brow.

"Do you also collect Beast things?" Barclay asked Abel. "Is that what your cards are?"

A look of horror crossed his face at the comparison.

"I collect champion cards! They're very different." He rummaged for his deck in his pocket and then spread the cards across the table. "These are different competitors in Dooling. It's a sport where Lore Keepers fight alongside their Beasts. The tournament is hosted in the Jungle every year—"

"A *sport*?" Barclay repeated, aghast. *That* was exactly the barbaric behavior he expected from Lore Keepers.

"Barclay doesn't know much about Beasts," Viola said, shooting him a warning look to be polite.

The twins' eyes widened. "What do you do for fun?"

"I . . . I like books."

"Oh great," Abel mumbled, looking between the three of them. "I'm outnumbered."

Ethel, meanwhile, clapped her hands in delight. "What are you reading, Viola?"

Viola lifted up the cover of *A Traveler's Log*, which depicted a giant lamprey the size of a sea monster with electricity running through its body. Barclay couldn't see what page she was on, but judging from how closely she'd been studying it, he guessed it had to do with Gravaldor.

"That's one of my favorite books!" cooed Ethel. "I've read it at least ten—"

"She used to sleep with it," said Abel, sounding bored. "Like a pillow."

"At least *I* never cried when my champion card of Clifton Langer got a bend in it."

"That—that was one time! And his Griffin's fire Lore lets him *rain fire from the sky*! He's a local hero. Besides, I don't see how you can still like that book when—"

"Conley Murdock was a genius, though!"

Indeed, Viola was now reading it so closely she didn't notice Mitzi biting her earlobe.

"What's so great about him?" Barclay asked.

Ethel looked astounded. "He once swam into the mouth of a Hookshark to treat its toothache! He rode a Pterodragyn! And he's cataloged more information on Beasts than any other Lore Keeper alive—over one thousand species."

"Do you think his book can help me study for the exam tomorrow?" Barclay asked bitterly.

"Probably not—it's a bit advanced. But you can always start here."

Ethel slid Barclay her stack of books.

Barclay had never seen a more welcome sight. Books? This he could manage, if only he had enough time. Unfortunately, Ethel's books were each monstrously large, with wispy thin pages and words so small he needed to squint.

"I've taken the exam before," Viola said, pausing her chapter to hold Mitzi down as she tried to drink Viola's mug of pear cider. "They only ask really basic things. Like who the first Grand Keeper was, and what a common use of a Petalmill is, and what the names of the six Legendary class Beasts are—"

"Basic?" Barclay squeaked. "But I don't know any of that!"

Abel shrugged. "That stuff only matters if you want to be a Scholar sort of Keeper. Not us."

Barclay remembered Mandeep explaining the different types of Lore Keepers. "What kind do you want to be?"

"Guardians, of course. They're the ones who protect the towns from wild Beasts. They're always the most famous and powerful, and their assignments have the highest rewards. There are only a few Guardian Masters at this Exhibition, but I think we'll be selected."

"You'll jinx us!" Ethel hissed.

Abel smirked. "You worry too much."

Barclay, however, was certain he hadn't worried *enough*. He poured over the opening of a book called *The Wilderlands, Volume 1: The Woods*. Then he made Viola tell him the answers to all the questions she had mentioned. The first Grand Keeper was Faiza Asfour, who supposedly bonded with all six Legendary Beasts and used her Lore to keep them contained within the Wilderlands. The common use of a Petalmill was a cure for the Summer whooping cough. And the names of the six Legendary Beasts were Shakulah, Dimondaise, Raajnavar, Lochmordra, Navrashtya, and Gravaldor.

"You don't need to know all this!" Abel said. He stretched and yawned. "The best thing you can do is get a good sleep."

Barclay very much doubted he would sleep tonight. He better stay up all night studying. Because even if Abel didn't need to worry, even if there were several Guardian Masters at the Exhibition who would select him, Barclay didn't have Abel's experience or his options. He *had* to win. And failing the first exam didn't seem like a good start.

Hours later, after Viola had finally convinced him to let her pay for their two rooms, Barclay lay in his bed upstairs in the Ironwood Inn and read by candlelight until his eyes strained and his head ached. And then he read some more. He scribbled notes into a journal, and even though the last thing he wanted was to become a Lore Keeper, studying like this still felt good. It felt normal. He could almost imagine Selby sleeping in the other corner of the cramped room or hear Master Pilzmann's snores shaking the entire inn.

He fell asleep with his cheek pressed against the page, and it was the most comfortable night he'd had since he left home.

THIRTEEN

The written exam took place at sunrise in the Guild House, though it didn't look the same as when Barclay had last entered. A large stage had been set up by the fireplace, where over sixty adults sat, each one dressed more strangely than the next. The walls were decorated with dusty banners embroidered with trees and Beasts. A chandelier of branches and moss had been hung from the ceiling, and strange Beasts like massive lightning bugs perched on it, emitting an earthy glow.

"Students, please take your seats," High Keeper Erhart told them. Because Barclay had only seen him sitting in an armchair, he hadn't realized how short he was. He was shaped like an upside-down acorn, all round with brittle, tiny legs.

The two hundred students swarmed to the tables. Barclay,

Ethel, and Abel managed to find seats next to one another near the front, giving them a good view of the Masters onstage. Runa was among them, near the back. She gave Barclay a small nod.

Barclay's chair jolted, and he whipped around to face Tadg. Tadg whistled and stared at his parchment.

"Before we begin," said High Keeper Erhart, "I'd like to offer a round of applause for Soren Reiker, who has generously donated the funds to renovate the Guild House here in Sycomore."

Barclay's heart tightened in panic as Soren, seated on the end in the front row, stood up. His blond hair was cleanly slicked back, and he wore an expensive coat with fur trim. Nearly all of the students and Masters clapped.

Soren had noticed Barclay too. As Soren took his bow, his eyes widened with something that looked like excitement, like a predator who had once again spotted his prey. Barclay quickly averted his gaze and slid down in his seat, his palms sweating.

"And now, to pass it off to the first exam's proctors," Erhart said, "Mandeep Acharya and Runa Rasgar."

Mandeep and Runa stood up, and the students' excited whispers swelled at the mention of Runa's name. They made an intimidating pair, Mandeep in his scholarly copper glasses and Runa in her chainmail jacket.

"You'll all notice a brooch in front of you," Mandeep said. Barclay reached forward and grabbed the pin placed before him. It was the ugliest brooch he'd ever seen—rather than a gem, the dull rock looked like any found on a riverbed or in the dirt. It glowed with a cool green pulse once he touched it. "This brooch will turn red if you cheat. No Lore will hide it, so best to keep that in mind."

Barclay nervously pinned it to his shirt.

"You'll have sixty-two minutes to complete the exam," Runa said. "Good luck."

At that, Barclay and the other students opened their packets and began.

What is the largest Beast in the world?

Barclay's thoughts were hazy from not sleeping, but he did remember this one. A whale dragon known as a Silberwal. Barclay scratched the answer down in the clawlike Lore Keeper script, finding that the writing came as naturally to him as the alphabet he had used in Dullshire—so easily that it was a tiny bit eerie.

His confidence grew—he could manage this test. He wouldn't fail.

In what city is the Guild of the Tundra headquartered?

He didn't know that one.

What are the seventeen life stages of a dragon?

What is the only Beast capable of immortality?

How many Lore Keepers, throughout all of recorded history, have bonded with a Legendary Beast?

Barclay didn't know any of these questions either. He scanned the rest of the exam and filled in the few he did know, and then, with fifty minutes of the test to spare, had nothing to do but sit and panic.

He was going to fail. He wouldn't come in first. Runa would never tell him how to break his bond.

When he glanced at the stage, Runa wasn't looking at him. Soren looked nowhere else *but* him. Barclay felt so nervous, he could burst.

I could cheat, he thought. He'd never cheated in his life, but he was desperate enough now to try. Except the brooch would turn red, and Mandeep and Runa would disqualify him for sure. That was worse than failing.

And so Barclay sat there for the rest of the exam, planning out his miserable future as a Beast poop-cleaner.

At the sixty-two-minute finishing mark, Mandeep called, "The time has expired! Students, please return your exam booklets and brooches to the Masters. Your tests will be graded and the results posted this evening."

Barclay turned to Ethel to moan about his failure, but before he did, he noticed her brooch had gone red, like a piece of fiery coal.

He turned around. Nearly every student's brooch was red. The only ones that weren't belonged to him . . . and Tadg.

Erhart even wrote this exam himself, Ethel had told him. Barclay realized it didn't matter if you cheated. All the brooches did was tell the proctors that you *had*. There would be no disqualifying. No consequences.

He turned in his exam feeling worse than foolish—feeling pathetic.

Abel and Ethel waited for him at the door. Ethel looked rather pale, but Abel yawned and stretched his arms behind his head.

"I'm ready for a nap," Abel told them. "You look like you could use one too, Barclay. And a mug of pear cider."

"You couldn't mean Ironwood Inn cider, could you?" a cool voice asked from behind them. It was Soren.

Barclay took a frightened step backward. "I . . . No . . ."

"Yes!" Abel said brightly. Barclay recognized a grown-up-pleasing face when he saw one, though he wouldn't have expected one from Abel. "Best in town. That's why we're staying there."

Barclay could have kicked him. Now he'd have to fear Soren trying to murder him in his bed.

"How charming," Soren said, smiling his all-too-pleasant smile. He held out a wicker basket. "Please return your brooches."

Barclay shakily dropped his inside, as did Abel and Ethel. He barely breathed again until Soren moved on to another student.

"What's wrong?" Ethel asked him.

"That man . . ." Barclay lowered his voice. "He attacked me! He tried to steal my Beast."

Abel furrowed his eyebrows. "Why would he do that? What sort of Beast do you have?"

That didn't strike Barclay as the right question to ask, but before he could say so, he was distracted by Soren's voice once more.

"Being honorable won't get you anywhere, Mr. Murdock," Soren said coolly behind him.

Barclay turned in time to see Tadg return his brooch.

"Murdock?" Barclay hissed to Ethel and Abel. "Like Conley Murdock? The man who wrote *A Traveler's Log*?"

"We thought you knew that!" Abel said. "Tadg is his son. Why do you think everyone around here worships him?"

"I thought they just liked his Mythic class Beast," Barclay answered. "You know, his Mark does look a lot like the Beast on the cover of the book."

"That's Murdock's Nathermara—he was famous for it," Ethel said excitedly. "It's a Mythic class Beast from the Sea, where Murdock is from."

Before Tadg could respond to Soren, Runa appeared at Soren's side. "I wouldn't be so sure of that, Soren. I take honesty into account." She tore the stack of papers from Soren's hands. "As a *proctor*, I mean," she added curtly.

Soren glared at Runa for a moment, then turned to Tadg. He jerked his head toward the door. "Run along, then."

Tadg stalked past Barclay, Abel, and Ethel without so much as an insult or a shove. He stormed out into the snow, leaving his usual posse behind him.

Abel snorted. "Probably thinks he's above all this. He doesn't need to cheat if he has Soren, does he?"

"What do you mean, 'has Soren'?" Barclay asked.

"Soren Reiker and Conley Murdock used to be partners—they were writing the sequel to Murdock's book together before Murdock died," Abel explained. "So of course Soren will make sure Tadg does well. That's probably why he tried to steal your Beast, Barclay! You're the only other student with a Mythic Beast—he must think you'll hurt Tadg's chances."

It was possible, Barclay supposed, though he hadn't ever told Soren he planned on entering the Exhibition. But it didn't surprise him that Tadg and Soren could be working together. Unpleasant people always had a way of finding one another.

Abel sighed. "Must be nice to be rich like that. And to travel. I've been stuck in the Woods my whole life." He kicked at the edge of a loose floorboard.

"Never mind that," Ethel said, sounding worried. "Do you really think Runa will take honesty into account?"

"Shouldn't she?" Barclay asked. "I mean, how can you award first place to someone who doesn't deserve it?"

Abel shook his head. "I wouldn't worry about it. Erhart wrote the test, and he purposefully made the test too hard to pass. Because it's important to be resourceful and crafty, not just to be smart."

"But what about to be *good*?" Barclay pressed.

Abel gave him an inquisitive look. "Is it not like this in the towns beyond the Woods?"

Barclay shook his head bitterly. "No. Nothing is."

* * *

The exam results were posted later that evening on a long roll of parchment pinned to the bulletin board outside the Guild House. A crowd of students milled around it, each shouting in despair or glee when they spotted their names. It took Barclay, Abel, and Ethel ages to make it to the front of the masses, Viola hovering nervously behind them.

Even though it was freezing outside, Barclay was sweating so much, his hair was plastered to his neck. He better start preparing his application as a poop-cleaner.

"I placed seventh!" Ethel squealed. "Abel, you got twenty-ninth!"

Abel grinned and stretched his arms behind his head. "See? Nothing to worry about."

Being so short, Barclay had to squeeze his way past the others to see the scores. And his shoulders fell in relief when he spotted his name.

Second place.

His happiness was short-lived.

"Barclay Thorne?" a student sneered beside him, jabbing his finger on the score list. "Who's that?"

"Isn't that the Elsie?" someone else asked.

"But that's not fair! There's no way he did better than I did. My parents quizzed me for weeks."

Viola squeezed Barclay's shoulder and steered him out of the crowds. "You did amazing, Barclay!"

"But I . . . I barely knew anything!" he said, careful to keep his voice down.

"Runa must've convinced Mandeep to go against Erhart. After all, everyone else cheated!"

Though Barclay wasn't exactly proud of his achievement, Viola's words did make him feel like less of a fraud. Even Ethel and Abel, as competitive as they were, gave Barclay congratulatory smiles.

"Second?" someone smirked behind them.

Barclay turned and scowled. He should've known Tadg wouldn't be without his admirers for long.

"You must be feeling pretty lucky, Elsie," Tadg laughed. "Because we're taking bets for the next round. The odds are two hundred to one that you don't make it out alive."

Barclay could think of nothing to say. After all, Tadg was right. He was hopeless.

"I'd bet on him beating *you*," Viola mumbled under her breath.

Tadg snorted, and Viola seemed to shrink under the scrutiny of him and his friends behind him. "Well, if the daughter of the *Grand Keeper* thinks so . . ."

When Viola looked away nervously, Barclay demanded, "What gives you the right to act so full of yourself? What slot did you get, anyway?"

Tadg smirked and nodded at the parchment. His name was at the top. First place.

He hadn't cheated either.

Tadg took a step closer to Barclay, and Barclay wondered if he should've kept his mouth shut. After years dealing with Falk, he knew all goading ever got him was a black eye. Especially when Tadg clearly liked putting on a show—all the students had stopped their whispering to glare at Barclay. Maybe Runa thought Barclay deserved second place, but obviously, the other apprentices did not.

Tadg stabbed a finger into Barclay's shoulder.

"Prove it, Elsie. Place in the top thirty in the practical, and I'll lay off. I will. Even if I'm only telling you the things you need to hear."

Tadg held out his hand.

When Tadg had shaken hands with Ethel yesterday, he'd hurt her in some way. And so Barclay was ready. He wouldn't be tricked. And he wouldn't lose.

When they grasped hands, Barclay thought, *Wind!*

A gust roared past in response, sweeping Tadg right off his feet. He landed on his back in the snow, his expression furious.

"I think I'll keep my bet," Viola said brightly.

Tadg muttered something to himself, then stomped off, his admirers whispering behind him.

Viola, Ethel, and Abel broke out into howls of laughter.

Barclay only basked in his glow of victory for a few moments. After all, he'd only gotten the better of Tadg because it'd been a trick.

He turned to Viola. "You've done the Exhibition before. You're an apprentice."

She nodded hesitantly.

"If I'm going to have any chance of beating Tadg and placing first," Barclay said, "I need to get better. I need you to train me to be a real Lore Keeper."

FOURTEEN

The next morning, barely after sunrise, Viola had gathered Barclay and the twins on a crowded main street in Sycomore in front of an apothecary shop called Bottles and Brews. Red ivy crawled up its entire front, making it difficult to find the front door amid the prickly leaves and vines.

"The practical exam will test you on a wide variety of topics," Viola explained. "You'll need to be able to defend yourself against different types of Beasts, to identify Beasts, and to know how to take care of Beasts."

Abel slapped Barclay on the back. "So, you know, not much."

"But why are we here?" Barclay asked. "To go shopping?"

"In a way," Viola answered.

They entered the shop. It was full of rickety, slanted

shelves, each of them stacked with clay pots. They had strange labels like *Invisible Sap* and *Twelve-Leaf Clovers*. Everything smelled of pungent flowers, and the vibrantly green carpet on the floor was actually a thick layer of moss.

"Dried plants and such are useful," Viola said, "but not during the practical exam. If you need them, you'll have to forage for them yourself."

She led them through a back door to the greenhouse. Inside was pleasant and warm, with plants ranging from blossoming flowers to fruit trees to—Barclay noticed with delight—various clusters of fungi.

Viola bent over the first mushroom. "I thought you might like to start with this."

Barclay had never seen a mushroom like this before. It was small and white, and it rocked back and forth gently. It grew in cluster formations, all nestled together.

"These are Stoolips," Viola told him. "They're Trite class."

"These are Beasts?" Barclay asked incredulously.

Ethel cooed at one and tickled its stem. To Barclay's shock, the mushroom giggled, and beady green eyes blinked below its top. "They're so cute." She rushed to her backpack for her pencil and sketchbook.

While the Stoolip laughed, Viola plucked its cap off, as though it were a hat. The Stoolip didn't seem to mind being without it. It only snuggled itself closer to its companions and fell back asleep.

"They grow near rivers and streams," Viola explained.

Then she stuck the top of the mushroom on Abel's forehead. He let out a yawn far longer than his usual yawns, and his eyes went droopy.

"Its cap suctions to the skin and induces sleep," she continued. "One Stoolip top is worth a nap for a human, maybe two tops if the person is really big."

While Abel collapsed on the tiled floor, asleep, Viola led Barclay around the greenhouse, pointing out every mushroom, fern, and fruit. Barclay took detailed notes, and like a proper student, asked plenty of questions and recited everything back to her when she finished, surprised to find that he was actually enjoying himself. Viola's lessons were detailed, and Barclay marveled at how much she knew from memory. Even Ethel often scribbled down Viola's words in her journal.

Viola was clearly an excellent Lore Keeper student—a great one, even. She was a better and more patient teacher than Barclay ever had been with Selby. It made him wonder about what had happened between Viola and Cyril, but he didn't want to upset her, especially when she was sacrificing time teaching him that she could have spent preparing to face Gravaldor.

"This one smells like you, Barclay!" Ethel pointed out a beetlelike Beast clinging to a head of skunk cabbage.

This left Barclay glowering as Viola took them to their next stop, the town grocer. While Ethel and Abel each bought large jugs of spiced pear cider, Viola led Barclay to the butcher's section.

"Beasts live in stasis when within their Marks," she

explained, "but once in the normal world, they'll grow hungry and sleepy. You'll probably need to use Root during the practical, so we're going to train with him. Which is why you need to learn to feed him."

"Are we really calling it Root?" Barclay grumbled.

"Well, it's better than nothing."

Viola pointed at a number of bloody steaks behind the glass.

"Root is a carnivore," she said.

"Naturally," he muttered.

"We'll buy a few things to figure out what he might like."

"What if it likes human meat?"

Viola shrugged, as though nothing about the thought was bothersome. "I don't think human meat is good—very tough and dry." At the horrified look on Barclay's face, she laughed. "I'm just joking. But no, I don't think Root is going to like human meat. No Beasts do, according to *A Traveler's Log*. That's just an Elsie myth."

"You're still reading that even though Tadg is Murdock's son? And Soren, his partner?"

Viola fiddled with her golden pins, which Barclay realized she did whenever she was flustered. "I-it's very informative! And it's all still so hard to believe. Conley Murdock was so nice! You can practically hear in his voice on every page how much he loved Beasts."

"Yeah, probably enough to steal them," Barclay grumbled under his breath.

Nevertheless, on the book's recommendation, they exited the grocer with bags of wrapped elk, goat, squirrel, and hog meat in hand. They took their meaty feast to the edge of town and stopped amid a snowy patch of trees. While Ethel and Abel collapsed onto a log to watch and organize their card or notes collections, Viola launched into another lesson.

"Lore Keepers inherit several abilities from each of their Beasts, and those abilities depend on what sort of Beast you have, like how I can do light Lore like Mitzi," she said. "Why don't you try out some of yours?"

Barclay only knew of two abilities he'd gained from Root: he could run even faster than he could before, and he could summon wind.

He tried running first, though it was hard in the snow, and it made him nervous to have an audience. He slipped on an icy stone and face-planted onto the ground.

Abel laughed so hard, he choked on his cider. "That'll show Tadg."

Barclay grimaced and stood up. "But did I go fast?"

"Sure," Ethel told him encouragingly.

"Faster than the wind?"

"If you say so," Abel chirped.

Barclay pursed his lips and turned to Viola. "What am I doing wrong? I've done it before."

"Only in dangerous situations, when you were acting on instinct," she told him. "You still barely know your powers, just like you still barely know your Beast. You'll be stronger if you summon Root from his Mark."

Barclay knew, eventually, he would need to do that. If he hoped to place first in the Exhibition, he'd need to do exceptionally well in the practical. He'd need to use the Lufthund.

But the whole reason he wanted to remove his Mark was because he didn't want to *be* a Lore Keeper.

"Let me try something else first," Barclay told her.

He raised his arms like when he had faced Tadg or Soren.

Wind!

The wind came when called. It tore across the Woods, making icicles clack together and snow sweep off branches in billows of dusty white.

Ethel clapped politely. Abel yawned.

"It isn't bad for a first try," Viola said gently.

Barclay pouted. "I thought it looked pretty good."

"But there's no control. Which direction do you summon the wind from? Where do you aim it?"

Barclay hadn't considered any of that. When he called, the wind came. In Dullshire, he hadn't even meant to do it. It felt simple—thoughtless. Thus far, he'd never needed it to be more precise. He didn't control the wind. The wind simply *knew*.

Still, he gritted his teeth and tried again.

Wind!

And again.

And again.

And again.

Each time, the wind came from a new direction to a new target. It didn't matter how much Barclay focused. The wind went where it wanted to go. It wasn't until a particularly strong gust swept Viola off her feet that she told him to stop.

"You can't avoid it," she told him. "You need to summon Root from your Mark."

Barclay knew she was right. He took a deep breath to calm his nerves. Viola, Ethel, and Abel didn't seem afraid—they were Lore Keepers; they could take care of themselves. And maybe not all Beasts were terrible, but the Lufthund wasn't like the ticklish Stoolips. He was dangerous. Even if he *had* helped Barclay escape Soren.

Come out, Barclay told it, hoping this wasn't a huge mistake.

The wind answered. A breeze cut across the trees, making Barclay shiver from his head to his toes. The Lufthund appeared at the edge of the grove, its black fur harsh against the white snow.

Abel hollered and stood up. "Barclay! You didn't tell us your Beast was a Lufthund! They're wicked powerful."

"And *beautiful!*" Ethel called, frantically flipping through her sketchbook for a blank page. "He even looks like you, Barclay!"

Barclay didn't answer. He was too preoccupied *with* the Lufthund, who had crouched down and was watching

Barclay as though preparing to attack. Its tail gave a sudden, violent swish.

It leapt forward.

Barclay screamed and darted away. The sound made the Lufthund freeze, its black eyes suddenly narrowed, uncertain and wary.

"Careful," Viola said sharply. Mitzi appeared from her Mark and stood on alert on Viola's shoulder. "Don't startle him. Try to feed him."

Barclay carefully reached into his bag to grab some of the meat. His movements startled the Lufthund, who let out a low, throaty growl that made Barclay's heart stutter to a near stop.

"I'm just getting you some food," Barclay told it. He grabbed the elk meat and slowly unwrapped it. He held it out. "Here."

When the Beast prowled closer, Barclay had to restrain himself from stepping back. Even if the Lufthund ate the meat, there was nothing stopping it from taking a bite of Barclay's arm along with it.

And so, once it got close enough, Barclay tossed the meat into the snow in front of it.

"There you go," Barclay offered, his voice hitched.

The Beast watched Barclay the entire time it ate, as though it would rather be eating *him*.

That night at the Ironwood Inn, Viola, Ethel, and Abel all pummeled Barclay with advice.

"You need to be his alpha," said Abel. "He's like a wolf, isn't he? He needs to respect you."

"If you keep feeding him, I'm sure he will grow nicer," Ethel told Barclay. Then she paused and added, "And maybe a bit heavier, but I'm sure that's fine."

"You just scared him a little," said Viola. "You only need him to trust you. You're his partner. His Keeper."

As she said this, Mitzi scampered onto the table and lunged for Viola's mug of cider—Mitzi had developed an obsession with the drink. She stuck her wing in it and dumped it all over the table.

Viola scowled and wiped away the puddle. "On second thought, maybe you *should* be his alpha. Maybe then he will *listen to you.*" She shot Mitzi an annoyed look.

Mitzi squawked defiantly and tore at Viola's napkin.

But even though Barclay knew the three of them understood way more about Beasts than he did, he didn't think any of them were right. His Beast hadn't seemed defiant or mean or suspicious when they'd escaped from Soren. It'd seemed . . . impatient, maybe. Like it was waiting for something.

But that was then. Now he had no idea what to make of the Lufthund.

Barclay miserably laid his head against the table. "Tadg is right. I'm going to die during the practical. If anyone should feel scared, it's me. You saw how the Lufthund looks at me! I'm not its alpha or its partner. I'm its dinner!"

"What happens if you *can't* remove your Mark, Barclay?" Ethel asked him.

"I think Soren will do it for you," Abel said darkly.

Viola frowned and squeezed Barclay's shoulder. "We won't let that happen."

"Even if you don't come in first," Ethel said cheerily, "a Lore Master could still take you on as an apprentice! Then you could join the Guild, like us."

Even though Ethel's words were meant to be comforting, they only made Barclay more depressed. Unless he managed the impossible and beat Tadg to claim first, he had no choice: he'd have to remain a Lore Keeper forever. He'd never return to Dullshire. He'd never see Master Pilzmann or Mrs. Havener again.

It was true that Barclay had once longed for an adventure, but even then, he had never wanted one like this. What he really wanted was to make his parents proud, and the last thing his parents would've wished for was for Barclay to live in the world of Beasts when they'd been killed by one.

"I have a great idea!" Ethel squeaked. She reached into her backpack and pulled out a crumpled flyer. "Lecture Day is coming up—it's the day before the second exam, when the Lore Keeper Masters put on presentations for the students, so that students can hear more about the instructors and the different subjects they specialize in. We could all go together and find you a Master!"

Unable to take another second of their enthusiasm, Barclay stood up. "I need some air," he declared, and he walked out into the Winter night.

* * *

A half hour later Barclay pressed his back into a tree trunk and held out the squirrel meat. "Take it! Just take it!"

The Lufthund sniffed it suspiciously. With its black fur, the Beast was nearly impossible to see in the darkness. It was reckless, Barclay knew, to spend time alone with it. There was no one around, no sounds but the hoots of owls. No one to witness if Barclay got eaten.

But Barclay didn't want a backup plan, like Ethel had suggested. In order to win the next exam, he'd have to take risks. To do whatever it took.

With the Beast's fangs dangerously close to his hand, Barclay once again tossed the meat into the snow. This time the Lufthund didn't even eat it. It sniffed it, then wrinkled its snout like it was actually picky about what food it ate.

"You *will* obey me," Barclay told it. "Because you are a Beast and I'm your Keeper. And I need you to. I don't care what they say—I can't be a Lore Keeper forever."

While the Lufthund was distracted with inspecting the squirrel meat, Barclay tried once again to summon wind. He'd placed a pine cone on the remains of a rotted tree stump, and he aimed to topple it over. A wind appeared, though far above Barclay's head, rattling the branches. The cone remained in place.

Barclay collapsed onto the stump and stared at his Beast. The Beast let out a loud huff from its nostrils, and its tail twitched. Like it was laughing at him.

"I'm no good at this," Barclay grumbled. "Even if I did stay here, I'd make a terrible Lore Keeper."

The Beast huffed again, as though agreeing with him.

"Think I'm funny, do you?" Barclay asked. When the Lufthund padded closer, Barclay reached into his pocket for his Beast-warding charm. The Lufthund eyed it curiously, even when he should have been shrinking away.

"Viola was right. This doesn't work, does it?"

The Beast sniffed it and made a disgusted face. Then it scrunched its nose and licked it.

"Was the taste worth it? Just to make me look stupid?"

The Lufthund lifted its chin up, snobbylike, as if to say it had been. On top of being dangerous, Barclay's Beast seemed a snide sort of know-it-all.

Barclay sighed and tossed the charm into the snow. He should've known Dullshire's charms didn't really work, like Viola had told him.

"You know what I don't understand?" he asked. "How did I even bond with you? Because it doesn't sound like anyone can bond with a Beast by accident."

The Lufthund's dark eyes met his, and Barclay got the sense that it was trying to tell him something. But, of course, he didn't get a response.

"This place is turning me bonkers," he muttered. "It's not like you can talk to me."

The Beast's face wrinkled, as though affronted.

Barclay put his hands on his hips. "Don't look at me like that. I didn't ask to be bonded with you."

It sat down and lifted its front paws, mimicking Barclay.

"Don't do that." Barclay dropped his hands.

The Lufthund did too.

"You know, everyone in Sycomore already makes fun of me. I don't need it from you."

Barclay kicked at the snow. The wind picked it up and scattered it in flurries, and the Lufthund barked and ran after them, its tail wagging. Once the snow settled, the Beast turned around, watching Barclay eagerly, as if this were all a game.

Barclay sighed. Without his charm, Barclay resorted to the only other thing to help him think—running. It didn't matter that it was freezing, or late, or dark. He needed to move. He needed to move *fast*.

Come back, Barclay thought, trying to send the Lufthund back to the Mark.

The Beast whined.

"So you're being stubborn, then?" Barclay asked. Viola had told Barclay he needed to know his Beast, and so far, he didn't like him.

The Beast whined again, and it was such a sad sound that Barclay suddenly felt rather bad for it. Viola had said that Lufthunds weren't pack animals, but maybe this one got lonely. As an orphan with few real friends, Barclay knew the feeling.

"Fine," Barclay told it, trudging to the closest street. Lightning bugs filled the lanterns dangling from the trees, lighting the path. He didn't know his way around Sycomore, but the winding alleys called to him, urging him to run, no matter if he got lost.

But still he hesitated. *No running. No filth. No wildness.* It was hard to shake off Dullshire's rules, even if he wasn't in Dullshire anymore. But then a breeze rushed past, as though asking him to join it. And Barclay realized there was something to like about Sycomore after all.

He took off.

It felt so good, the wind in his hair, his heart pounding. He knew every corner and cranny of Dullshire, and he was surprised by how much he loved the feeling of getting lost in Sycomore. Every turn meant a new discovery. A small adventure.

The Lufthund caught up and ran beside him. Barclay considered stopping—the Beast was *not* helping him clear his head. But the Lufthund looked more content than Barclay had ever seen it, its tail wagging, its jaws open like a smile. It clearly loved this as much as Barclay did.

So Barclay decided to let the Beast stay beside him. To keep running.

It couldn't hurt, just for one night.

FIFTEEN

Barclay didn't tell the others about his night running with the Lufthund. He didn't want them to think he was second-guessing his decision to go back to Dullshire, because he wasn't. His life had changed so much in the past week that he just needed a moment to think.

That didn't mean he'd betrayed his parents.

But if that was true, then why did he feel a little bit guilty?

The next morning the four of them registered for Lecture Day. It was required for Barclay, Ethel, and Abel—but the rest of Sycomore was invited to attend as well. Barclay registered for all the Masters he recognized—except for Soren, of course.

When Barclay spotted Tadg's name on the list, he wasn't the least bit surprised to see he had registered for Soren's lecture over Runa's.

With several days to wait until Lecture Day, Barclay still had plenty of time to train for the second exam. The four of them ventured out to a field where other students sat on benches surrounding a bonfire, passing around champion cards and playing with their Beasts. The air smelled like any good Winter day should, like smoke and pine and fresh cider.

"What is it?" Barclay asked, catching Viola staring at him.

"You stopped combing your hair flat," she said. "It looks much better."

"And you don't smell like skunks anymore," Ethel added.

He stiffened, suddenly self-conscious. "I—"

"Don't you think Barclay looks less like an Elsie now?" Ethel asked her brother.

But thankfully, saving Barclay from more scrutiny, Abel wasn't paying attention. He shuffled through his deck of champion cards.

"Do you think someone would trade with me for a Runa Rasgar card? I'd like a Sanjit Varma card. Or maybe Aoife Kearney . . ."

"You'd trade your Runa card?" Ethel asked. "But she's our top choice for a Master!"

"Yeah, but I have almost ten of them," Abel muttered.

"Runa was a, um, Dooling person?" Barclay asked, looking up from the textbook Ethel had lent him.

Abel gaped at him. "It's called a *Dooler*. And Runa was champion *six times*."

"She has two Mythic class Beasts," Ethel said dreamily. "I'd love to see them in person and draw them. Mythic Beasts are so rare—you're so lucky, Barclay."

If Barclay was "lucky," he'd still be in Dullshire right now. Or he'd find a way to make what had happened during the first exam blow over. You'd think *he'd* cheated from the way the other students still glared at him, not the other way around.

"I'd love to see Runa's Beasts *fight*," Abel gushed.

Viola rolled her eyes. "Dooling isn't that respectable. It's a sport. If you're going to rave about Runa, at least rave about her real accomplishments. She's also a world-famous Guardian Keeper."

"You just think that because your family is noble," Abel told her.

"We're not *noble*," Viola retorted.

"Wasn't the Grand Keeper before your father his mother? And her father before her?" Ethel asked.

"Yes," Viola replied.

Abel smirked. "Yeah, that's called noble."

Suddenly Abel fumbled, as though smacked on the hand, and his deck fell to the ground. He hurriedly scooped it up out of the snow.

"Stop doing that," he grumbled, at what seemed like no one.

Barclay wondered again if his friends were a little bit strange.

He wanted to focus on studying so that he could prepare for the practical, but it was hard, surrounded by so many students and Beasts. His eyes roamed over the crowds. Some of the kids sat in clusters, others with their parents who'd traveled with them for the Exhibition. The Beasts roamed freely, playing in the sparse patches of snow. Their magic—their *Lore*, Barclay corrected himself—made their paw prints harden to ice, or weeds sprout up in the frost, or colors bleed into the white.

Watching them, Barclay's Mark began to prickle. It didn't sting, like it did when danger was nearby. It felt more like an itch. And when Barclay stretched down his collar to examine it, the Lufthund padded across his skin, his tail wagging.

"Do your Beasts ever try to tell you something, when they're in their Marks?" Barclay asked the others.

Viola nodded. "Your Beast can communicate with you a little bit when they're in the Mark, like you can sense each other. My Mark tends to tickle when I walk past something shiny. It gets Mitzi excited."

"I think mine warns me when there's danger. Or when . . ."

When it wants to play, Barclay was going to add, realizing immediately that that was what the Lufthund wanted, why it was wagging its tail. But his Beast wasn't a companion, like Mitzi. He couldn't just let it wander in such a large crowd—it might attack someone.

"What about yours?" he asked Abel and Ethel.

"I guess they do, but we almost never keep our Beasts in their Marks," Ethel said, furiously scribbling notes about the Beasts around them.

"They're out now," Abel said, shrugging.

Barclay furrowed his eyebrows. He didn't remember them ever having Beasts with them. "Which ones are they?"

"They're right there." Ethel pointed toward the grass beneath the trees.

Barclay and Viola exchanged a dark look. There was nothing there.

Maybe they were only joking, since they'd said they wanted to keep their Beasts secret. But then Viola asked, "Um . . . Are you sure they didn't run off?"

"They're invisible to other people," Ethel explained, which did nothing to make Barclay feel better. "Unless you have a—"

"You couldn't be referring to Doppelgheists?" a slick voice asked from behind them, and the four of them turned around to face Soren and Erhart.

Barclay's hand instantly reached for his shoulder, as though to protect his Mark. The others tensed. Mitzi rose from Viola's lap to let out a low growl.

"Yes. I mean—" Abel started nervously, then stopped when Soren reached down and picked up Ethel's notebook. Soren flipped to the first page and stared at something Barclay couldn't see.

"Amazing Beasts. Wouldn't you agree, High Keeper?" Soren asked, showing Erhart what Barclay guessed was a sketch of Ethel's and Abel's Beasts.

Erhart didn't seem to be paying attention, distracted from staring at the expensive fur trim of Soren's coat. "I . . . Oh yes. Quite amazing."

"Prime class. Quite common, really, but I've never heard of a Keeper bonding with them, on account of how difficult they are to find—"

"Don't get any ideas," Barclay bit out.

Erhart's gaze shot to Barclay. "To speak like that to a Master!" Then his eyes narrowed. "You're the registrant from the Elsewheres, aren't you? Well, you wouldn't understand the contribution that Mr. Reiker has made to our Guild chapter. No more will Sycomore pale in comparison to the cities of the Desert, the Mountains, the Jungle! No more will the Woods be the punch line of the rest of the Wilderlands! Why, look how many students we have this year. A record amount! Even with the Exhibition being moved early!"

Viola snorted. "You only have this many students because Runa Rasgar is one of the Masters."

Erhart's face reddened, and he swayed like he might topple over. "Really, I would never expect such insolence from you, Miss Dumont."

Viola stiffened, as though she too couldn't believe what she'd just said. She straightened her lopsided gold pins.

Erhart continued, "And if you knew the uglier sides of Miss Rasgar's reputation . . . Mr. Reiker has filled me in on *quite* a story. I'm second-guessing even allowing her to come to this Exhibition."

Fear seized Barclay—Runa was the only person in Sycomore who knew how to help him.

"You can't send Runa away!" he shouted, loudly enough to make other students' heads turn. Many of their eyes widened.

Erhart cleared his throat. He must have thought Viola's earlier comment was true, because he said, quite loudly, "You misheard! I'd do no such thing." Then, once the crowd looked appeased, he lowered his voice. "I don't want to hear any more of this about Soren. Not from you, or from Miss Rasgar."

"Yes," Soren purred. "I think that's quite enough. It was nice to meet you." He handed Ethel back her notebook. Then, with one last vicious smile, he led Erhart to the other end of the field.

Once they were both out of earshot, Barclay moaned to the twins, "Now Soren will be after your Beasts too!"

Ethel glanced at the first page of her notebook and swallowed. "I'd like to see him try."

"What do you think Erhart meant by the 'uglier sides of Miss Rasgar's reputation'?" Abel asked. "That didn't sound like he meant Dooling. . . ."

"Well, Soren and Runa must know each other," Viola said.

She pulled out her copy of *A Traveler's Log* and turned to the final pages.

"In the acknowledgments, Murdock thanks Soren as a beneficiary—seems like Soren helped pay for a portion of Murdock's travels. He calls him 'a fellow enthusiast of the incredible Legendary Beasts,'" Viola read. "That makes sense—everyone knows Soren was helping Murdock write his sequel, which he never finished. Then, later, he writes: 'And to my dear friend, Runa Rasgar, without whose support I never would have written this record down.'"

"So they both knew Murdock," Abel said.

"Do you think Runa was somehow involved in Murdock's death?" Viola asked, anxiously stroking Mitzi's back.

Abel shrugged. "I don't know, but I don't feel too sorry for Tadg, the way he acts. Real full of himself, isn't he?"

"Um, Abel—" Ethel squeaked, looking over Abel's shoulder.

"Well, I wouldn't be if I only had my Beast because my dead father—"

"*Abel—*" Viola cut in.

"Gave me *his*, would I?"

Behind them, someone cleared their throat. Barclay and Abel whipped around, and Tadg stood there, his face redder than the top of a Mourningtide Morel.

"I won't feel too sorry either"—he growled—"when I send you back to your no-name village in pieces."

Abel stood up and pushed Tadg away. Barclay's eyes widened. He didn't put it past either of them to start a fight.

"Try it, then," Abel snapped. "I dare you. Let's see that Beast you brag so much about."

Tadg's fingers curled into a fist, the golden Mark of the Nathermara coiling over his skin. He glanced at Barclay, Viola, and Ethel, all frozen on the bench behind Abel, as though considering his odds, four against one. Tadg's eyes fell on Ethel's open notebook and narrowed. She hurriedly snapped it closed.

The fire in Tadg's eyes faded, and he turned back to Abel. "You don't know what you're asking. You collect cards and toys, but my Beast isn't a plaything. There's a difference between a companion and a monster."

"Your father didn't seem to think so," Abel shot back.

"Stop. Talking. About. Him."

The other students—and some of the parents, even—had formed a circle around their group. Tadg's admirers, in particular, cheered for him to unleash his Beast.

"Let's see it!" they called.

"Don't let him off easy!"

"Show us what it can do!"

Tadg, usually happy to oblige his fan club, went pale. Meanwhile, Abel dug his boots into the ground, preparing to lunge.

But before he could, Tadg shook his head. "You don't know what you're asking," he murmured one last time. Then he turned around and walked away. The crowd booed, but they parted for him and let him pass.

"I didn't think so," Abel said smugly, sitting back down.

"You shouldn't have said that, about his father," Viola scolded him. "I don't like Tadg either, but it was no wonder he got mad."

Barclay agreed with her. Falk and his gang had made fun of his dead parents on more than one occasion, for no other reason than to make Barclay feel terrible.

But then he remembered Tadg's name on the lecture list and how he'd registered for Soren's, and he stopped feeling bad.

Abel leaned over and grabbed Barclay's textbook. "Maybe I *will* study. Maybe I'll study so I can beat him."

For the rest of the afternoon, Viola took turns quizzing them. But whenever Barclay tried to focus, his thoughts kept drifting. To Soren's slimy smile. To the rumors about Runa. And especially to Tadg's words: *There's a difference between a companion and a monster.*

Hours later, once night had fallen, Barclay returned to the grove where he had trained the day before, and he'd tried to knock over the pine cone more times than he could count. There were only five more nights until the second exam, and at this rate, he'd come in dead last.

He collapsed into the snow in frustration while the Lufthund watched behind him, snorting from time to time as though mocking him. A flurry of snowflakes swirled around Barclay, burying him. Barclay was almost miserable enough to let them.

"Viola must be wrong," Barclay huffed. "I don't think the wind *can* be controlled. It's not light, like her Lore! It's not precise. It's . . . wild."

The Lufthund nodded. Or perhaps Barclay imagined it.

"With Falk and Soren and Tadg, I managed it," Barclay said. He yanked off his gloves, soaked from the snow, and examined his hands, as if trying to figure out the Lore they wielded. He frowned and picked at the dirt under his fingernails, then stopped when he remembered Master Pilzmann wasn't here to scold him for it. "Why could I do the Lore right then but not now?"

The Lufthund padded over to him. Barclay tensed as it approached, and he froze altogether when it stood over him. But rather than attack, the Beast gently placed its paw on Barclay's forehead, then it lifted it and pointed to itself. Like it was trying to tell him something.

He remembered yesterday how Ethel had said that the Lufthund looked like him, and Barclay could reluctantly admit that it did. Its wild black fur resembled Barclay's long hair. Their eyes matched, irises so dark, they blended into the pupil. There was even a similarity to their expressions—equally stubborn, equally wild.

"'There's a difference between a companion and a monster,'" Barclay repeated Tadg's words under his breath. Looking at the Lufthund, he wasn't sure. There was something untamable about it, like the wind. But that didn't make it a monster.

He shakily reached his hand up to touch it, wondering if the action would lose him a few fingers. But the Lufthund didn't bite him. Instead, Barclay's fingers ran through its shaggy fur.

"Root," Barclay murmured. "Your name is Root."

Root gave a light bark of approval at his name, then he nodded to the right, toward the streets where they had run the previous night. Barclay's heart gave a thrilled thump. In Sycomore, there was no one to punish him for wild things. For running in the dark of night. For the tangles in his hair, the dirt beneath his fingernails. Barclay was no one here. He was free.

But then a rush of memories returned to him, the kind so precious and painful that he normally kept them locked away. Like his father reading him to sleep each night. How his parents' house used to smell, like the sage and thyme that grew on the windowsill, like the logs burning on the fire. He remembered his mother's hair—it was long and black, much like his own. How much they'd loved Dullshire, even with its many, many rules.

And he remembered who he really was: Barclay Thorne, a mushroom farmer's apprentice and townsboy, the last person who'd ever want to go on an adventure.

Come back, Barclay told him, and Root ignored him, wagging his tail and once again motioning toward the road.

"We're not running tonight," Barclay told him bitterly.

Root woofed and padded excitedly in a circle.

"I said *no*," Barclay groaned.

Root's tail fell in disappointment, and this time he didn't fight returning to his Mark. Barclay stood up, dusted the snow off his coat, and trudged back to the Ironwood Inn. His cheeks were flushed, like they were when he lied. But there was no one around to lie to but himself.

SIXTEEN

On Lecture Day, the day before the second exam, Barclay found himself seated in a crowd in the snowy grass at the edge of Sycomore. Mandeep gave the first presentation of the morning, but Barclay only paid attention to Viola beside him, who continued to quiz him for the practical. She had two open books on her lap: a textbook Ethel had lent Barclay and Murdock's *A Traveler's Log* beside it.

"Where would you find a Tadpike?" Viola asked.

"At this time of year, probably buried near freshwater. It's too cold for them to be in the river yet," Barclay answered, and Viola gave him a distracted nod.

After several moments, impatient for the next question, Barclay hissed, "Viola."

"Sorry, sorry. I'm just interested in this chapter Murdock

wrote about bonds between a Keeper and Beast. You might want to read—"

"Will you two be quiet?" Ethel snapped from his other side. "I can't hear."

"I thought you and Abel want to be Guardian Keepers," said Barclay. "So why listen to Mandeep? He's a Scholar."

"It's still really interesting!" Ethel said, flipping to a new page in her notebook.

Abel rolled his eyes. "You think everything is interesting."

"I'm an interesting person," she huffed. "I have *interests*."

"I just don't understand why you need a license to be a Scholar," he said. "You don't need to be part of the Guild to go to the library."

"Certain texts are forbidden to anyone without a license," Viola explained. "Being part of the Guild is important, even in some of the non-Lore-Keeper world. It's why the Exhibition is so difficult. And apprenticeship is even harder. Only a small percentage of Lore Keepers are licensed by the Guild."

"What sort of texts do you think are forbidden?" Ethel whispered, a glimmer in her eyes. Even Abel, who had thus far only studied to beat Tadg in the practical, quieted to listen to Mandeep's presentation.

"All three of my last apprentices went on to great universities, including the University of Al Faradh and the Meridienne College in Halois," Mandeep said. He paused as though expecting a round of applause, but no one clapped except Ethel.

"My mother teaches at the University of Al Faradh," Viola told them proudly.

Barclay furrowed his eyebrows. "But I thought your parents lived in the Mountains."

"They're not with each other anymore—they don't really get along much. Mom lives in the Desert. That's where she's from," Viola explained. It was no wonder Viola was such a good tutor if her mother was a professor. "You know, Mandeep sounds really impressive. He could be a good Master for you, Barclay, if you—"

"Don't bother," he grunted, turning his attention away from Mandeep and back to the notes on his lap.

The Apothecary Masters presented next, and the group relocated to the Ironwood Inn for Floriane's lecture. Unlike Mandeep, who had merely drawled on for an hour, Floriane had a table set up full of interactive supplies, so Barclay had no choice but to participate.

"Does anyone know what this is?" Floriane held up a tub of something sappy and as blue as sea glass. It oozed as she poured some of it into a beaker. Similar beakers with the goo sat at the workplaces of all the students.

Viola's fingers twitched, and she bit her lip, as though swallowing down the instinct to raise her hand. None of the other students did, but Barclay supposed she didn't consider herself one of them, since she already had a Master. She did hate to stick out.

In the silence that followed, Barclay resisted the urge to

touch the goo. It was made from Beasts, after all, but it did look pretty interesting.

Then Abel shrugged and lifted his beaker to sniff it, but Viola grabbed his arm. "Don't smell that!"

But it was too late. Within moments, a rash erupted across his face, bumpy and dark like a blackberry. He lifted his fingers to touch his cheeks and let out a word that was forbidden in Dullshire.

"Well, Miss Dumont," Floriane said, sighing. "Would you like to inform your friend what he just smelled?"

"It's Glowsap," Viola answered, even as whispers circulated the room at the mention of her name. Barclay often forgot, until moments like these, how famous his friend was.

"Dumont like Leopold Dumont?" someone murmured.

"Daughter of the Grand Keeper—"

"Cyril Harlow's apprentice?"

Viola's face flushed, but she continued, raising her voice so Floriane could hear her. "Glowsap is honey made by Stingurs, a beelike Trite class Beast. The Stingurs glow in the dark, which makes their honey do the same. It's used as a lure to summon certain Beasts, because lots of Beasts love its taste and smell. It's toxic for humans, though."

"Toxic?" Abel moaned, rubbing at his skin.

"But not deadly," Floriane added. "You'd still best go see the doctor."

Across the room Tadg let out a loud snort. "I guess they

don't have common sense in the middle of nowhere in the Woods. Can't say I'm surprised—I heard they don't even have outhouses."

A round of snickers spread across the inn, and Ethel shot Tadg a mean look and led Abel outside.

"Well," Floriane said, shaking her head, "if any of you learn anything today, I hope it's not to sniff something when you don't know what it is." This earned laughter all around. "Now, if you could put on your gloves, we're going to make a lure for Trite and Familiar class Beasts. Traps are handy for all Lore Keepers, but especially for those like me, who need Beast by-products but don't always want to go searching for them in the Woods. We'd rather the Beasts come to us."

Floriane passed out a number of flower-infused waters and oils to combine with the Glowsap. Within minutes the innkeeper let out a screech.

"Anthorns! Murrows! Arachadees!"

The students all stopped their work to look. A swarm of antlike Beasts with gold bodies swept across the room's floor toward their tables. Mice like the kind Barclay had seen with Selby at the Woods' edge scurried beneath barstools. Spiders descended from webs along the ceiling, white as snowflakes.

Many of the students screamed and dashed out of the Beasts' paths as they made for the Glowsap mixtures. The innkeeper swatted at the mice with her broom.

"What were you thinking, letting vermin into my restaurant?" the innkeeper shouted at Floriane, who was pulling spiders out of her tangled hair. "You only told me you were brewing potions! I would never have agreed to this! High Keeper Erhart is going to hear—"

With many apologies, Floriane ushered the students and their beakers of Glowsap outside, all sorts of Trite and Familiar class Beasts following in eager pursuit. By the time they'd dumped all the Glowsap in a cider barrel and sealed it, three students had fainted. Several had spilled the concoction on themselves, making their skin swollen like Abel's but worse—letting out a bright, eerie glow. Barclay and Viola grew sweaty lunging away from Murrows.

Few students paid attention during Athna's lecture that followed, as they were all still shaking Anthorns out of their coat sleeves. In the commotion, Barclay had left his textbook in the Ironwood Inn, and so he and Viola whispered instead of studying.

"It's a shame," Viola said. "Floriane is very well-known! Her tinctures and potions have done a lot of good. I considered apprenticing to an Apothecary Master—I've always been good at traps—but Dad would never have dreamed of it."

"Why not?" Barclay asked.

"Oh, the Dumonts have all been Guardians. It's the family trade, and it's what I wanted in the end, anyway." She gave him a sly smile. "But an Apothecary Master might be a good fit for you! I'm sure there's lots of crossover with mushroom farming—"

"Stop doing that," he snapped. "Stop trying to make me a Lore Keeper."

"Oh, you're not fooling me. I've seen you slipping out at night to spend time with Root."

Barclay glowered. Viola was as sneaky as she was smart.

"We're only training. I need to win, in case you've forgotten. I'm not going to beat Tadg by getting enough sleep."

"Or could it be that you don't hate Root *or* Sycomore as much as you thought you would?"

Barclay crossed his arms and pretended to listen to Athna's presentation about fossilized remnants of forgotten Beasts.

"So you're going to brood and ignore me now?" Viola asked.

He didn't answer.

"At least talk to me about *something*, so I don't have to pay attention to everyone still staring at me."

Barclay struggled not to smile, preferring—as Viola had accused—to continue brooding. "It must be so exhausting having people give you things and be so polite all the time, Your Highness."

She elbowed him in the side. "They're not being polite. They think I ran away."

"Well, did you?" he asked. Viola didn't strike him as the sort to abandon her teacher.

She sighed and stood up. "I think it's better that I not go to Runa's lecture. But Abel and Ethel should be back by then." She handed him her copy of *A Traveler's Log*. "Just . . . just read the page that I bookmarked. I think it might help you."

Before Barclay could protest, she left, and his bitter mood soured further. He did *not* like Root. He did *not* like Sycomore.

Thankfully, Ethel and Abel did return for Runa's presentation—Abel with a strange green ointment on his face, but otherwise well. Tadg was gone, which suited Barclay fine—he didn't want to see Tadg and Abel stir up another fight. Then he remembered that Soren, also a Guardian, was giving his lecture at the same time as Runa. So Tadg had left to spend time with his future Master. Well, they deserved each other.

Runa held her presentation in the Guild House, and even though it was the town's largest building, students were crammed inside, filling the tables, standing along the sides, and seated on the beer-sticky floor.

While Abel described the gory details of what had happened to him in outrageous exaggerations ("The sap *exploded* all over my face! I was *covered*. Hot like *lava*."), Barclay opened *A Traveler's Log* to the page Viola had marked.

It's a common misconception to believe that a bond between Keeper and Beast is only ever initiated by the

Keeper. It's true of Familiar class Beasts and almost always of Prime class. These Beasts don't have the power to forge a Mark. But on rare and remarkable occasions, I have heard of or witnessed Mythic class Beasts casting the bond themselves.

Why? Well, that is the question! But I believe the Beast recognizes something in their would-be Keeper. They see someone else of their kind. Of their Lore. Of the wilds.

A hush fell over the room as Runa entered, and Barclay tore himself away from his book. As always, Runa's long blond hair was tightly braided, and she walked like a soldier, menacing, nimble, ready to strike. Even Barclay, who had little in common with the other students, was eager to hear what she had to say.

"Many of you already know who I am," she began, taking a seat on her usual leather armchair by the fireplace. "My name is Runa Rasgar, though some refer to me as the Fang of Dusk. As many of you also know, it's the power of the Legendary Beasts that keeps the other Beasts within their Wilderland. But that power is imperfect, and it often slips. I consider it my job to protect the world from the most vicious of Beasts, because not all Beasts are useful or cute or friendly. Some Beasts are dangerous. Some Beasts aren't meant to be tamed."

At her first pause, someone took advantage of her silence and shouted out, "Could you tell us more about Dooling? What was it like to be champion for six—"

"After my apprenticeship ended, I spent some time as a Dooler, so that I could meet Keepers and Beasts from all over the world. I won champion six years in a row."

Beside Barclay, Abel let out a huff. "There's a lot of people full of themselves around here, don't you think?"

"I thought Runa was your top choice," Barclay hissed.

He and Ethel both shrugged. Barclay wanted to ask more about their change of heart when another student spoke up.

"But if you could tell us more about—"

"There's nothing more to say. I won't be competing in the Dooling tournament this year," Runa said sharply. "As I've decided to take on apprentices instead."

The room quieted, realizing that offending Runa could ruin their chances of becoming her student. Barclay wondered why Runa wouldn't share more about the sport that had made her so famous—it was obviously what all the students wanted to hear about. Maybe her memories of Dooling had been bad ones. Maybe that was how she had gotten that scar.

This time someone raised their hand, rather than shouting. "What was it like to be apprenticed to the Grand Keeper?"

Barclay elbowed Ethel in the side. "Runa was Viola's father's apprentice?" he asked.

"Well, yeah," she said. "Didn't you know that? So was Cyril Harlow, who's also a Guardian Keeper."

No wonder Viola had been nervous to go talk to Runa the first time they met.

Runa didn't seem to like this question any more than the last. "I learned a lot," she said, and left it at that.

When she didn't continue, the same person pressed, "But . . . Is that when you met the Horn of Dawn? Maybe you could—"

"I don't wish to elaborate on my relationship with Cyril Harlow. Any other questions?"

Barclay didn't know a lot about Guardian Keepers, and with Runa refusing to answer anything, he doubted he'd know any more after this presentation ended. What was the point of giving a lecture if she refused to speak?

"Soren Reiker said you used to know Conley Murdock, that you all worked together studying Lochmordra—"

"He told you that?" Runa growled, looking up with a fire in her glare. A hush descended over the students.

The girl who'd spoken seemed to shrink several inches. "I . . . Yes. That's what he said after the first exam. I don't . . . I mean . . ."

Runa's gaze traveled over the room, as though she was looking for someone. Each of the students straightened, hoping her eyes fell on them, but she didn't seem to find who she was searching for. Then she grimaced and stood up. "You're all dismissed."

And she walked out the front door.

Almost no one moved. "Do you think she'll be back?" someone asked.

"No. What do you think 'dismissed' means?"

"I wanted her to sign my champion card!"

While the students at last filed out, Abel asked, "Am I the only one who found that a bit strange?"

Ethel's brown eyes narrowed shrewdly. "It sounded like she had something to hide."

Barclay agreed that the lecture was strange and her leaving abrupt, but he couldn't help but feel loyal to Runa. She was the only person who hadn't laughed at him when he told her he'd bonded with a Lufthund. She was the only one who could help him get back home.

"Something to hide?" Barclay repeated. "I thought you said Conley Murdock was killed by the Legendary Beast of the Sea. What is there to hide?"

Abel shrugged. "For all we know, she could've had something to do with it too."

"And either way," Ethel continued, "she can't be that good of a teacher, can she? Not after a performance like that."

Barclay didn't want to fight with his friends—he barely even knew Runa, and they *did* know more about Lore Keepers than he did. But he still felt guilty, talking about her like this.

So he stood up and muttered, "I'm going on a walk," and he left the Guild House.

He'd only wanted to clear his head, but it was hard to get the lectures out of his mind. How Scholars could read books banned from the general public. How Apothecaries brewed medicinal tonics or traps, and Surveyors mapped out places never before discovered. And especially Guardians, who protected vulnerable towns like Dullshire from the Beasts . . . even if Dullshire didn't realize it.

The world of Beasts was more fascinating than he'd ever imagined it.

And then there was the matter of what he'd read in *A Traveler's Log*. That maybe Root had not bonded with him by accident. Maybe that was exactly what Root had been trying to tell him.

As he turned down a cobbled alley, still lost in his thoughts, he spotted Runa in the distance, dragging Tadg with her.

"You need to stop this. Stop going to him," she snapped at Tadg. "It won't change anything."

Tadg ripped his arm away from her. "I don't have to listen to you. What happened was your fault too."

They're talking about his father, Barclay realized with shock.

"That's not fair." Runa's voice nearly shook from anger.

"Then tell me I'm wrong."

When Runa didn't answer, Tadg growled, "I thought so."

Then he turned around and stormed away. Barclay, not wanting to be caught eavesdropping, ducked around the corner, his back against the crooked stone wall.

"I don't want to hear about you going to the Bog's Inn again!" Runa shouted after him.

"Then stop listening!" Tadg called back.

Tadg passed Barclay without noticing him, and Barclay let out a strangled breath. If Tadg was visiting the Bog's Inn, then that proved that Tadg and Soren were working together. Which meant it didn't matter what Barclay thought about Root or the world of Lore Keepers.

Surviving the second exam could be just as hard as passing it.

He ran the entire way back to the Ironwood Inn, as though he could sense a monster chasing him.

SEVENTEEN

The morning of the second round of the Exhibition, all the students and the Lore Masters gathered at the edge of Sycomore. The sky was gray from an oncoming blizzard, and snow whipped across the street, stinging Barclay's already sleep-deprived, bloodshot eyes. This exam's proctors, Floriane and Athna, distributed pieces of parchment and canvas bags while Erhart spoke at the crowd's center.

"The second exam is a scavenger hunt," he told them. He was bundled up so heavily that only his blue eyes were visible between his wooly hat and scarf. "You will have three hours within the Woods to collect the items on that parchment. Stow them in your bags, and return to this spot for the proctors to count them. Speed and correctness are important. You must finish quickly, and you must try to collect as many items as you can. Fewer items will result in a lower score."

Ethel locked arms with Barclay. "We should work together!"

"We can do that?" he asked incredulously.

"Of course we can," said Abel. "There aren't rules, remember?"

After an entire night worrying about Soren and Tadg plotting his demise, Barclay's hope rekindled. Ethel and Abel could protect him—they wouldn't let him die, or fail.

When Floriane handed Barclay the list, his spirits lifted further. Viola had done a good job teaching him. Already he guessed the proper places to find all the items. And Soren, who usually watched him menacingly across the crowds, was nowhere to be seen.

"What are you smiling about?" Tadg asked Barclay as the students queued up at the starting line. "Eager to die, are you?"

Barclay's skin prickled at his words. Ethel and Abel shot him suspicious, knowing glances. Last night Barclay had told them everything he'd overheard between Tadg and Runa.

"We'll be waiting for you at the finish, fish food," Abel told him.

"I told you to stop calling me that," Tadg growled. Barclay realized Abel must've done so when he'd first overheard Abel and Tadg fighting in the Exhibition registration line.

Considering how Tadg's father had died, it *was* a pretty mean thing to say.

"Make me," Abel goaded.

Before Tadg could, however, Athna cleared her throat. With a voice surprisingly powerful for an old woman, she shouted, "Begin!"

The students sprinted into the forest. Even in the thick of the blizzard, Barclay was one of the fastest. Ethel and Abel panted to keep pace.

"Do you know where to find a river? Or a creek?" Barclay asked. "We can find the Stoolips, Tadpikes, and Garneeli by water."

Ethel held up her arm to block the snow pelting her face. "I think there's one to the north."

They trudged through the snow. The weather made it difficult to see *and* hear, so they didn't notice they were nearing the stream until their boots were wet. Chunks of ice floated down the water.

"I found a Garneeli," Ethel exclaimed, bending down and scooping up a crayfishlike Beast burrowing into the cold, muddy riverbank. She dug around for two more and placed them in their bags.

Abel searched the ground for any Tadpike holes, while Barclay scoped for Stoolips. He quickly spotted a cluster nestled between a pile of rocks. He tickled three of them and gently popped off their tops.

They dumped their findings into the bags. "Only twelve

more items to go," Abel declared. "We're going to win this, no problem."

Except there was a problem. Nearing the end of the exam, they encountered five other students, and Barclay recognized them as Tadg's usual admirers, even though Tadg was—thankfully—not among them. The group blocked their path.

"If you give us your Tadpikes and Petalmills, we won't hurt you," one of them said. It was an older boy—one of the oldest of all the students. He was tall and pimply, like an Autumn gourd.

"Not a chance," Abel growled.

"It's five against . . ." One of them smirked, looking at Barclay. "Two." Barclay's cheeks heated in anger and embarrassment.

"You'll still lose," Ethel warned.

Vines shot up out of the earth, vibrant green even in the dead of Winter. They latched around Barclay's and Ethel's ankles, rooting them in place. Abel managed to scramble out of the way to avoid them, but he quickly collided with a foxlike Beast. Though small, it pinned him to the ground. He groaned and wrestled with it as the others went for his bag.

"This is cheating!" Barclay shouted.

One of them—the fox Keeper girl—laughed. "As if Erhart will care."

As two others reached for his and Ethel's bags, Barclay

desperately summoned wind. A gale blew through the thickets of trees, and though it succeeded in knocking the fox from Abel's chest, it did nothing to help Barclay and Ethel with the vines. And the vines were growing steadily up their bodies and slithering around their waists and wrists, tight enough to bruise.

Then a curious thing happened. The number of people in the area suddenly jumped from eight to sixteen, and Barclay realized that a massive mirror had appeared ahead of them, forming a long wall. He blinked at his reflection, his body covered in vines and his hair whipping wildly across his face.

Abel jumped to his feet and ran to the mirror. Barclay braced himself for a crash, but instead of colliding with the glass, Abel leaped *into* the mirror, as though he'd merged with his own reflection.

"What the—?" one of the students started.

Then, in an instant, Abel ran and made it to the other end of the mirror. He lunged out of the glass and tackled the student to the ground.

The vines on Barclay's and Ethel's legs sank back into the snow, and the two of them stumbled free. They immediately targeted the two students closest to them, Ethel deftly sweeping one of them off their feet, Barclay summoning a wind to do the same.

"What *was* that?" Barclay asked. He retrieved his fallen bag, and he and Ethel joined Abel at the giant mirror.

Abel's eyes twinkled. "Mirror Lore. Though it's better when—"

"We use it together," Ethel finished bitterly. "But I was a bit tied up!"

The students watched them more cautiously now, as though realizing that five against three didn't necessarily mean they had the upper hand. The gourd boy staggered to his feet and leaned against a nearby tree to steady himself.

Something rumbled beneath their feet, and Root's Mark stung painfully in warning. A thunderous groan echoed through the Woods.

"No!" Barclay called out. "Don't lean on that tree!"

But it was too late. The rootlike tongue of a Styerwurm shot up from the earth, and the head followed, its mouth open wide like a dark tunnel. The gourd boy screamed and scampered out of its path.

"Don't just watch!" Barclay shouted, grabbing at Abel's and Ethel's hands. "Run!"

The Styerwurm, distracted with shaking the fox girl, didn't notice them escape. Several more screams echoed throughout the trees, the Woods once again reminding Barclay how dangerous it was. In the hazy blizzard of white, it was impossible to see. They collided painfully with thorn bushes, fell and stumbled down hills, and tripped over logs. The barren trees seemed to sway and move in the darkness.

"Which way is Sycomore?" Barclay asked.

"I have no idea," Abel breathed.

Ethel shakily looked up at the sky, hoping for the sun to provide direction, but it was swallowed by the storm.

Silhouettes approached around them, each different shapes. Some were tall and wide, others crouched and predatory. There could be Beasts far more dangerous than Styerwurms wild in this forest.

The three of them stood in a circle, back-to-back.

"How many items are left on the list?" Abel asked hoarsely.

"Only one," Ethel answered. "The Hasifuss."

A roar shook the Woods around them. They cringed and pressed closer together.

"We could split up," Ethel suggested.

"Bad idea," Abel squeaked.

"We could go back to town," she said. "No one would blame us in this blizzard—"

"I'm not giving up," Barclay said determinedly, and Abel nodded. No matter what wild Beasts attacked them, they weren't helpless. They could still finish this.

Then a silhouette took form through the falling snow. The Beast looked like a mountain lion, only giant, with gray fur and two heads. Each face bared its fangs, growling menacingly.

"It's amazing," Ethel said in her usual awe.

"It's terrifying," Barclay corrected.

"Barclay, we're going to distract it with a mirror," Abel said. "Then we all run."

Barclay nodded, grateful they'd settled so quickly on a plan.

Another long mirror appeared among the trees, so sudden and clear that Barclay didn't notice anything had changed until he saw his reflection staring back at him.

The Beast ran forward, striking the mirror and shattering it. Barclay, Abel, and Ethel screamed, their hands over their heads. A sharp piece fell and sliced Barclay on his wrist, making him shout out in pain. But he was so scared, no sound even came out.

The Beast raced toward them, and the three of them took off running. Normally, Barclay could have run faster, but his legs suddenly felt heavy, like something was tugging on them. Yet when he looked down, there was nothing there.

So intent on fleeing the wild Beast, Ethel and Abel didn't notice him lagging as they charged ahead.

They ran.

And ran.

And ran.

Suddenly Barclay lost sight of them in the distance.

"Ethel! Abel!" he tried to call, but no matter how loud he shouted, no sound came out.

He froze. He remembered that Lore.

He turned around and faced the Ischray, its smoky white body barely visible in the whirls of snow. Barclay's scream wisped through the air, and the Beast ate it whole.

Then Barclay looked down and saw rusty chains

materialize around both of his feet, as though they'd been there for a while, invisible. No wonder it'd been hard to run, with them dragging him down. His eyes followed them to where they ended, and he saw them shackled to the legs of the mountain lion.

Barclay had not noticed earlier, but all four of the eyes on its two heads were a cloudy white. It was blind.

"It's impressive, isn't it?" a voice asked. "Lore that plays with your senses."

Another silhouette appeared from the trees, only this one was not a Beast.

"Hello, Barclay," Soren said, smiling viciously.

In his hand, he carried a scalpel.

EIGHTEEN

D o you like this recent addition to my collection?" Soren asked Barclay. He petted the mountain lion behind one of its four ears, the keys to the chains swinging from his belt. "A Nitney, a Prime class Beast. They're blind, but they can trick your sight Lore. With the Nitney, I can make you miss things that are really there. It pairs well with my Ischray's sound Lore, don't you think?"

Soren gave a fond look to the haunting Ischray, which now pinned Barclay's arms behind his back. Barclay squirmed in its grip and opened his mouth to yell at Soren, but it was no use. Until Soren snapped his fingers and Barclay regained his voice.

"If something happens to me, if I don't come back—" Barclay started.

"Everyone will assume you died. You're just an Elsie, after all. One very much in over his head."

Soren nodded at the Ischray, which unfastened Barclay's heavy coat. It fell into the snow, leaving him shivering in only his sweater. Soren placed the scalpel against Barclay's shoulder, prepared to cut through the wool.

"Viola will tell her father. He's the—"

"Grand Keeper, yes," Soren said dismissively. "Something tells me the Grand Keeper will be much more concerned about his only child wandering in the Woods alone without her Master. She's not here to spectate the Exhibition. She's here to *hide*."

If that was true, maybe Viola couldn't help him at all.

"Why are you doing this?" Barclay asked him. "Is it for Tadg?"

Soren's eyebrows raised. "Tadg hardly needs my help. Do you know how hard Mythic Beasts are to find? No? Well, I'll tell you—they are far easier to *take*." Soren grinned maliciously. "My real interest lies in the Legendary Beasts, and once I have my apprentices . . . Well, the opportunity to claim a Mythic Beast was still too good to pass up."

"They can't be that hard to find! I mean, I didn't even *mean* to bond with—"

"Do you think it's easy?" Soren spat. "A powerful summoning trap or not, a Mythic Beast will nearly always attack the Keeper who summoned it. It's a wonder you even survived."

His words reminded Barclay of what Conley Murdock had written in his book. How a Mythic Beast sometimes chose its Keeper.

"How lucky I am to have found someone like you," Soren continued, licking his lips. "You have no one watching out for you. No home. No *idea* what you could be capable of."

The scalpel was ice against Barclay's skin.

Come out! Come out! Barclay desperately called into his mind.

Soren paid little concern to the wind that swept across the forest, to the figure of the Lufthund as Root appeared behind him.

"Its class might be powerful," said Soren, unlocking the chains that bound Barclay to the mountain lion, "but even my Nitney can handle one so young."

Soren was right. When Root pounced, the Nitney quickly pinned him to the snow. He writhed and barked as the Nitney raked its claws at his side.

"You're hurting him!" Barclay growled.

Soren smirked. "Beasts heal faster than humans. You should be more concerned about yourself."

And with that, he sliced through Barclay's skin.

A week ago Barclay might have been happy to give Soren his Beast. *Take it,* he'd have told him, without a fight. But Barclay did care about Root. It wasn't just that they'd run together, that Barclay understood him better—it was that Root had chosen him when no one else ever had, even if Barclay didn't know why.

And so Barclay writhed the best he could beneath the

Ischray's grasp—for Root's sake as well as his own. Nevertheless, Soren cut with a steady hand, like he'd done this before. It scared Barclay to think that if he was left in the snow, he might never be found.

Unfortunately, the only two abilities Barclay could manage—running fast and summoning wind—were impossible without the use of his legs or arms. Which meant he'd have to think of something else to do, and quickly.

It was Soren himself who'd told Barclay what Lufthunds were capable of, when they'd first met at the Bog's Inn.

Apart from flying Beasts, they are the fastest species in the world. They've been known to dissolve completely into wind. Their howls can conjure storms.

As Root moaned louder from beneath the Nitney, Barclay looked up into the sky, into its endless stretch of gray and white, and he howled. The sound of it seemed to come from his very core. From the place inside of him that loved unearthing a mushroom from fresh, damp soil. That kept his hair long to better feel the wind in it. That didn't like anything as much as running—running and knowing no one could catch him.

His howl did nothing to change the storm, and Soren let out a strained laugh. "Did you think your own howls had power?"

"No," answered Barclay, "but Root's do."

As though in response, Root let out a howl of his own. Barclay felt it inside of him, echoing around his ribs, thumping against his heart. It shook its way up the trees and into the sky, and the sky answered.

The winds, already fierce, picked up speed. Their sound was a roar too. Thunder and lightning cracked above, and the flurries of snow transformed into shards of hail.

The gusts grew stronger and stronger. The Ischray quickly dispersed somewhere deep in the Woods, and the Nitney was blown against the trunk of a tree. Soren let out a curse, muffled in the noise of it all, as Barclay tore free from his grasp.

Barclay stumbled back, his eyes squeezed shut against the ice and wind. Without his coat, he was so cold, he felt numb all over. He peeled one eye open in time to see Root staggering to his feet. His dark eyes met Barclay's own.

Just as Soren lunged forward to grab Barclay, he ran.

And when Barclay ran, Root followed.

The snow that had slowed him down before no longer bothered him. His legs moved so fast, they merely seemed to skim the ground. The trees flew past in a dark blur. Everything was so brutally strong—the wind, the hail, the speed—that Barclay quickly lost his balance. He grabbed onto a fistful of Root's fur to steady himself. And when Root offered no disagreement, Barclay hoisted himself over Root's back and hugged his arms around the Beast's neck.

In that moment, the wind slowed to barely a tickle against his skin. Then to nothing at all.

They were running faster than the wind.

No—it was more than that. The edges of Barclay's fingers were wisps, and Root's black fur had the look and feel of smoke from a forest fire. They spun in spirals and curls. The sky and the ground seemed to infinitely change places.

This was Root's power. His *full* power.

They had become the wind.

Barclay let out a second howl, this one of delight. And the entire world seemed to answer. The wilds recognized one of their own.

Within moments, it came to a stop. Barclay and Root collapsed at the edge of Sycomore, a crowd of people around them. Everyone gasped when the pair of them appeared, tumbling and leaving bloody streaks against white snow. Barclay was still clutching Root's neck when strong arms hoisted him up.

"My boy!" Erhart rasped, his hands hot as he patted Barclay's cheeks. "We all thought you were dead!"

Root stood up and crouched over Barclay protectively, and the onlookers stepped back to give him space. Even Erhart paled to be so close to him.

Barclay looked around, bewildered, at the other faces. Viola came charging through the crowd, and she threw her arms around him. Her face was streaked with tears.

"The exam's been over for almost an hour! I wanted to go look for you, but—"

"It's fine," he assured her. "We're both fine."

"You're not fine! Look at you!" She examined the blood

on his shoulder. But as much as she fussed, the cut from Soren's scalpel didn't look deep.

More faces appeared in the crowd. Abel and Ethel stared at him, wide-eyed.

"B-Barclay!" Ethel choked, her face flushed. "How did you make it out?"

"We didn't know we'd lost you!" Abel said.

But of them, no face looked more stricken than Tadg.

"We all bet you were dead," he said, his voice strangely hoarse. His gaze fell on Barclay's shoulder. "Who did this to you?" Barclay noted he asked "who," and not "what."

"Don't you already know?" Barclay asked him coolly, and Tadg stiffened. "Soren attacked me and tried to carve off my Mark."

Nervous titters swept across the crowd. Barclay was shocked that many other Masters, like the woman who had once pointed him in the direction of the Bog's Inn, looked far more disgruntled than aghast. Clearly, Soren's wealth had bought him many friends.

At the mention of Soren's name, Erhart's face grew even paler. "How unfortunate!"

"How unfortunate?" Viola echoed furiously. "He's here as a Master! He attacked a student!"

"Y-yes, well, you see, how can I be expected to believe—"

"Enough!" Runa said, stepping forward. "Of course you can believe it. And given Soren's reputation, this is really no surprise."

"That's conjecture," Erhart shot back. "And ironic, I might add—coming from you, whose reputation is by no means clean. It's only this boy's word against Soren's. Really now, Soren isn't even here to defend himself."

"That's because I ran away from him!" said Barclay. "He's still in the Woods!"

"That's impossible, when Soren was doing very important business for *me*," Erhart said.

Barclay squeezed his hands into fists. Of course, thanks to Soren's donation to the Guild House, the High Keeper would willingly lie for him.

"How else would Barclay have gotten such an injury?" Runa demanded.

"He isn't the only injured student to return from the Woods," Erhart answered flatly. He then stalked off into the crowds, and Barclay angrily kicked at a mound of snow.

Beside him, Tadg knelt down in front of Root. He was the only person—student or Master—who dared to approach the Mythic class Beast. Then Tadg gathered up the fallen items from Barclay's bag and handed it to him.

Barclay was too startled to say thank you, and Tadg didn't wait for it. He stood up and walked away.

Floriane stepped forward and cleared her throat. "Now that the final student has arrived, the Masters will count the items in each of your bags, and Athna and I will issue the exam rankings."

Barclay's stomach sank as he got in line. He was still

missing the Hasifuss, *and* he had returned far after the time limit. His ranking was sure to plummet.

It was Runa who checked his bag for him, and he held it out to her with shaking hands.

"Why so nervous?" she asked him.

"Because I'll just come in last place, won't I?" he asked.

"I wouldn't be so sure about that. After all, everyone had to face Beasts and other students in the Woods—you were the only one who faced a Master."

Barclay's face broke out into a smile. Soren had not ruined his chances.

"Besides," Runa continued, a twinkle in her gray eyes, "I haven't seen one other student return with all the items yet. But you have."

"What?" Barclay asked, taking back his bag. "That can't be—"

Runa raised her eyebrows. "Are you suggesting I counted wrong?"

"N-no, I just . . ." Barclay dug through his bag, and sure enough, the Hasifuss was buried amid the other items, its green slime smeared across the Stoolip top, smoking slightly. How did that get in there?

Barclay wanted to run off and tell his friends about the good news, but then he hesitated.

"I don't believe Soren," he told Runa. "I don't believe you had anything to do with what happened to Tadg's father."

Runa's expression faltered, replaced by one that looked

like guilt. "I appreciate you telling me that, Barclay. That's very good of you." But she didn't tell him whether or not he was right.

Deciding to reflect on Runa's reaction later, Barclay shook off his questions and rushed over to Viola to show her the Hasifuss. "I collected all the items!"

Abel, however, was far less happy. "My Hasifuss was gone! It disappeared!"

Barclay wondered if their items had somehow been exchanged, but that couldn't be right. He had gotten split up from Abel and Ethel before they'd found the Hasifuss, and once Barclay had returned, Abel's bag had been nowhere near his. And Runa couldn't have slipped it in either. He would've seen.

It took several mugs of pear cider to cheer up Abel, but that was before the rankings had been posted. The four of them visited the Guild House hours later—after Barclay's shoulder had been stitched up and Root had been bandaged—to look at their scores.

"Ethel, you came in first!" Viola said excitedly.

Ethel's face lit up. "But Abel and I were hardly the first ones back."

"But you were one of the only ones with all the items. Abel, you got seventh—that's still quite high. And Barclay! You got—"

But Barclay had already spotted his name. He should be thrilled, he knew. Relieved. But instead, a knot twisted in his stomach.

"*'Second'?*" Abel read, too loudly. "The proctors must really like you, Barclay."

"He was attacked," Viola said flatly. "And he was the only other student with all the items."

But the damage was done. The other students reading the scores turned to glare at Barclay.

"He's some sort of cheat, isn't he?"

"He *does* have a Mythic class Beast."

"Still, Tadg deserved better than third."

Viola narrowed her eyes at Abel. "Now you've done it," she snapped, ignoring Abel as he stammered apologies and leading Barclay out of the cloud of scorn.

But while the others returned to the Ironwood Inn to discuss the day's exam, Barclay made up some excuse and headed straight for the grove with Root. He needed to think about what had happened out in the Woods between him and Root, because something had definitely changed.

Sure enough, when he summoned wind, the pine cone soared right off the stump.

Barclay gave a triumphant holler. Root barked, as though telling him, *That's it! You've done it!*

His chest swelling with pride, Barclay knelt and stroked Root along his back. Root's tail wagged appreciatively.

"I understand it now. What you've been trying to tell me," Barclay breathed. "You bonded with me because we're the same. We're both alone. And fast, and smart, and wild. And we could . . ."

In an instant, his exhilaration drained out of him. All

he could picture were his parents—and there was a worse memory, one Barclay never dared to think about. The way the ground had shaken with each mighty footstep. The way the fallen beams had trapped him, and he hadn't been able to see. But he could hear. The roar of Gravaldor. The sound of his father screaming. The silence of his mother, who had never answered him.

Barclay couldn't want to be Root's Keeper. He couldn't want anything to do with Beasts.

"No," he murmured to himself. "I'm still going home."

He returned Root to his Mark, left the clearing, and in the next week that passed until the third exam, he didn't visit again.

NINETEEN

Despite being injured, Barclay did everything he could to prepare for the third and final exam. He took notes on whatever Viola told him. He drank all sorts of questionable Lore tonics—from Scaromilk to Mendijuice— to heal his shoulder and restore his strength.

But under no circumstance did he practice Lore. It didn't matter that he and Root had saved each other in the Woods or that Root had chosen Barclay, the orphan no one else wanted. It didn't matter that Barclay got a sick, guilty feeling in his stomach whenever he thought of Root cooped up in his Mark. It didn't matter that Lore felt natural, freeing, and not at all terrible. Barclay had decided. He would perform the best he could, and then he would go home. No matter what.

The snow from the blizzard had melted within the week.

For the third exam, Erhart gathered the two hundred students and sixty-two Masters in a park in Sycomore's center, the only spot in town where the trees had been cleared away, with nothing to block the sunshine. A number of spectators had joined as well. They sat on wooden chairs and quilts along the dead grass. Some even sold food and drinks—the air smelled sweetly of pear cider.

A large chalk rectangle had been drawn on the field.

"Soren Reiker and I will be the proctors of the final exam," Erhart declared, and Barclay stiffened as Soren joined Erhart in the front the crowd. Tucked beneath his arm, Soren carried a wicker basket. "The last exam of the Exhibition is simple. It is also the longest of all the exams, and it will take the entire week."

Barclay's heart pounded, trying to imagine what sort of test could take so long. Would they ask them to cross the Woods to Dullshire and back? To go searching once again for something rare and powerful, with even more dangers to face? Knowing Soren, he'd likely concocted something horrible.

"In this basket," Soren explained, "are two hundred slips of paper with each of your names. When your name is drawn, you will face another randomly selected student in a battle of power and skill. The objective is to be the first to capture your opponent's flag, which ties around your arm."

He held up two black strips of fraying fabric.

"The match will also finish if either Keeper or Beast are

unable to continue, if one of the Keepers surrenders, or if either Keeper steps out-of-bounds. You may win by any means necessary."

A buzz of excitement swept across the crowd, with more than one mention of Dooling and champions—Abel loudest among them. The conversations quieted quickly as Erhart drew two pieces of parchment from Soren's basket.

"Fergus Maciver! Ethel Zader!"

Ethel jolted at hearing her name called.

"Good luck!" Viola told her brightly.

"Be careful," warned Barclay.

"Go for the eyes!" Abel said. "Or the—"

Abel's advice was cut off as the other students hurried to the edges of the field to claim the best viewing spot. The three of them sat at one of the corners, and Barclay wished they'd brought blankets like the other attendees. The grass was quite damp, and out in the open, there was nothing to stave off the Winter chill.

"Have either of you ever fought like this before?" Barclay asked them.

Viola and Abel both nodded.

"It's standard training if you want to become a Guardian Keeper, since they often need to subdue or battle dangerous Beasts," Viola answered. "Or sometimes even dangerous Keepers themselves."

"It's like Dooling, though those matches are all-out brawls." Abel rubbed his hands together. "You know,

Barclay, with a Lufthund, you could compete in them! You don't need a Guild license to—most champions don't have one. You could—"

"Yes, the world is my oyster, I get it," Barclay said grumpily. "Except the oyster spits out toxic phlegm instead of pearls."

"Gross," Viola said, wrinkling her nose. "You're so dramatic."

Abel shrugged. "I don't know, toxic phlegm sounds kind of neat."

Ethel's opponent, Fergus Maciver, was a stocky, pale boy with red hair. He summoned a Beast that looked like a turtle, except its shell was made of prickly, pink stone that looked like coral.

Ethel didn't bother to summon her own Beast. A long mirror appeared in the field, earning the claps and cheers of the audience. Much like Abel had in the Woods, she slipped within the glass—to gasps of surprise all around— and jumped out at another point behind Fergus. So disoriented, Fergus fumbled as he tried to block her. But Ethel was faster. She reached out and snagged Fergus's flag.

At her victory, Abel jumped to his feet and hollered.

"What kind of Lore is that?" Viola asked. "I've never seen anything like it."

"It's mirror Lore," Abel told her. "We can conjure mirrors and hop in and out of them. When we're in one, we're faster, like light speed, so it makes it easy to leap out behind you and attack."

Viola nodded, then turned to Barclay. "You look almost green."

He swallowed. "I'm nervous."

"Don't be! You'll be—"

"Did you forget, Viola? I did the math. The only way I have any chance of winning the Exhibition is placing first in this round. Otherwise, I'll be a Lore Keeper forever."

Viola studied him carefully—and maybe a bit sadly. "Would that really be so bad?"

Barclay hugged his arms to his chest, frustrated, with no idea how to answer.

Tadg's fight occurred in the afternoon, against a boy named Knut Wetzel. The entire audience quieted, eager to see Tadg's famous Mythic Beast, but they were disappointed. Within moments of starting, there was a faint spark of light, so fast that Barclay nearly missed it. Then Tadg's opponent let out a sudden mangled shriek and dropped unconscious.

Barclay could scarcely believe his eyes. "He attacked him!"

"But did you see it? Did you see what happened?" Abel hissed.

"Not at all," replied Ethel.

"Maybe Knut got scared and faked it," said Abel.

Viola rolled her eyes and pointed to the cover of *A Traveler's Log*, to the lampreylike Beast on the cover. "Nathermaras can use lightning and water Lore. Tadg probably electrocuted him."

Abel let out an annoyed huff. "Seems cheap."

When Barclay's name was called, he shakily climbed to his feet and walked to the center of the field. His opponent was a boy named Simon Specht, who had bushy brown hair and horn-rimmed glasses.

"Go on and shake hands," Erhart told them hurriedly. It had already been a long day of matches, and there were still over fifty to go.

They did so, even though Barclay's hands were clammy. Soren watched with a hungry gleam in his eyes. And almost equally nerve-racking, Barclay felt the stares of the crowd hot on his back, and he heard more than one voice call him a cheat.

He would prove them wrong.

But I won't summon Root unless I have to, he told himself. It wasn't that Root wasn't healed—after being bandaged, Root had healed nearly overnight from his scratches he'd earned from Soren's Nitney. It was that Barclay didn't think he could face Root again and disappoint him a second time.

Simon, however, summoned his Beast immediately. It was a small squirrel-like thing, with greenish fur probably meant to blend into grass in the Spring and Summertime. Its eyes were red like cranberries.

The Beast sprang forward and darted across the field. It opened its mouth wide, exposing dozens of tiny jagged teeth.

Barclay dodged it easily and ran toward Simon. In one second, two, three, he'd made it across the field, his powers from Root making him especially quick. Simon didn't even have time to react as Barclay snatched his flag. The crowd gasped.

"He was so fast!"

"I barely saw him!"

"It's already over?"

Barclay squeezed the fabric in his fist, his heart pounding with a surge of excitement. He'd won. And he hadn't even needed to summon Root.

Barclay, Viola, Abel, and Ethel celebrated their advancement that night with a round of pear cider. The number of students in the bracket had been halved, leaving one hundred competitors remaining.

The three days that followed went much like the first. Barclay faced Huan Yu, a boy from the Mountains, whose batlike Vampirwing let out a screech so piercing, it made Barclay dizzy . . . but it didn't slow him down. Then there was Neela Das with her Arachadee, whose spidery silk web tangled up on Barclay's legs but tore easily with a gust of wind. The Calamear gave Barclay a little trouble at first, until he'd kicked his way out of its slimy tentacles and nabbed Bryn Kelley's flag.

By the end of the fourth day of the tournament, Barclay had managed to place within the top eight competitors, which included Barclay, Abel, Ethel, Tadg, and four others.

All students with a Familiar class Beast had been eliminated. Barclay had been watching the fights for long enough to know the matches ahead would be far more challenging than any he'd faced before.

"Klara's Beast is a Hocus," Ethel said, referring to one of the other students. "She has illusion Lore. She can make you see things that aren't real."

"I think Emilie will be difficult," Abel said. "She has a dragon!"

Viola nodded and scratched Mitzi's head. "Never underestimate a dragon."

"I'd like to see Tadg's Beast," Abel muttered. "I hope I face him next."

"So you've figured out how he's attacking people now, have you?" Barclay asked. All Tadg's competitors, much like the first one, had collapsed within moments of the fight's start.

"No, but I won't be taken out that easily," Abel said. He yawned and stretched out his arms, the picture of ease and confidence.

"What about *your* Beast, Barclay?" Ethel asked. "It's all anyone can talk about now. They don't even mind that you got second twice, now that they know you're powerful."

"It's better that I don't summon him," Barclay grumbled.

"Better? Or *easier*?" Viola asked pointedly.

At this, Barclay's Mark gave a sudden twitch. He didn't even have to look at it to know what Root was doing—

cocking his head, being snide and teasing like he normally was. But Barclay wasn't playing a game. He couldn't be a Lore Keeper. He needed to go home.

He barely slept at all that night, knowing only three more victories separated him from first place. And worse, it had only just occurred to him that those victories might be against his friends.

The next day, Abel got his wish. His match with Tadg was the first that morning. Even though it was raining, the final battles of the Exhibition had still managed to draw a large audience.

Abel barely waited for Erhart to begin the match. He quickly conjured a wall of mirrors and leaped inside.

Barclay cheered, expecting one of Abel's usual quick victories. However, after Abel hurtled out to grasp at Tadg's flag, he sprawled back in pain.

"What happened?" asked Viola.

"Did Tadg hit him?" asked Barclay.

"He electrocuted him!" Ethel said. "That's what he does when he touches you. It zaps!"

While Abel clambered to his feet, Tadg crouched on the ground and placed both of his palms on the grass. Something bright shot across the field, so fast that Barclay couldn't tell what it was. Abel dodged out of the way and fled back into the safety of the mirrors, but then there was a loud crash. And all the mirrors shattered.

The audience gasped.

Abel was gone.

Barclay jumped to his feet. "He's not . . . He can't be *dead*, can he?" The other students around him looked equally as shocked and whispered among themselves.

Soren called the match for Tadg, who strutted off the field into his cheering band of admirers. He grinned widely, and Barclay feared that whatever he'd done to Abel must've been truly horrible.

Ethel, however, didn't look as concerned about her brother's disappearance. "He's just stuck as a reflection," she said simply.

"He is?!" Barclay asked, aghast. "Can you save him?"

"He just needs to run off and find some other mirror, like in a nearby house or inn."

"But *you* can conjure mirrors."

She shrugged. "Yes, but he'll be so grumpy that he lost to Tadg. Let's leave him as a reflection for a bit."

The next match was between one of the opponents Barclay didn't know well and Emilie with the dragon. She did summon the dragon for this match, and it looked nothing like Mitzi. It was tall—nearly fully grown—with brown scales and eyes that glowed like firelight. When it roared, everyone in the crowd picked up their umbrellas and seats and moved back several paces.

The eaglelike Beast of the other opponent was no match. Even as it surrounded the dragon's head in a gale of glittery gusts, the dragon swung its tail and batted it to the ground like it was little more than a fly. With its Keeper coughing in the haze, Emilie had an easy opportunity to seize her flag.

Barclay's name was drawn next, along with the name of a student called Klara. Barclay had seen her matches before, and apart from Abel and Ethel, she had been the person he was least keen to fight. Her illusion Lore had forced all of her opponents into forfeiting their matches without so much as a scratch on them.

He nervously shook her hand.

And the match began.

Suddenly the daylight began to fade, as if a shadow had descended over the sky. The audience members disappeared, as did Klara. Barclay was alone as his surroundings fell into complete blackness. It was the deepest sort of darkness, without even the stars or moon.

He could still hear and feel the rain, which he assumed were real and not part of her illusion. Soren had also used similar tricks against him, but Soren had used multiple Beasts for different senses. If this was anything similar, then the girl could only fool his sight.

He could still hear her.

Lights began to appear in the darkness. No, not lights—eyes. Dozens of them. His heart thundered as they neared, even when he reminded himself they weren't real.

Barclay felt something graze his arm—Klara's hand, reaching for his flag. He dashed in the opposite direction, feeling lost and clumsy without his sight.

As the illusionary Beasts crept closer, Barclay tried a different tactic.

Wind! he thought. Then a gust tore across the field, so strong that Barclay struggled to maintain his balance.

He heard a splash behind him.

As he swiveled around to go after Klara, the illusion around him changed. Instead of many Beasts, there was only one. The darkness had brightened into a dim glow, allowing Barclay to glimpse the outline of its massive form. The Beast was larger than a five-story building, with wild, patchy brown fur the color of earth. His face reminded Barclay of a bear.

A jolt of fear shot through him. This wasn't simply a Beast. It was Gravaldor, the Legendary Beast of the Woods, exactly like the descriptions from Dullshire's tales. He was staring into the eyes of the Beast who had murdered his parents, with all his most painful memories returning to him. Gravaldor had crushed his home under a single paw, crushing his mother along with it. He had bent over the wreckage and eaten Barclay's father within his own living room. And he had left Barclay, a small child, to be dug out from the rubble.

Barclay had never hated anything more in his life.

Reacting on a mixture of panic and instinct, Barclay summoned another wind, this one far more forceful than the last. It swirled around him like a storm, pelting him with rain and bits of debris, even more powerful than the one he'd accidentally conjured in Dullshire. Screams chorused around him, which he realized came from the audience.

"Stop!" a voice bellowed. "The match is over! Stop!"

The image of Gravaldor flickered and vanished in an instant, transporting Barclay back to the field. All around him, the park was in disarray. Picnic blankets had been blown into the trees, food carts and lawn chairs knocked over, onlookers deliriously stumbling to their feet.

"Klara Hagen was blown out-of-bounds," Erhart called, his clothes disheveled and covered in mud. Beside him, Soren frowned and swatted a brown leaf out of his hair. "The match goes to Barclay Thorne."

At the edge of the field, Klara huffed and stood up. Her Beast lay beside her. It was small, wrinkly, and hairless, with a wide body and stubby legs.

Viola, Ethel, and Abel ran out onto the field to congratulate him.

"That wind was *incredible*!" Abel told him. "You blew Erhart right over."

Barclay was still shaken—trembling even—and it took him several moments to collect himself. Then he managed, "I thought you were stuck as a reflection, Abel. How did you escape?"

"Oh, I found a mirror in a bathroom nearby and jumped out of it. Scared Mandeep half to death. He almost fell in the toilet—"

"I want to know more about the match!" Viola interrupted. "We didn't know what was going on. You were stumbling around, looking all strange."

"I saw . . . I saw Gravaldor." The memory of it sent another shudder through him. He needed to lie down.

"Her Hocus's illusion Lore is amazing," Ethel cooed. "And look at it! It's so cute!"

"It looks like a turnip," said Abel flatly.

Other students began to crowd Barclay as well, bursting with questions about his wind Lore and his Lufthund. Ethel had been right—none of them teased him for being an Elsie, not anymore. And unlike Dullshire, no one treated him like a rulebreaker or a burden. They treated him like he *belonged*.

Barclay hadn't felt that way in a very, very long time.

You were never meant to stay here, Master Pilzmann had told Barclay the day he'd fled town. Barclay was starting to understand what he had meant, that there was something wild and adventurous inside of him that would only be squashed in Dullshire.

But that only made his heart hurt all the worse. Barclay had finally found the place where he belonged, but he couldn't stay. It wasn't right, after the way his parents had died.

There was no way around it. He would win this Exhibition. He would say goodbye to Root. And then he would go back to the place that no longer seemed like home.

TWENTY

With only two days of the third exam remaining, the audience had grown to an all-time high. Many of these travelers, Barclay learned, had also journeyed to Sycomore from all over the Woods to celebrate the Midwinter holiday, and the town's festivities put Dullshire's to shame. What had begun as a few pear cider stalls had grown into rows of feasting tables piled high with spicy bratwurst, syrupy pastries, and great goblets that drinkers actually set aflame. Paper snowflakes and Beast treats on strings decorated all the trees. There was caroling, dancing, and no matter where you roamed in Sycomore, it always smelled of bonfire.

While Ethel and Abel hurried through the makeshift markets before the lines grew long, Barclay caught Viola frowning at the decorations.

"What's the matter?" he asked her. "You don't like Midwinter?"

"It's not that," Viola answered, sighing. "It's that Midwinter is one of the only times Gravaldor wakes without being summoned. Since I couldn't trap him, Midwinter is my last chance . . ."

"If you want to bond with him," Barclay finished for her.

"If I don't leave tonight, I'll never make it to the center of the Woods in time. And so I have to . . . I need to . . ." She fiddled with her leather bookmark in *A Traveler's Log*, and Barclay recognized the look of someone torn. "But I want to see the rest of the Exhibition. And yesterday, when you saw Gravaldor from Klara's illusion Lore, you looked so frightened. And I'm scared that all along I've been making a mistake."

Barclay had always thought Viola's plan to bond with Gravaldor was a mistake, but he didn't think it nice to say that. So instead, he told her, "I hope you stay."

And that was all he got to say. Because a moment later, Erhart had fished two slips of paper out of Soren's basket.

"'Ethel Zader,'" Erhart read. Ethel stiffened beside them. "'Barclay Thorne.'"

Barclay avoided Ethel's gaze as they met at the edge of the field. Barclay had hoped, more than anything, to avoid fighting Ethel, who wanted to win nearly as much as he did.

Before Barclay could take a nervous step toward the proctors, Ethel grabbed him by his scarf and yanked him aside.

"Look, Barclay. I know how much first place means to you," Ethel told him fiercely. "But it means something to me, too. And so I'm not going to let you win."

"I never expected you to," he said.

Her brown eyes glimmered mischievously. "And don't think you need to take it easy on me either, like you did everyone else. I'd love to see you and Root in action."

That wasn't the reason Barclay never summoned Root for a match, but he didn't have a chance to tell her so. Abel impatiently pushed them both onto the field.

"Good luck," Barclay told her.

Ethel grinned. "Keep your luck. You'll need it."

On the grass, Erhart and Soren whispered to each other. Erhart's face, normally flushed pink from the cold, had gone very pale.

"Surely you must be overreacting, Soren. I'd heard rumors about her and Cyril, of course. But this . . . It's unthinkable!"

"I . . . I don't think I am," Soren said gravely, his voice sounding fake and dramatic. He paused and glanced at Barclay and Ethel, as though he had forgotten that he and the High Keeper were in the middle of proctoring a match.

"What's unthinkable?" Barclay asked coolly. "We already know you're not above attacking students."

"*Really*, now," Erhart blustered. "I could disqualify you, you know." But, seeing all the expectant faces around them, Erhart seemed to think better of that idea. He handed

Barclay and Ethel their flags, then led Soren out of their way and raised his voice over the buzz of the crowds. "Begin!"

Ethel wasted no time readying herself. Just as Barclay had now seen in many of her matches, she conjured a giant mirror, stretching from one edge of the field to the other. Barclay didn't even have a chance to run for her flag before she leapt into the glass and became one with her reflection.

He already knew Ethel's strategy—in less than an instant, she'd jump out in front of him and deliver a quick chop to the side of his neck, knocking him down and snatching his flag. But he wouldn't be beaten that easily.

And so Barclay did what he did best—he ran. As far from the mirror as he could.

I won't attack like her past competitors, Barclay thought. *If she wants me, she'll have to come and get me.*

Then something solid pressed against his back, and to Barclay's horror, a *second* mirror had appeared behind him, just as massive as the first. And Ethel was now right behind him.

She lunged out of the new mirror, her hand outstretched to swipe the flag tied around his arm. He ducked away, but only just in time. Before he could counterstrike, Ethel fled back into the glass.

And that was how it went for several minutes. In the mirrors, Ethel was faster—as though she were the speed of light. And so wherever he dodged, she easily followed.

But whenever she did leap out of the glass, she lost her speedy advantage. Every kick and swipe ended up short, and Barclay's few attempts at attacks of his own had her fleeing back into the safety of her reflection.

Soon they were both doubled over, panting. Ethel in the mirrors, Barclay on the field. Barclay shed his scarf and tossed it aside, overheating even though his breath still fogged in the Winter air.

She'll have to come out again eventually, Barclay thought. *And if I can grab her, then—*

Suddenly another reflection appeared in the glass. It was foggy to look at, even if the rest of the mirrors were clear. It looked a little like Ethel, if Ethel had colorless gray skin, shapeless clothes, and strange, undefined facial features— as though she'd been drawn two-dimensionally.

That can't be her Beast, he thought. *It looks just like her!*

It was clearly some other type of trick. And besides, like Ethel, it would need to come out to land a blow on Barclay.

Then something solid struck him in the back of the head. He whirled around, but there was nothing there. Then something tripped him, and he fell to the damp grass.

In the mirror, the real Ethel hadn't moved. But the Ethel-looking Beast pinned him down beneath its boot, and Barclay could *feel* it. As if it were really there.

We almost never keep our Beasts in their Marks. . . . They're invisible to other people, Ethel had told him about her and Abel's Beasts. Barclay remembered all the instances when Ethel and Abel had dropped things, as though they had been knocked aside, glaring at or scolding things that weren't even there.

Then Barclay realized it. The Beast was invisible.

Except for its reflection.

Barclay's heart raced as he struggled underneath the Beast's boot, but he didn't need to get up in order to defend himself. He stretched his other arm up, to where the Beast stood over him.

Wind!

When the vortex came, it looked as though he had attacked nothing. However, the Ethel-looking Beast in the mirror writhed. He'd been right—it wasn't in the mirror with her. It was really out here, with him.

Once the Beast had been struck down, the mirror disappeared, and the real Ethel stumbled onto the field. She raised her hands, still out of breath, and called, "I forfeit! The match is over!"

Barclay called off the wind, and Ethel ran to take care of her Beast.

"You can only see it with a mirror," Barclay said with surprise.

"It's called a Doppelgheist. I'm surprised you figured it out so quickly. Most people don't." Her voice was tight, and Barclay hoped she wasn't angry with him. But then she turned to him and smiled. "You know, you'd make a great Lore Keeper, Barclay. If you wanted to be one."

Barclay's own smile faded.

"I *don't* want to be one. So just . . . just stop. You can all stop."

He grabbed his scarf off the ground and stormed away, hoping to hide the telltale flush in his cheeks.

Viola must've heeded Barclay's words, because she didn't leave that evening. Instead, she stowed *A Traveler's Log* away in her bag and rented a table for their friends. A rusty chimenea crackled with fire behind the four of them, casting a comfortable warmth beneath the tent alongside the exam field, where much of Sycomore had gathered for the Exhibition and holiday celebrations. On each table stood large glass jars filled with fireflylike Beasts called Zaplings, which Mitzi poked and snarled at. Chandeliers of evergreen branches hung overhead, drooping with garlands of cranberries and ornaments of twine and cinnamon sticks.

For the first time, Barclay was aware of Ethel's and Abel's Doppelgheists out of their Marks. The grass beside the table was dented where they sat, a bowl hovering midair in their invisible grasps as they devoured maple-flavored Beast treats.

It made him feel guilty that Root wasn't joining them, but Barclay only had one more match separating him and first place. He couldn't afford to question his decision now.

"I mean, you're my friend," Abel said, slapping Barclay

on the back so hard, he choked on his sip of pear cider. "But now I don't just want you to win. I *need* you to win. If Tadg gets first in the Exhibition, I'll . . ."

"You'll what?" Ethel asked, arching her eyebrows.

"I'll jump into a mirror and never come back," Abel declared miserably. When Barclay gave him a horrified look, Abel laughed. "It's not bad in there. I call it the mirror world. Lots of glittery reflected light. I can travel nearly anywhere I want in barely any time, so long as there's a mirror to jump out of. Quite nice, really—"

"You don't need to pressure him," Viola snapped. "Barclay has enough to think about. *Don't you*, Barclay?"

Barclay dodged her pointed look, his face reddening. If Viola had changed her mind about going after Gravaldor, then maybe he could change his mind about being a Lore Keeper, too.

No, he thought, thinking of his parents. His situation was different.

"It's not pressure," Abel said. "It's just . . . very strong support. I just don't want to see fish food win."

Someone grabbed Abel by the shoulder and spun him around. It was Tadg, seething. He let go of Abel and cracked his knuckles.

"If you like it so much," Tadg growled, "I'd be happy to send you back to your mirror world."

Abel jolted and spilled his mug all over the table. "Why do you keep doing that? You stalking us now?"

Tadg ignored him and met eyes with Barclay. "I was wondering if I could speak with you in private."

Barclay didn't like the idea, but he doubted even Tadg would try something the night before the final match, especially in such a public place. His friends, however, shot him warning looks.

"Whatever you want to say to Barclay," said Viola coolly, "you can say in front of all of us." Mitzi nodded and squawked in agreement.

"It's fine," Barclay mumbled, not wanting to cause a scene.

He followed Tadg out of the tent toward the field. It was so crowded with people stargazing on quilts and shopkeepers selling sparkler sticks and peppermint bark that it was difficult for Barclay to picture battling Tadg here tomorrow.

Like Barclay, Tadg had won all his matches without even needing to summon his Beast.

"Um," Barclay said awkwardly. "Whatever happens tomorrow, I—"

"The annual Exhibition is in the Spring every year. Did you know that?" Tadg asked. Barclay vaguely remembered Erhart mentioning how they'd moved it earlier, but he didn't have a chance to respond before Tadg grumbled, "I mean, why would you? You're from the Elsewheres."

Barclay's attempts at politeness quickly died.

"I get it—I don't know anything about Lore Keepers! I'm not from a Wilderland! But I made it to the final match, just like you. I'm not—"

"The matches are just a show. They don't matter," Tadg spat. "Why do you think the Exhibition was moved to Midwinter?"

"I don't . . . I don't know," Barclay hissed. "What do you mean, that the matches are just a show?" Tadg was fidgeting, agitated. He wasn't making any sense.

"Do you really think you'd get this far if they weren't? Some of the students already have Masters, and the Exhibition isn't even over."

At that, his gaze shifted to the tents behind Barclay. Barclay turned to see what he was looking at, and he spotted Soren, drinking with Erhart and several other Masters. Barclay stiffened.

"Are you threatening me?" Barclay asked him. "Well, you and Soren—"

"Me and Soren, what?" Tadg took an aggressive step closer.

"You're working together, aren't you? Like how he and your father were writing his next book together? *You* already have your Master."

Tadg jabbed his finger into Barclay's chest.

"Whatever you think you know, you're wrong. I can't say anything or he'd find out. And I don't trust any of your friends. But if I were you, I'd leave Sycomore tonight and go back to that town of yours. If you warn them now, maybe you can—"

"And let you win tomorrow?" Barclay scoffed. He saw exactly what Tadg was doing.

"To be clear," Tadg said flatly, "you wouldn't win."

"We'll find out."

"To be *clearer*," Tadg hissed, "I'm warning you: if you compete tomorrow, you'll regret it." He lowered his voice. "Run off and mention this to Runa if you want, but she won't be able to stop me."

And with that, Tadg stalked off, leaving Barclay furious and alone on the field. He would *not* be scared out of competing tomorrow. He had a Mythic class Beast, just like Tadg. He had come this far for Runa, and he wouldn't back down now.

"What happened?" Ethel asked when Barclay rejoined the table.

"He was trying to convince me not to fight," Barclay said. "In fact, he said I should leave Sycomore."

"That coward. I knew it," Abel muttered.

"There's more—I think you're right. I think he's already Soren's apprentice."

Viola furrowed her eyebrows. "Did he say that?"

They already knew that Soren and Conley Murdock used to be partners. And when he thought about it, Tadg had been shocked when Barclay had returned from the Woods after Soren attacked him . . . very shocked. As though he hadn't thought he'd come back at all. As though he *knew* he wouldn't.

And then there was Runa forbidding Tadg from going to the Bog's Inn, how he'd gone to Soren's lecture over hers . . .

"He tried to deny it," Barclay said, "but it was obvious what he was doing. He wants me to leave. He's scared of losing."

"If he really *is* Soren's apprentice," said Viola carefully, "then maybe you should tell someone. Like Runa. You could be in danger tomorrow during the match."

"Erhart won't call off the match," Abel said, "even if Runa wanted him to."

"Of course not! Erhart practically worships Soren." Barclay nodded at where they were seated together across the field, drinking from those flaming goblets. "Tadg even said Runa 'won't be able to stop me.'"

"I don't like this," Viola murmured.

"You *have* to fight," Ethel told him.

"You have to *win*," Abel finished.

Barclay had every intention of winning. He had not journeyed across the Woods, nearly getting himself killed or eaten on multiple occasions, only to back down because of cruel threats. This was the one time in Barclay's life that he would *not* run.

He would get his life back. The life that his parents had wanted for him.

Barclay raised his mug of cider. "To victory," he said.

"To victory," the others echoed, smacking mugs.

The next morning, when Barclay returned to the field, he expected all the festivities of the night before, if not more.

It was the day of the final match *and* the day before Mid-winter, yet the area was almost deserted.

With furrowed eyebrows, he approached Erhart. A small crowd of Masters gathered around him, shivering in the cold. Barclay noted with relief that Soren was not among them.

Then, when they saw Barclay, they started clapping. It was an uneasy sort of cheer—most of them frowned.

"What is it?" asked Barclay. Viola, Abel, and Ethel beside him looked equally as bewildered.

"We have our victor," Erhart announced.

He reached forward and shook Barclay's hand, though he didn't look too pleased about it.

"Victor? Where's Tadg?" Barclay asked.

"Mr. Murdock left Sycomore last night and hasn't returned. He has therefore forfeited." The Masters once again started a quiet, pitiful round of clapping. "Congratulations, Mr. Thorne. You've won first place in the final exam."

TWENTY-ONE

don't understand," Barclay hissed at the others. Once Erhart and the Masters had stopped congratulating him, he and his friends had hurried back into town. "Why would Tadg leave?"

"He's a coward," Abel said. "I told you."

Barclay might not have liked Tadg, but Tadg didn't strike him as a coward. In fact, Barclay might have interpreted everything Tadg had said to him last night totally wrong. Tadg had told Barclay that he was warning him, not threatening him. But warning him about what? It all left a dreadful knot in his stomach.

"We should talk to Runa," Viola said warily.

"We should be celebrating," Abel countered. "You got first place, Barclay! Of course, the awards aren't until tomorrow, but—"

"Viola is right," Barclay interrupted. "There's something wrong about this."

"Maybe Runa will show you how to remove your Mark now," Ethel told him hopefully.

Barclay nodded, but his thoughts were somewhere else. He was replaying every piece of his conversation last night. Tadg had mentioned that the Exhibition was in the Spring every year—why had he brought that up?

"Maybe he ran off with Soren," Abel suggested. Ethel shot him a sharp look.

"What? Is Soren gone too?" Viola squeaked.

"I didn't mean . . . I mean, he wasn't with Erhart just now, was he?" Abel turned to lead them back to the Iron-wood Inn, but Barclay stopped.

"I'm going to the Guild House to talk to Runa," he declared.

"I'll come with you," Viola said.

"We'll meet you back at the inn," Ethel told them, but Barclay and Viola were already running off.

The inside of the Guild House was mayhem. The rest of the Masters were gathered here, arguing at each of the tables. The Beasts along the ceiling squawked and roared back and forth. Barclay searched everyone's faces and saw that, indeed, Soren was not among the havoc.

"Do you see Runa?" Barclay asked her.

Viola shook her head. "Should we ask them?"

She pointed to Mandeep, Floriane, and Athna. They were

once again seated alone at a table covered in Athna's mugs of ale, Mandeep and Floriane bickering with each other. Barclay agreed, and they strode toward them.

"Ah," Mandeep said, sighting them and grinning. "The champion of the third exam! What can we help you with?"

"He's not the real champion just because the Murdock boy left," Floriane grumbled. "I'm worried about him. Where did he go? He isn't from the Woods."

"He keeps a Nathermara," Mandeep said. "There isn't much in the Woods more fearsome than that."

Floriane's lip quivered. "But it's a Sea Beast. And Midwinter is tomorrow. . . ."

"Do you know where Runa Rasgar is?" Barclay asked them.

"I would check the High Keeper's office," Mandeep said.

"I believe her words were 'Then I'll wait here until he decides to return and do his,' um . . ." Floriane glanced nervously at Barclay and Viola. "'His job.'"

Somehow Barclay got the sense that Runa's words had been more colorful than that. "Thank you," he told them, and he ran off, Viola behind him.

Erhart's office was in the corner of the room, with a golden plaque on the door with his name. Barclay knocked until Runa answered.

"The High Keeper isn't here right now," she grumbled without looking at him. Then her eyes drifted down to the pair of them. "I thought you'd come find me. Come in."

Barclay and Viola slipped into Erhart's office. It was

filled with a collection of books and antiques. Runa sat on his desk as comfortably as if it were her own. She gestured at the two seats in front of her.

"Is it true that Tadg's gone?" Viola asked.

"I'm afraid so. It's dangerous for any Lore Keeper to wander around the Woods, especially at this time of year. And Tadg is only a student." Runa shook her head. "No one will go after him now, of course. It's much too—"

"And Soren? He's gone too?" Barclay asked.

"What?" Runa asked sharply. "I thought he was with Erhart."

"He isn't. We were just with him," Viola told her.

Runa furrowed her eyebrows. "That greedy, incompetent man," she muttered. "I told him this would happen. Moving the Exhibition to Midwinter . . ."

"Tadg also mentioned that the Exhibition had been moved," Barclay said. "Why is that important?"

"Midwinter is one of the two times each year that the Lore of the Woods—of any Wilderland—is at its strongest. It means Gravaldor will wake from his rest in his home in the center of the Woods. If the Woods are calm, he returns to sleep, but if not . . . he will attack anything in his path, eating and gathering energy and Lore to feed the forest. Can you guess the other time of the year he does that, Barclay?"

"Midsummer," he murmured. The day his parents had died. "But what do Midwinter and Gravaldor have to do with the Exhibition?"

"All the Lore Keepers in the Woods are here. Those who are normally tasked with keeping tabs on Gravaldor at this time of year are going to find it very difficult to do so. It gives Soren the opportunity he wants."

Soren had told Barclay that his real interest lay in Legendary Beasts. He'd told him during the second exam, in the Woods. The idea of Soren adding Gravaldor to his collection terrified Barclay.

"Can't he just summon Gravaldor?" Barclay asked.

"He can't," Viola answered. "The ingredients for the trap are almost impossible to find. I should know—they took me *ages*. And the Mourningtide Morel can only be foraged before the first snow. His window to try it passed."

"What happens if Soren bonds with Gravaldor?" Barclay asked.

Runa gave him a dark look. "The Legendary Beasts control all the flow of magical power in the world, which is what has made them so coveted throughout history. If Soren bonded with Gravaldor, he would have power greater than the Grand Keeper. And who's to say he will stop there? This isn't the first time Soren has attempted to go after a Legendary Beast. If Conley Murdock hadn't let Soren join him to study Lochmordra over Midsummer, Conley would still be alive today. Why do you think Tadg and Soren hate each other?"

"H-hate each other?" Barclay sputtered. "But Tadg is his apprentice!"

"His apprentice!" Runa barked out a laugh. "Tadg is *my* apprentice. Or he was going to be, had he not charged into the Woods after Soren before the Exhibition ended."

Barclay's stomach did a painful somersault. Tadg's conversation last night made far more sense. He hadn't told Barclay to go back to his town to avoid the fight—he'd told Barclay to go back to warn them.

"Then why would he leave?" Viola asked.

"I never saw what happened out in the Sea between Conley and Soren. Even though Tadg warned me not to trust Soren, I still stayed behind to focus on my own work there and let Conley and Soren go after Lochmordra. But Tadg went too—snuck out when I wasn't paying attention. It was how he bonded with Conley's Nathermara. After Conley died and the bond broke, Conley's Nathermara chose Tadg over Soren—as Mythic Beasts can sometimes do. Tadg was stalking Soren at his lecture, trying to confront him, sabotage him. This whole time, I thought he'd been confused about what happened that night, and I never listened to him. Not then, and not now."

Barclay remembered when Tadg had told Runa that what had happened to his father was "your fault too." The dark look on Runa's face made Barclay think she'd taken his words to heart.

"What will happen to Dullshire if Soren finds Gravaldor?" Barclay asked quietly.

"If Soren manages to bond with him, probably nothing,"

Runa answered. "But Soren's failed to bond with a Legendary Beast before. It's likely Gravaldor will be angry at being woken up by someone trying to control him, and when he's angry like that, he's been known to be destructive. Even to leave the Woods."

"Then what do we hope for?" Viola asked frantically. "If Soren bonds with Gravaldor, he could kill my father! And if he doesn't, then Gravaldor could destroy half the towns outside the Woods!"

"When Erhart returns, I'm going to request to send out a search team to retrieve both Soren *and* Tadg." Runa sighed and rubbed her temples. "Barclay, I'm sure you have something else to ask me?"

In all the commotion about Soren, Barclay had nearly forgotten that the Exhibition was finished. And he'd placed first, just like Runa had asked.

"Will you tell me how to remove my Mark now?" he asked.

"Do you want me to?"

Barclay's face reddened, no matter how hard he tried to stop it. "What? Of course!"

Runa took a deep breath and lowered herself to look Barclay in the eyes. "I'm afraid I haven't been honest with you. You see, removing a Mark has nothing to do with your own strength. I'd hoped your weeks spent in Sycomore with your friends would change your opinion about Lore Keepers. It seemed a shame to let such a promising student make such a hasty decision."

Barclay couldn't believe her words. All these weeks had been a *lie*? Even if his opinion about Lore Keepers had changed, even if *he*'d changed, it didn't matter. He had to go back to Dullshire. He had to.

"So it's impossible, then?" Barclay seethed. He squeezed the armrests of his chair until his knuckles whitened.

"Marks can be removed using a Beast of a higher class," Runa explained. "But yours is a Mythic Beast. I'm afraid for you, it's not possible."

Barclay bit his lip to prevent a curse—or worse, tears.

Runa's face softened. "I'm sorry about lying—I really am. My intentions were good. In fact, I never thought you'd do as well as you did. To progress to the final match in the bracket with so little time with your Beast. To escape from Soren—twice! I can't offer you a way home, but I can offer you something. An apprenticeship with me, if you'd want it."

"*Your* apprentice?" Barclay repeated, stunned. He was already someone's apprentice. Master Pilzmann's.

"You as well, Viola," Runa added.

"I already have a Master," Viola said, echoing Barclay's thoughts.

Runa turned to her. "I know full well that isn't true. Cyril would never let his apprentice wander alone the way you have." Viola swallowed and looked at her shoes. "I don't know if it's any help to you, but I don't think you could find a Master more different from Cyril than me. Or anyone who hates Cyril as much as me." She smiled at Viola cheerily.

Viola didn't return it. "I can't—"

The door to the High Keeper's office swung open. Erhart stormed inside, followed by a herd of other Masters. He pointed a shaking finger at Runa.

"You're under arrest! For the murder of Conley Murdock."

Barclay and Viola shot up from their chairs and exchanged a dark look. Soren had been spreading rumors about Runa and Conley for weeks, but surely, Erhart didn't have any proof.

Runa gritted her teeth in frustration. "You're delusional. I'm not the one who killed him. If you listen to me, I can tell you who did. The perpetrator is fleeing Sycomore as we speak—"

"Nonsense! Soren flees because he fears for his life! And I have the evidence."

Erhart waved a leather notebook through the air, then he hurriedly flipped through the pages. Barclay recognized the messy, scratchy handwriting as belonging to Conley Murdock.

"These are the notes Conley was keeping from his work with Soren! Listen to what he writes! 'Runa has begun following me, and I don't know why.' 'I think she's planning something terrible.' 'I'm becoming more afraid, both for myself and my son—'"

"Those are forged!" Runa snapped. "Why would Soren hold on to this evidence for two seasons if he'd had it all along?"

But Erhart wouldn't hear sense. He shoved Barclay out of his path. And the potted plants around his desk suddenly grew, and their vines twisted around Runa's wrists like shackles.

"I read some of Sycomore's old lawbooks and decided that there will be a trial!" Erhart proclaimed. "I've already contacted someone to speak on behalf of your character. He'll be in Sycomore this evening."

"And who might that be?" Runa asked. She didn't struggle against her restraints, but the sound of her voice was icy.

"Cyril Harlow."

Runa took a deep breath and wore a smile so terrifying, Barclay's skin prickled. "How charming. Then if I'm to be imprisoned, who will leave to find Tadg?"

"L-leave?! It's almost Midwinter! The Beasts are at their most dangerous!" Erhart blubbered. "I won't be sending people out to their deaths! If the boy had any sense, he wouldn't have left. Little did he know his father's murderer was here all along." Then Erhart turned his attention to Barclay. "You both! Get out of my office! The Exhibition award ceremony and the trial will be tomorrow!"

Barclay and Viola were shoved out the door into the Guild House, which was now deadly silent. The other Masters had all crowded around the door to eavesdrop.

"Arrest the Fang of Dusk?" Mandeep said. "That's absurd!"

"Wasn't she Murdock's friend?" Floriane asked.

"Of course she was, you two turnips!" Athna huffed. "I don't know what Soren said to convince Erhart, but if Soren's plans go wrong, Gravaldor could murder us all before the end of the Midwinter."

Barclay and Viola stumbled through the crowds to the Guild House's door. The cold air forced Barclay's muddled thoughts to clear and made him more alert.

"Tadg's gone after Soren to *stop* him," Barclay groaned, "not to help him."

"But it doesn't make sense!" Viola said. "If Soren only came to Sycomore to seek out Gravaldor, why would he wait through the entire Exhibition? He could've left earlier and given himself more time. Even if he left last night, he'd have to rush to make it to the heart of the Woods by Midwinter."

Barclay admitted that she had a point. But then he remembered something.

"When I was in the Woods with Soren, he told me that he wanted to find apprentices."

"Apprentices? As in, more than one?" Viola asked. "Who would they be?"

The dread in Barclay's stomach knotted tighter. Abel had already known Soren was gone.

Barclay grabbed Viola's hand and ran to the Ironwood Inn. They charged up the stairs to Abel's and Ethel's rooms on the top floor, but the only person they found inside was a maid.

"Where did they go? The people staying in these rooms?" Barclay demanded, panting.

"They already left," she told them. She huffed as she stripped the sheets off their beds. "In a bit of a hurry too. Left so many bits and baubles. Didn't even leave a cleaning tip."

It wasn't like Ethel and Abel to leave behind any of their collectibles, but sure enough, he spotted a few of Abel's champion cards and one of Ethel's notebooks on the bureau. Barclay flipped to the first page of the book, his hands trembling.

There was a detailed sketch of Ethel's Doppelgheist, notes scribbled along the margins. Except there was one piece of handwriting that didn't belong. It was cold and precise, its ink bleeding red through the paper. Written, Barclay guessed, before the second exam, when Soren had examined Ethel's notebook.

I'd like to make you an offer.

Barclay exchanged a dark look with Viola. "No wonder Tadg didn't trust us. That was who he meant, when he said some Masters had already taken on apprentices. He meant *Soren* had taken on apprentices . . . Ethel and Abel."

TWENTY-TWO

I t was them," Barclay breathed, dropping the notebook and slapping a hand against his forehead. Beside him, Viola looked equally stricken. "Soren didn't just trap me in the Woods—they led me to him. Maybe when Soren overheard us talking about their Beasts, he was interested—not in *taking* their Beasts—but in teaching them."

"He could've killed you in the Woods that day!" Viola squeaked. "But why leave now? Why not leave last night with Soren? The center of the Woods isn't close. They'll never catch—"

"They will. Abel said they can move faster in mirrors," Barclay said.

"And the way Soren planted Conley's notebook to frame Runa . . . I don't think it was a coincidence. He probably got the idea from Ethel!"

The room spun around him. Soren had left, and so had Ethel and Abel. Tomorrow was Midwinter. Tomorrow Soren and the twins would greet Gravaldor while he emerged from his lair, and Soren would attempt to bond with him. Whether Soren succeeded or not, the entire Woods was in danger.

"Then we need to find Tadg," Barclay said hurriedly. "Tadg left to stop him. We need to help him."

The maid cast each of them a stern look. "And *I* need to clean." She ushered them out of the room and into the hallway, but Barclay and Viola were already sprinting downstairs.

"How far is it to the center of the Woods?" he asked Viola.

"At least two days," she responded.

"Do we have enough supplies?" Barclay asked. He hadn't been prepared to travel, so his bags weren't packed.

"We might, but we'll never make it in time. Neither will Tadg."

"We will if we run fast."

Soon Barclay and Viola had bundled themselves in their heaviest clothes, thrown as many supplies as they could into their bags, and raced down the streets of Sycomore. Shopkeepers had decorated their storefronts with candy icicles and glowing Zapling lanterns. The town was loud with carolers and bell chimes and the hisses, caws, and growls of various Beasts.

It wasn't until they reached the quietness of the clearing

that Barclay summoned Root. His black fur looked like smoke in the pulsing lantern light.

"It's been awhile," Barclay told him. Nearly two weeks had passed since he'd last brought Root to this grove, since he'd last summoned Root at all. Root let out a low huff, like he was well aware of how much time had gone by.

"Barclay . . . ," Viola said nervously. "What are you planning?"

Barclay knelt in front of Root and ran his hand through Root's fur. "I'm sorry. I have a favor to ask," he murmured.

Root's dark eyes watched him, wary. If Root had trusted Barclay once, he didn't anymore.

The thought made Barclay's stomach clench with guilt, and even disappointment. It didn't matter what Runa had offered him. It didn't matter what Barclay really wanted. All that did matter was stopping Soren before what had happened to Barclay's parents happened to others.

But another idea—a tiny, quiet one—pinched in the back of his mind. Runa had said that Marks could only be removed with a Beast of a higher class. She'd assumed because Root was a Mythic Beast, that was impossible.

But if they were about to confront Soren, if they were about to face Gravaldor . . . maybe that wasn't quite true.

"It's one last favor," Barclay said softly.

Root must have understood, because his head sank lower.

"We need to find Tadg and reach the center of the Woods fast," Barclay continued. "Will you take us there?"

Root let out a low whine, but then he nodded.

Swallowing down his feelings, Barclay climbed on top of Root's back, between the bones of his protruding spine. He reached out to Viola. "Come on."

Viola's eyes widened. "Are you serious?"

"Do you want to stop Soren or not?"

She took a deep breath and grabbed his hand. He hoisted her behind him, and she wrapped her arms around his stomach. "How fast will Root—" Her words turned to a startled shriek when Root took off.

Barclay and Root had run this fast before, but then Barclay had been too afraid of Soren to pay attention. As Root picked up speed, Barclay felt the exact moment he went hollow. When the wind whipped through him, through his skin and between his bones. When they moved so fast, the entire world went still around them.

They ran for hours. As they traveled deeper into the heart of the Woods, the blurry surroundings around them began to change. The white of snow became the reds of Autumn and the greens of Summer. Barclay's Winter coat and layers of sweaters suddenly felt hot. The sounds of Beasts surrounded them. He could feel the roars and howls quake within his stomach, the screeches and caws echo in his ears. The air even smelled like the magic of the Woods, like the scent of the earth after it rained.

Eventually Root slowed to a stop within a grove. The trees around them were vibrantly green, drooping with long tangles of leafy vines, and insects buzzed within their canopies.

A small squirrel Beast, which had been busy digging in the dirt, froze as the Lufthund loomed over it. It made a squeak and fled up a nearby tree.

"Why have we stopped here?" Barclay asked Root.

Viola hopped onto the ground and shrugged off her coat. When Barclay followed her, Root let out a whimper.

"What is it?" he asked him.

"Barclay," Viola choked, pointing at the ground.

A hand lay in the dirt.

Barclay's stomach gave a violent turn. A golden Beast Mark stretched over the hand's fingers in the shape of a serpent's tail.

"Is that . . . ?" he asked, and Viola nodded.

The two dropped to the ground and, with their hands, began to dig him out.

Finally they freed Tadg's head and chest. Viola felt for his pulse, and her shoulders relaxed. "He's not dead."

"I don't even think he's injured," Barclay said. His sweater was covered in dirt, but not blood. Clutched in Tadg's other hand was the cap of a mushroom. It was suctioned to his palm, and Barclay recognized it instantly as part of a Stoolip. He pulled it off, and it made a popping sound.

Tadg's eyes fluttered open, as though he'd been having a pleasant dream. Then he looked at Barclay and Viola with a lopsided sort of frown, like he wasn't sure if he was awake or not.

"What's going on?" he asked, his voice slurred.

"A squirrel Beast buried you," Barclay told him. "Like a nut."

"Didn't you come in third in the practical?" Viola grabbed the top of the Stoolip and threw it at Tadg's face. It bounced off his forehead and fell into his lap. "How could you be so careless?"

He stared at it blankly for a moment before jolting up. "Soren—how long have I been—when did you both—?"

"Midwinter is still tomorrow," Viola assured him. "But we do need to get moving if we're going to catch him."

"Why did you both come and not Runa?" he asked.

"Runa was arrested for your father's murder," Barclay blurted out. Viola shot him a sharp look, and Barclay knew there were probably softer ways he could have put that, but they didn't have the time.

Tadg shot Viola an annoyed glance. "Your father really knows how to pick High Keepers. Erhart is going to get Sycomore and every town beyond in the Woods destroyed."

"Not if we stop Soren," Barclay said determinedly.

Tadg staggered to his feet and gave them a strangled laugh. "You're not coming. You'll only get in my way."

"You'd still be buried if it wasn't for us!" Viola growled.

"Neither of you know Soren like I do. What he's capable of—"

"Don't I?" Barclay snapped.

"You don't know Legendary Beasts like I—"

"I've studied Gravaldor for *ages*," Viola countered.

Something dark crossed Tadg's face. "You're friends with his apprentices! For all I know, your father is in league with Soren—and I don't trust the Horn of Dawn either—"

"We're not friends with Ethel and Abel," Barclay said.

"And Cyril isn't my Master," Viola finished.

Barclay wasn't surprised by *what* Viola said, only that she finally admitted it. He wanted to ask her about it, and by Tadg's expression, it looked like he did too.

But both were stopped by a huff. That was the only word for the sound, like something letting out a great deep breath.

The three of them turned and came face-to-face with a set of nostrils.

They looked up. The Beast in front of them was nearly fifteen feet tall. Barclay counted four legs, three tails, and two giant tusks sharp enough to pierce a man through.

It was a boar, if boars were as large as buildings and had pelts rougher than mountain rock. Bugs buzzed and crept all over its skin—some normal fleas and ticks, others small Beasts.

It let out a second huff, and all three of them cringed from the smell of its breath.

Root whimpered again.

They took several careful steps back.

"Time to run," Barclay rasped.

"We're not running," Tadg snapped. "Then it will think we're food."

The boar treaded forward and sniffed them.

"I'm pretty sure it already does," Barclay said.

"Step back," Tadg commanded, and Barclay and Viola happily obliged.

The ground softened below them as water bubbled up to the surface. It crept across the grass in a puddle below the Beast. Then Tadg, the same way he'd done during all the matches of the Exhibition, placed his palm in the water. Bright currents sparked out of his fingertips, and the Beast gave a disgruntled sort of snort.

Tadg frowned and tried a second spark.

The Beast pounded its feet into the mud, as though preparing to charge.

"Why isn't it working?" Tadg grunted.

"Look at its tusks. Look at its hooves," Viola said. "They're stone. They don't conduct electricity."

Tadg's gaze flickered to Root. "We're not all going to fit on the back of that Lufthund."

"I can run beside Root," Barclay told him.

"Didn't you hear what I said about it thinking you're food?" Tadg asked.

"It won't catch me."

Seeming to like what it smelled, the boar opened its jaws wide to take a bite. Viola screamed and narrowly missed becoming an appetizer. She and Tadg scrambled onto Root's back, and all of them took off, Barclay dashing alongside them.

Though they didn't run as quickly as earlier, they still moved fast. The boar's footsteps thundered behind them.

Birds flocked out of trees. Smaller rodents and Beasts ducked for cover.

And larger Beasts came looking.

Erhart had been right about one thing—at only one night left until Midwinter, the Woods crawled with Beasts. Eyes watched them as they passed. Shadows crept through the trees around them, branches reached for them. It was as though the Woods itself had teeth.

When the trio finally stopped, it was late in the evening. Barclay and Root, exhausted, both collapsed under a giant tree with violet sap leaking out each of its knots.

"We should keep moving," Tadg said. "Soren and the others could be close by now."

Barclay shot him an annoyed look and scratched Root behind the ear. "He means, 'Thank you for the ride,'" he mumbled to Root.

"So you're willing to let us come along now?" Viola said. "Or did we get in the way of you being eaten by that Eberock?"

Tadg sighed. "We'll stop to eat and rest for the night, but only because we'll be at a disadvantage in the dark. And we *will* leave at sunrise."

"We want to stop Soren as much as you do," Barclay told him.

His eyes flashed. "I doubt that."

Leaving Tadg to be grumpy by himself, Barclay and Viola set out in search of food they could eat. Barclay was pleased to uncover several clumps of white mushrooms at the base of nearby trees.

"If we make it back to Sycomore alive," Viola asked him, "would you accept Runa's offer?"

Viola sounded hopeful, and Barclay didn't want to disappoint his friend. So he avoided the question.

"That depends," Barclay answered. "Will Runa still be imprisoned for murder when we return?"

"I'm being serious." She reached onto the ground and scooped up several green walnuts. "You could be a great Lore Keeper, you know."

Barclay *did* know that, and that was what made it so hard. He could become the apprentice to an incredible, famous Master with the Guild, and he could travel the world. His life would be one adventure after the other. Or he could return to Dullshire, a town that had never wanted him anyway. He'd have to be forever on his best behavior. No running. No dirt. No being who he really was.

"Runa said that it takes a Beast of a higher class to remove a Mark," Barclay murmured, finally revealing his true thoughts. He gave Viola a pointed look.

"Barclay, Gravaldor isn't a regular Beast! And without a Keeper, it's probably impossible."

"You don't know that," he countered.

"Is being a Lore Keeper really such a horrible thing?" she said, her voice rising. "Are we all just as terrible as you thought we were?"

That wasn't it—that wasn't it at all. But he was frustrated, so he snapped back, "We *are* in a race to stop a Lore Keeper from destroying the Woods or becoming so powerful that he *could* destroy the Woods, if he wanted to."

"Yes, but—"

"And up until yesterday, didn't you want to summon Gravaldor for the same reason?" he asked.

She gaped. "I wanted to bond with Gravaldor, yes, but not for the same reason Soren does. How could you even think that?"

"Then tell me the real reason," he challenged.

"Because Cyril fired me as his student," she said bitterly. "It didn't matter how well I did in my Exhibition—I wasn't good enough for his standards. I need to prove to him that I am."

Barclay's anger sobered. He'd suspected something bad had happened, but it didn't make him feel any better to hear her say it. "Why not just find a new Master?" he asked.

"Because I didn't pick him—my father did. That's why I can't find another Lore Keeper Master. I *need* to convince Cyril he made a mistake. I'm the daughter of the Grand Keeper. Failure isn't an option. Not in my family."

Barclay didn't pretend to be an expert on family, but Master Pilzmann was the closest thing to a father he'd ever had, and he couldn't imagine Master Pilzmann being so cruel. And Viola might not have been entered in the Exhibition, but Barclay knew she was one of the most exceptional students in Sycomore, Tadg included. How could anyone think she wasn't enough?

"My father has *three* Mythic class Beasts. He's the most powerful Lore Keeper in the world. Nothing I've done has ever measured up, and I thought bonding with a Legendary Beast was the only thing to convince him that I was enough."

"The way I see it," Tadg said behind them, making both of them jolt and turn around. Barclay spilled his armful of mushrooms. "If a person or a town is willing to cast you out, then maybe they don't deserve to have you come back."

Barclay bent down to pick up his dinner and stow it—this time—in his satchel. "How long have you been standing there?" he grumbled.

"Long enough," Tadg answered.

Tadg might not have been Soren's apprentice, but that didn't mean he'd ever been nice to Barclay. In fact, Tadg could have saved everyone a lot of confusion and trouble last night had he only explained the truth to Barclay without insulting him every other word.

"That's big of you to say," Barclay said gruffly.

Tadg sighed and held out his hand. "Maybe there's been a misunderstanding. That day in the park, I saw the message Soren left Ethel on her notebook, and I thought *all* of you were working for him, up until after the practical when Soren attacked you. Who do you think stole Abel's Hasifuss and put it in your bag?"

Barclay eyed Tadg's hand warily. He'd seen Tadg once

convince Ethel into shaking it only to trick her with Lore.

"That was you?" He did remember Tadg gathering the fallen items out of Barclay's bag. That must have been when he added in the Hasifuss.

"I wanted to get back at him for calling me fish food. And I would've explained myself better, but I didn't want you telling Abel and Ethel by mistake and for Soren to know I was coming after him."

Barclay supposed that made sense. He reluctantly shook Tadg's hand, as did Viola.

Tadg looked down into Barclay's satchel. "What is that? Is that for dinner?"

"They're mushrooms."

Tadg frowned. "Mushrooms taste like dirt." Then he turned and started back toward camp.

Barclay shot an annoyed look at Viola. "I still don't like him."

He bent down to tickle several Stoolip tops—he wasn't foraging just for food. It wasn't like he'd be getting any sleep tonight naturally, being near the heart of the Woods the night before Midwinter. He stuffed several into his bag.

"He's not wrong about mushrooms," she mumbled, following after Tadg. "Don't look at me like that. We could be eaten by Gravaldor tomorrow. I get to be picky about my last meal."

TWENTY-THREE

The center of the Woods reminded Barclay more of a stomach than a heart. On Midwinter Day, the farther they walked, the more every tree branch began to resemble fangs. The canopy above them was an intricate web of knots, making it so dark and tunnel-like that Viola had to lead them using Mitzi's light Lore. The noises of a thousand different bugs and animals sounded like gurgles. The wind carried a nasty sour smell.

"Are you sure we're going in the right direction?" Tadg grunted. "We've been walking for hours, and everything looks the same. I'm certain we've passed that tree before."

He pointed at a tree with a spiral trunk covered in fruits as brightly colored as jewels.

"It does look familiar," Barclay admitted.

"We have to be getting close," Viola said. "It's almost noon."

"Gravaldor could be waking at any moment." Tadg kicked an acorn on the ground, and it soared through the air.

And with a loud *clunk*, hit what appeared to be nothing.

"Did you see that?" Tadg asked sharply.

Viola walked to the fallen acorn and picked it up. Then she threw it in the direction Tadg had kicked it. Once again it struck against nothing, against *something*, and fell to the ground.

"What's going on?" Barclay asked.

Viola carefully crept forward and held out her hand. Eventually she smacked something hard. "There's a wall here. We just can't see it." A grim expression flashed over her face. "We've probably been walking in circles, and we didn't know it."

"It's not invisible," Tadg said. "It's a mirror."

"Abel and Ethel," Barclay breathed.

"But we don't have reflections," Viola pointed out.

"Ethel and Abel *lied*. Think about it—they'd traveled from the middle of nowhere in the Woods to find a Master. They were probably thrilled when Soren offered! After all, they collect things, don't they? Just like he collects Beasts," Tadg said. "In the third exam, Abel barely attacked me before he let me finish the fight. And Ethel waited until it looked convincing to forfeit her match. Do you think she'd have lost to an Elsie otherwise?" He glanced at Barclay. "No offense."

"Too late," Barclay muttered.

"Ethel and Abel probably didn't intend to stay for the

final match—they'd planned to leave with Soren," Tadg said. "Just because we beat them then doesn't mean we know what Lore they're really capable of."

Tadg pressed his hand against the glass, and droplets began to trickle down from his palm. Then a spark swept across the mirror and shattered it. Behind it was a new path deeper into the Woods.

And blocking that path were two figures, side by side.

"We were hoping you wouldn't notice our trick," Abel called.

Barclay, Viola, and Tadg walked toward them, Root and Mitzi creeping at their sides. Once they got closer, Barclay saw a wall of mirrors behind the twins, where their Doppelgheists lurked. Barclay had never realized how creepy Abel and Ethel's Beasts were until this moment, the way they looked so similar to them yet so . . . wrong.

"We don't want to fight you," Ethel warned.

"Then you shouldn't have helped Soren," Barclay told her. It was hard to imagine that the two of them were the same friends who had helped him study and shared pitchers of pear cider.

"And you have fish food with you," Abel said, a smile stretching across his face. "You know, I've been wanting a rematch. A real one, this time."

"I'd be more than happy to give you one," Tadg growled.

"Careful—there isn't any water nearby. Your Beast is at a disadvantage."

They were *all* at a disadvantage, Barclay realized. Viola's light would only be reflected off mirrors. His wind wasn't strong enough to shatter the glass. Tadg might have a better offensive chance with Abel and Ethel's powers, but without his Beast out of its Mark, he would be the weakest among them.

"I wouldn't worry about me," Tadg threw back.

Suddenly several mirrors appeared around them, forming—not a wall—but a circular enclosure. Each of their reflections stretched out endlessly in every direction, as did the Doppelgheists'. As always, Abel and Ethel slipped inside the glass.

Viola, Barclay, and Tadg stood back-to-back. "How do we stop them from jumping out if they're *everywhere*?" Viola asked.

"You don't," said Tadg. "Whatever you do, don't let the water touch you."

Water bubbled up from the grass and seeped across their enclosed circle. Viola and Barclay nervously backed up to the glass.

"I wouldn't do that," Ethel told Barclay, directly behind him.

Tadg pressed his palm into the puddle and let out a spark of electricity. One of the mirrors shattered, but it was quickly replaced by another.

"You can't trap us in the mirrors when there are this many of them," Abel told him.

"And you'll electrocute Barclay and Viola if you're not careful," Ethel warned.

Tadg's expression darkened.

One of the puddles beside Barclay rippled from an invisible splash, and he looked at the circle of mirrors to see it was Abel's Beast advancing toward him. Barclay froze. The last time he'd faced one of their Doppelgheists, he'd run. But now he had nowhere to go, no idea how to fight against something you could only see through its endless reflections.

Root lurched forward and tackled it, and Mitzi pounced on Ethel's Beast on the other side of the ring. It was very strange to watch them wrestle with something invisible, as though they were thrashing in midair.

"If Root and Mitzi handle the Beasts," Barclay said lowly to Viola and Tadg, "then we only need to overpower Ethel and Abel."

"But how?" Viola asked.

As she spoke, Ethel darted across the mirrors. With so many of her reflections surrounding them, it was impossible to guess where she'd emerge.

Then she leaped out behind Viola and tripped her. Viola landed in the puddle, soaking herself. By the time she had gathered herself enough to grab at Ethel, Ethel had already jumped back into her reflection.

Abel darted out from the glass behind Barclay. Barclay whipped around in time for Abel to punch him in the stomach. He doubled over, and Abel fled right back into the mirror.

"We don't want to hurt you more than we have to," Abel said. "But Soren told us we can't let anyone inside Gravaldor's den. You can't win this. Surrender, and we'll let you live."

"Ow!" Viola yelped. Ethel had pulled one of her hair buns. Moments later Abel kicked Tadg behind the knees.

"One of you need to do something," Tadg grunted.

"Mitzi, try some light," Viola said to Mitzi, who was in the midst of struggling with Ethel's Beast. Mitzi bounced off it and opened her mouth, and let out a huge burst of light, so bright that Barclay needed to shield his eyes with his hands.

It must have been working, because Abel's and Ethel's jabs and punches momentarily stopped. But the light reflecting around them in every direction made it extraordinarily hot in their circle. Sweat broke out over his forehead.

"I think it's working," Viola told them.

"But I can't open my eyes," Barclay said.

"And you're cooking us," Tadg added.

"Then *you* two do something," Viola hissed.

Barclay didn't know what he or Root could contribute in this situation. But they were desperate and out of options, so Barclay reached his hands out and summoned as much wind as he could muster.

Gusts began to pick up amid their circle, swirling and whirling so fast, they needed to lock arms to prevent themselves from being dragged away.

"How is this helping?" Tadg yelled.

"Well, I'm dry!" Viola shouted.

"Yeah, and there's no water left to summon," he growled back. "If I had more, I could summon Mar-Mar. He's no good on dry land."

Defeated, Barclay called off the wind. Ethel and Abel watched the three of them smugly from the mirrors.

"There isn't anything you can do," Ethel told them.

"So you might as well surrender," Abel finished.

A roar tore through the Woods.

Not just any roar but the loudest and most frightening sound Barclay had ever heard. Everyone—even Abel and Ethel in the mirrors—covered their ears. Barclay heard the roar in his stomach. He heard it in the ground. He heard it in the trees around them.

The canopy above them rippled, as though the Woods was taking a breath.

As though the Woods was waking up.

"Gravaldor," Tadg said, ashen. Then he charged and threw himself at one of the mirrors. The mirror cracked slightly, but Tadg ended up collapsing onto the ground, clutching his shoulder.

Abel laughed and leaped out of the mirror at Tadg's left. He kicked him in the chest.

Tadg sputtered.

"Hard to breathe, fish food?" Abel asked him.

Viola groaned, and Barclay whipped around to find her

also on the ground. Ethel had one foot in the mirror and the other on the grass. She clutched Viola's arm and held a broken shard of glass against her throat.

"Just stay still," Ethel told her, "and you won't even get a scratch."

Another ripple swept through the trees. Gravaldor was waking up, and Soren could have found him by now. If they stayed here any longer, they wouldn't be able to stop him.

Barclay had never wished so desperately to be a more powerful Lore Keeper. There was nothing he could do to win this.

Nothing *he* could do.

The thought gave him an idea.

"How much water do you need?" he asked Tadg.

"Don't answer that," Abel said, pressing harder on Tadg's chest.

"Whatever it is," Tadg rasped, "just do it."

Barclay hesitated. If he acted, would Abel and Ethel hurt Tadg and Viola more? But no amount of pleading would save them now. No amount of pleading would save the *Woods* now.

And so Barclay howled, and in the moment of silence that followed, Barclay wondered if Root wouldn't listen like he had when they'd faced Soren in the practical. Maybe Barclay had broken their relationship beyond repair.

He met Root's eyes desperately, as if to say please.

Root threw his head back and howled as well.

The already dark forest went significantly darker. Thunder cracked through the sky, and it began to pour, the hardest rain Barclay had ever felt. His clothes were quickly drenched, and the circle of mirrors began to fill up like a bathtub.

"Make it stop," Abel growled.

"I can't," Barclay told him truthfully. This was Root's power, not his.

The water levels rose, soon above both Tadg's and Viola's heads. But while treading water, Ethel and Abel could no longer hold them, and Tadg and Viola slipped out of their grasps. The rain continued so hard that it hurt, the drops beating like hail against Barclay's skin. The pool rose and rose. Beside Barclay, Root had pushed Abel's Doppelgheist off him and had begun to tread, his head bobbing up and down at the water's surface. Barclay reached for him and mouthed, "Thank you," then he and Viola returned Root and Mitzi to their Marks.

"Is this enough for you?" Barclay asked Tadg.

"Almost," Tadg answered. He'd tilted his head up so he could still stand and breathe.

Abel and Ethel had disappeared back into their reflections, but the mirrors remained.

"How is this not enough?!" Barclay shouted at him.

"Mar-Mar will shock you if you're still in the water," Tadg said. "You need to wait for the mirrors to fill up so you can spill over."

Barclay didn't like the idea of wasting more time. But the pool filled up within only a few minutes, and soon both Barclay and Viola were able to hoist themselves over the ledge of mirrors and tumble the ten feet to the ground below.

Once they did, a terrible shriek pierced the forest. Barclay's Mark stung in warning, more painful than it ever had.

"Can you see anything?" Barclay asked Viola, wincing and standing on his tiptoes to try to peer over the glass.

Viola shook her head. "I can't."

Just then, a head emerged from the water. It rose up and up, so tall that it hunched beneath the forest's canopy. The Beast's face looked even more hideous in person than it had on the cover of *A Traveler's Log*: wide, flat at the top, and translucent like a fish. He opened his mouth to let out a second bloodcurdling shriek and revealed rows and rows of teeth.

A bright light began at the lamprey's eyes and spread down him in a pattern of scales and lightning. A sound like a rumble of thunder roared, and all at once, the mirrors shattered. Glass blasted in every direction, followed by the water bursting out. Tadg was swept across the forest floor like a limp piece of algae.

He coughed, clinging to the lamprey's side. Barclay could see what Tadg meant now, when he called his Nathermara a monster. He was massive and hideous and terrifying—not at all like Root.

The lamprey shrieked again. Barclay got the sense that he was shrieking at Tadg.

Tadg grimaced at him. The serpent writhed as he faded and returned to his Mark, and when he disappeared, he left the Woods eerily quiet except for the rain. Then Root let out a second howl, and the rain lightened into a drizzle and stopped altogether.

"Who names a monster like that Mar-Mar?" Barclay asked, wringing out his hair and clothes.

"My father," Tadg answered darkly. "Now let's go catch his real killer."

TWENTY-FOUR

The forest pathways began to slope downward, like they were descending deeper and deeper into the Woods.

Barclay would soon come face-to-face with Gravaldor, the monster who had killed his parents. Even if that was seven years ago, even if Barclay had never seen Gravaldor himself, he'd heard enough stories and had enough nightmares to imagine his face. Barclay knew he couldn't bring his parents back, that stopping Gravaldor wouldn't somehow save them. But it felt like it might.

Barclay's heart nearly stopped when another roar shook the Woods. His Mark stung. What if they were too late?

Then the forest path opened into a sort of cave, its walls and ceiling made entirely of gnarled trees and branches. Only the faintest light broke through its cracks, and as Barclay's eyes adjusted, he made out the shape of something in the enclosure's center. Something very big.

He roared again, and though it was still loud enough to rattle Barclay inside and out, much of his breath had transformed into a white smoke.

"There!" Barclay said, pointing to the edge of the den.

"Mitzi, light!" Viola said, and a flash swept across the cave—not so bright for Barclay to squint, but enough that he could see clearly.

He wished he couldn't.

Gravaldor loomed above them, taller than the tallest building Barclay had ever seen. Like in the illusion he'd seen fighting Klara's Hocus, Gravaldor resembled a bear, with mangled brown fur and legs the size of oak trunks. His eyes were an earthy green and sunken, with strange markings around them like the inner swirls and grooves of a tree. Large stone plates covered in moss lay across his back like armor. Of his many gigantic claws, one of them on his front paw gleamed of solid gold.

Barclay could scarcely believe any Lore Keeper had ever bonded with the Beast, even if only in legends. There was something ancient and wild about it. A power greater than anything he'd ever imagined.

Staring at it, Barclay waited for the rage about his parents to sweep over him, but it never came. It was like being angry at a storm, a blizzard, a drought. Gravaldor wasn't a monster—he was part of nature itself.

The realization left Barclay suddenly empty. His anger at

Gravaldor, at Beasts, at Lore Keepers faded, and it hurt to feel it all go. He'd clung to that anger for so long like he'd tried to cling to his parents' memory. But blaming Gravaldor felt like looking at a mountain and blaming it for a landslide. Barclay had spent his whole life cursing the broken land when he should have been building on top of it.

Soren stood dangerously close to Gravaldor. His two Beasts from the Woods flanked him, the Ischray and the Nitney, but there were others, too, that Barclay didn't recognize. Soren was right to call himself a collector—Barclay counted at least a dozen Beasts. How could he control that much power?

At the light, Soren whipped around. He locked eyes with Barclay and glared. But before Soren could react, Gravaldor roared and stomped his feet, making the entire ground quake.

Tadg rushed at Soren first, but the Beasts around Soren blocked his path. They were ugly things, carrion birds and animals that looked half-rotted and others covered in grime and filth.

"You will *not* do this again!" Tadg screamed at Soren. "I won't let you!"

Soren ignored him. He motioned to the two Beasts at his side.

Gravaldor roared again. Barclay realized for the first time that he wasn't trying to frighten anyone—he was scared himself. Soren's Beasts could make you see and feel and hear things that weren't there—it was no wonder he'd taken a liking to apprentices like Abel and Ethel, whose powers complemented his own.

"Surrender, Gravaldor!" Soren called. "Surrender to the Mark!"

Gravaldor swiped out his paw, and it collided with Soren. He flew through the air and landed on his back several yards away. Viola screamed, making Mitzi's light flicker in and out.

Gravaldor advanced. The Beasts around Tadg raced out of Gravaldor's path, but he stood frozen.

"Tadg!" Barclay shouted. "Tadg, you need to run!"

Tadg didn't seem to have heard him. He was perfectly still.

Gravaldor opened his mouth.

Barclay ran forward, tackling Tadg to the ground. They both rolled through the dirt into a heap against a boulder.

Then Gravaldor stepped on the boulder, crushing it. He bent low and roared at full power, directly over them, with so much force that the ground beneath their backs caved inward. Barclay held his hands over his ears, certain his skull would shatter.

Mitzi's beam of light shot directly at Gravaldor's forehead. He groaned and backed away. Barclay and Tadg dizzily clambered to their feet.

On the other side of the cave, Soren's Beasts had disappeared. Gravaldor's claw had torn a large slash down his shirt, and it hung on him in bloody strips, exposing much of his chest and back. His skin was covered in thrashing Marks, but unlike the golden color Barclay was used to, they were each gradually turning black.

Soren staggered up. His back arched in strange, unnatural directions, and he seemed to grow several feet taller. Tufts of patchy fur sprung out over his arms. Scales started to protrude from his face. He screamed as a horn sprouted out of his forehead, leaving an oozing trail of blood down his cheek.

Viola reached down and pulled Barclay out from the crumbled pit of stone.

"What's happening to him?" Barclay asked in horror.

"Remember those stories in Dullshire about Lore Keepers being eaten by their own Beasts and their Beasts attacking a town?" Viola asked him. "If you can't bear the weight of the power of all your Beasts, your bonds break, and the Lore consumes you. Those Beasts in the stories you heard didn't *eat* their Lore Keepers. Those Beasts *were* the Lore Keepers."

Soren had lowered himself onto all fours. His eyes, once a pale blue, had gone yellow.

And he was watching them.

"This is not good," Tadg said, crawling out of the pit.

Meanwhile, Gravaldor had stood up on his hind legs. The canopy of trees above them parted for him, as though bowing, and Gravaldor stood taller than the entire Woods when he roared.

"If he leaves," Viola called, "he could attack Sycomore. Or Dullshire. Or anywhere."

Barclay looked up and up at the Legendary Beast's face. He had never felt so small.

Soren let out a birdlike shriek and began running toward them. Nothing about him looked human anymore—especially not the hunger on his face.

Barclay, Viola, and Tadg leapt out of his path. Viola attacked first, sending out another blast of light that struck Soren in the side. He faltered, for only a moment, but then he lunged at Tadg. Tadg fell to the ground, holding Soren back with his hands against his face. A spark burst out of Tadg's palms, and Soren wailed and lurched off him.

Wind! Barclay summoned.

The vortex appeared, just as it had during his match with Klara in the Exhibition. Unlike in those matches, however, Soren wasn't just a student. He wasn't even human. He broke out of the vortex easily and stood face-to-face with Barclay.

Root appeared beside him—Barclay didn't even realize he'd summoned him. Though Soren was several feet taller than Root and many times more frightening to behold, Root didn't hesitate. He lunged at Soren and managed to sink his teeth into Soren's scaly shoulder.

Soren let out a terrible cry and threw Root off him. Root rolled across the dirt and, with a whimper, stopped at Barclay's feet.

"Are you all right?" Barclay shouted to Root, wrapping his arms around him protectively, but his voice was lost as Gravaldor roared again. The trees bent even lower in response, kneeling before their king. The clouds in the sky swirled above him in a sort of crown. The earth shook in thunderous applause.

Soren leapt forward. He bit Barclay hard on the arm, making him scream.

Someone shouted, and Tadg ran forward. He placed both hands on Soren's back, letting out a torrent of flashing sparks. Soren's jaws opened wide, letting Barclay go. And before Soren could fling them both aside, Barclay reached forward and slapped something on his forehead.

A Stoolip top.

Soren's eyes drooped. He swayed, but he didn't fall.

Barclay reached into his pockets and grabbed several more. He stuck the mushrooms all over Soren's mixture of scales and skin and fur, even while Soren thrashed against him. After several moments Soren let out one final shudder and collapsed onto the dirt, unconscious.

Viola rushed to Barclay's and Tadg's sides. Barclay winced, holding his arm limply.

"You did it!" she breathed. "But he bit you—how bad are you hurt?"

Tadg shook his head vigorously. "There's no time for that! Gravaldor will leave if we don't—"

"If we don't *what*, Tadg?" Viola snapped. "How are we

supposed to stop him? We need to get Barclay back to—"

"I agree with him," Barclay cut in. "If we don't stop Gravaldor, there might not be a Sycamore to go back to."

But Barclay didn't have any idea how to stop him. He couldn't stop a storm, or a blizzard, or a drought. For as many silly rules as he had broken, the first rule he had ever been taught was to be afraid of the Woods. And the heart of the Woods wasn't this cavern—the heart of the Woods was the Beast living inside of it.

Above them, the sky darkened to a stormy gray, and fierce winds tore leaves and twigs from the trees around them. It felt like the Woods was preparing for battle.

While Barclay, Tadg, and Viola crouched together, Root staggered over to the three of them and howled. It was not his usual howl to summon storms—it was far less ferocious. This howl was the sort of a wolf trying to call to his pack, but although Lufthunds might resemble wolves, they were not pack animals. Who, then, was he calling to?

Gravaldor didn't seem to hear. He wrenched his head up, and the plating along his back rose out, making him look—if possible—even larger.

Shoulders bent against the gusts, Root pressed closer to the Legendary Beast. He dug his claws into the earth and howled again.

This time the trees around them bristled and straightened upright, as though snapping out of a trance.

Gravaldor lowered himself back onto all fours, but he did

not crouch for attack. He stood tall. Root might not have had the power to summon him, but Root was part of the Woods. And when the Woods called, Gravaldor answered.

Still, with the trees pointing in the sky like spears, with the wind still dropping debris from above, the Woods felt wild and dangerous. But Root had changed something in Gravaldor, as though he had reminded Gravaldor who he really was, just like Root once had for Barclay. So while Viola and Tadg continued to back away, Barclay stepped determinedly to Root's side. He rested his hand on Root's head, and though it was too loud to speak, he ran his fingers through Root's fur and said, "I'm sorry I let you down."

Barclay didn't think Root had heard him, but he still stood beside him for several minutes—until the noise and wind around them faded at last.

Once they did, Gravaldor's gaze dropped onto Soren, sleeping and defenseless, at his feet.

Gravaldor lifted his paw, his claws extended.

Barclay squeezed his eyes shut. He expected a terrible thud, or a tear, or whatever sound was made when one monster ended another.

Instead, for several moments there was silence.

"Barclay," Viola hissed, and he opened his eyes.

Gravaldor had placed a single claw against Soren's body. The fur and scales on Soren had begun to recede back into his skin. The black Marks of his Beasts faded to gold and then to nothing at all. While Soren continued to sleep, his

Beasts began to appear beside him. They abandoned their Keeper and scattered off into the trees.

"He removed all of Soren's Marks," Barclay said, gaping.

"Not sure that's punishment enough," Tadg grumbled, but his expression was smug.

When Gravaldor finished, his gaze fell on the three of them. His eyes, once full of wilds and rage, now looked calm.

Barclay wasn't sure what made him step forward. Maybe it was the wilds in him answering Gravaldor's call. Maybe it was awe, the way it felt to look directly into the eye of a storm.

I was right, he thought. *He could remove my Mark.*

Root followed him, his head low and mournful, as though he sensed what was about to happen.

Barclay opened his mouth to speak to Gravaldor, to make his request. But no words came out. It wasn't like when the Ischray stole his voice from his throat, but rather like he didn't have the words in him. All those reasons he had hated Gravaldor and the Woods and Lore Keepers no longer mattered to him.

Barclay had wanted to remain in Dullshire so that he could follow the life he thought his parents had wanted for him. But he couldn't help but think that his parents would be disappointed in him if he went back, when he had found the place where he truly belonged.

He'd be disappointed in himself too.

And so Barclay crouched down and pressed his forehead

against his Root's, watching his expression with his matching black eyes. They matched in so many ways. Both stubborn. Both teasing. Both wild. Now that Barclay could stop blaming Lore Keepers for what happened to his parents, there was no reason to stop him from becoming one too.

"I never belonged there," Barclay told Root. "You knew that before I did."

Seeming to understand, Root's ears pricked up happily.

"Will you forgive me?" Barclay asked.

Root wagged his tail and licked Barclay's cheek, which Barclay took to mean yes.

Smiling, Barclay turned around to Viola and Tadg.

Tadg pushed Viola forward. "I thought you had a request."

"I *don't*! I . . . I'd already made up my mind, and I'm not changing it. I don't need Gravaldor to become a great Lore Keeper." She looked toward Barclay. Her clothes were dirty and wrinkled, and one of her hair ties had snapped, leaving a single lopsided poof with an indent in her curls. She smiled, and he nodded. They had made the same decision: to become great Lore Keepers together.

When none of them moved, Gravaldor lowered himself to the ground. The trees formed a cavernlike canopy once more, and the Woods was peacefully still.

"My father would have loved to see this," Tadg murmured, staring up at Gravaldor. Then he looked at Soren. "We should take him back—maybe Erhart can enforce his laws, for a change. Do you have more Stoolips, to keep him asleep until we return?"

Barclay nodded and patted his pockets. "I have plenty."

Viola let out a long breath of relief. "Then let's go back to Sycomore."

TWENTY-FIVE

Barclay, Viola, and Tadg returned to Sycomore three days after Midwinter ended—Soren still in tow on Root's back, fast asleep. With both the holiday and the Exhibition over, the town was quieter than Barclay had ever seen it.

In early morning in Dullshire, everyone would be awake. The streets would smell of fresh bread from the bakery opening its windows to beckon customers. Gustav would be huddled lazily near Master Pilzmann's fire. Mrs. Havener would be putting on an extra scarf or pair of mittens while restocking books.

The thought no longer filled Barclay with so much homesickness. In fact, it warmed him like a mug of pear cider. Had it not been for him, Viola, and Tadg, there might not be anyone left in Dullshire to wake and go about their lives.

Dullshire might not ever welcome him back. Barclay would likely never become a mushroom farmer like he'd once wanted. But he still liked to think that his parents would have been proud of him for saving the town and going on an adventure.

Though tired from traveling, the trio staggered to the Guild House. Inside was no longer filled with so many Masters—only a handful sat among the tables. Many had students, now apprentices, sitting beside them.

Two figures sat by the fireplace.

The first was Erhart, and next to him was a man Barclay had never seen before. He was pale and wiry, with bluntly cut dark hair and stiff clothes. Shiny pieces covered his shirt, much like Viola's. But unlike Viola's, these looked more like medals and achievements than pins and baubles.

Viola tensed at seeing him. "That's Cyril Harlow, the Horn of Dawn."

"Why is he wearing so many medals of honor?" Tadg asked, rolling his eyes. "No wonder Runa hates him."

They walked behind them. Tadg cleared his throat.

Erhart turned around, his face red and annoyed from being interrupted, then he let out a startled yelp. "Mr. Murdock and Mr. Thorne! And Miss Dumont! H-how could you all be alive?" His gaze drifted to Soren, limp on Root's back, and he gasped. "What happened?!"

"Where is Runa Rasgar?" Tadg demanded.

"She's imprisoned in the Ironwood Inn," Erhart

answered. Barclay could think of worse places to be trapped than the tavern with the best pear cider in town, but he supposed Erhart had let Sycomore's jail fall into disarray. "But Soren! Did he try to save you from going off into the Woods? What did—"

"Soren Reiker is the one who murdered my father, not Runa," Tadg snapped. "He tricked you into moving the Exhibition early so that the other Masters would be preoccupied while he tried to bond with Gravaldor. Runa is innocent, and I demand you release her at once."

"B-but what about the notebook? Conley's notebook?" Erhart asked.

Tadg shook his head, and when he spoke, his voice was tight. "My father always kept his notebooks on him, which means his real journal is probably at the bottom of the Sea. Whatever Soren gave you is a fake."

While the High Keeper was too stunned to say anything, Cyril narrowed his eyes at Viola coolly. "I heard you'd come here. Is it true you faced the Legendary Beast of the Woods?"

Viola lifted her chin higher. "It is."

"I would expect nothing less of my apprentice," he told her.

Viola stiffened. "I'm not your apprentice. I'm Runa Rasgar's."

Cyril's face contorted with a mixture of shock and disgust. "You must be joking. If you knew what Runa had done, then you—"

"I know you both hate each other more than anyone else in the world. And that's why I think she's the right Master for me." Viola glanced nervously at Tadg and Barclay. "I didn't deserve for you to send me away. And you don't deserve for me to come back."

Cyril's gaze swept over Tadg and fell on Barclay's disheveled hair and dirty clothes.

"And who are you?" Cyril growled at Barclay.

"I'm also Runa's apprentice," he answered. It wasn't the same as being Master Pilzmann's apprentice, but it was better, because he didn't want to be like the rest of Dullshire. He wanted to be like himself.

"We *all* are," Tadg added. "So will you release her or not?"

Erhart's face reddened. He looked like he wanted to argue more, but many in the room had begun to stare. "Fine. On *my authority*, Runa Rasgar is released, as she has broken no laws." Then he scrunched his face and sighed. "And also from this moment forth, the laws in Sycomore will be reinstated and enforced, so that Soren or someone like him won't be able to take advantage of people again. There will be a trial, and he can answer for his crimes."

Twenty minutes later Runa Rasgar and her three apprentices sat together at a table in the Ironwood Inn, sharing a pitcher of pear cider, and she told the story of what had happened in their absence.

"Cyril couldn't wait to come here and testify on the flaws in my character," she said. "Of course, he wasn't there when it happened. I wasn't either. I'd been at the shore when Soren led Conley—and almost you too, Tadg—to his death. And Cyril was in the Mountains! Because we make certain to never be in the same place at the same time, you see."

"Why do you and Cyril hate each other so much?" Viola asked her.

Runa gave a very fake, pleasant smile. "Why do any two people hate each other?"

Barclay felt the answer was obvious—for wrongs done to one another. But something about Runa's expression made him think she was joking and that they wouldn't be getting the real answer.

"I just wanted to say . . . ," Runa said, suddenly turning serious. "As you all know, I work as a Guardian Lore Keeper. I take jobs for the benefit and protection of those who are vulnerable to Beasts—whether or not they ever thank me for it. It's a dangerous but rewarding job. And as a Guardian, I could not be prouder that the three of you accomplished what you did at Midwinter."

The three of them flushed.

"I-it was the right thing to do," Barclay stammered.

"That's right. And as someone who comes from a place so different from ours, our way of life must look strange to you. But should Dullshire learn what you've done for them, I think they would be thankful for you *and* your Beast. After all, they have more than their skunk charms and prickly walls to protect them. They have people like you."

Barclay liked the sound of that very much.

She turned to Tadg. "Your father was reckless and made a lot of mistakes, but he would have been proud of you. I know he would."

Tadg took a very long sip of cider.

"And you," she said to Viola. "Your father and I don't get along anymore. But you already know that, don't you?"

Viola nodded.

"Either way, it is still an honor to work with you, especially when you managed to teach this one—" She nodded at Barclay. "So much so quickly. I've never had apprentices before, and I admit I'm a bit worried you'd be a better Master than I would."

"I—I . . ." Viola fidgeted. "I doubt that."

"And that leaves you," Runa turned once more to Barclay. "You know, I never expected you to work so hard and make it so far in the Exhibition. Are you naturally gifted at everything, or have you always had to rise to the occasion, because there was no alternative for you if you didn't?"

Barclay flushed. "I've, well, I've been an orphan most of my life. I've learned to do a lot of things. And I'm not good at everything. I break rules all—"

"Not naturally gifted at everything, it seems. You're a terrible liar." She sighed. "The first thing I'll teach all of you to do is take a compliment. You don't need to start covering yourself in medals of honor and flaunting them about, like our oh-so-dear Horn of Dawn, but you're allowed to be proud of yourselves when you've done well. You're all extraordinary."

Viola caught his eye and beamed at him. Tadg, who was now only half as sullen as usual, cast him a look almost like a truce. Barclay realized he'd done the thing he'd always dreamed of—he'd found a place where he belonged, and people he belonged with. Who appreciated him exactly as he was.

Runa waved down the innkeeper and asked for another pitcher of pear cider. When it arrived, the four of them refilled their drinks, and Runa offered up a toast.

"To a job well done," she said, and then clacked mugs. Barely any of them had managed to take a sip before she added, "Speaking of jobs, I'm afraid we won't be staying in Sycamore much longer."

"But we just traveled through half the Woods to get back here," Tadg grunted.

Runa made a pouting face. "You must be very tired, then. How inconsiderate of me."

Barclay relaxed and took another sip of his cider.

"If just two days of walking is enough to make you tired, then it seems I have a lot of work ahead of me," Runa said snidely. "We'll leave in an hour. And you better liven up— it's a long journey beyond the Woods."

"Beyond the Woods?" Barclay repeated, nearly choking

on his drink. He'd never been beyond the Woods before. He'd read about places in books, of course, and he knew neither Viola nor Tadg were from here. But the Woods had always been the great black mass covering what was already a very large map. It was his whole world. He'd never thought he'd get to see another one.

"It's a bit of an unusual job," Runa said.

"What kind of job?" Viola asked.

"The dangerous sort."

Tadg smiled. "How dangerous?"

"Potentially deadly."

"And where are we going?" Barclay asked.

Runa leaned forward, making all of them do so as well. "I'd tell you, but that would spoil the adventure."

If you had asked Barclay Thorne six weeks ago if he'd like to go on an adventure, he would have firmly, heatedly declined.

But, with the wind tangling his hair, with new friends beside him and a new life ahead of him, Barclay would have admitted it. Ironically, it had taken him an adventure into the deepest part of the Woods, face-to-face with two very different sort of monsters, for him to realize it. But it was better late than never.

Barclay Thorne wanted to go on an adventure.

And when adventure called, the wilds listened.

AN EXCERPT FROM

A TRAVELER'S LOG OF DANGEROUS BEASTS

BY CONLEY MURDOCK

ANTHORN

Wilderland: all

Class: Trite

Antlike Beasts with metallic bodies, whose exact color varies depending on which Wilderland they are from. Their burrows and hills often contain precious metals and minerals due to the deposits found in their eggs.

ARACHADEE

Wilderland: all

Class: Familiar

These white, twelve-legged Beasts resemble spiders, and though most only measure a foot long, a queen Arachadee (Mythic class) can grow as large as a human man. Their webs make such a powerful adhesive that they often get stuck themselves.

CALAMEAR

Wilderland: the Sea

Class: Familiar

The bubble Lore of these octopus-like Beasts make them excellent bath companions.

DIZZISNUFF

Wilderland: the Woods

Class: Familiar

Known for being exceptionally friendly, these guinea-pig-like Beasts will often leave their Keepers berries and flowers.

DOPPELGHEIST

Wilderland: the Woods

Class: Prime

Their appearances change to resemble their Keepers, and as they can only be spotted by their reflections, few records exist about what Doppelgheists look like in the wild.

DRAGON

Wilderland: the Mountains

Class: varies

A collective term for Beasts of a mixture of reptilian and avian natures, who vary in size, power, and type of Lore.

EBEROCK

Wilderland: the Woods, the Mountains

Class: Prime

Look out! These powerful boarlike Beasts weigh as much as three tons and can cause earth tremors when running at full speed.

FELSNIP

Wilderland: the Woods

Class: Trite

These skunklike Beasts, notorious for their powerful stench that can knock an entire town unconscious, have been hunted to near extinction—to which I say, a little smell never hurt anyone!

GARNEELI

Wilderland: the Woods

Class: Trite

These crayfishlike Beasts dwell in freshwater and eat dead skin, which can leave even the most calloused feet or hands baby smooth.

GRAVALDOR

Wilderland: the Woods

Class: Legendary

Resembling a massive bear, the Legendary Beast of the Woods slumbers for most of the year, and some Keepers credit hearing a low rumbling in the forest that could be his snores. When awakened, he has been known to destroy entire towns, especially when feeling threatened.

GRIFFIN

Wilderland: the Woods, the Desert

Class: Mythic

These flying Beasts thrive in Summer, when they use the heat and sunlight to make flames fall from the sky.

HASIFUSS

Wilderland: the Woods

Class: Trite

These slugs secrete a corrosive slime that can burn through grass, tree bark, and even skin.

HOCUS

Wilderland: the Woods

Class: Prime

Primarily found in graveyards, these Beasts project terrifying illusions based on intruders' fears in order to protect their homes. Wrinkly and stout, they are often mistaken for rotten vegetables or disembodied heads.

HOOKSHARK

Wilderland: the Sea

Class: Prime

The heads of these sharks resemble large hooks, which they use with their sand Lore to dig bottom-dwelling fish out from the seafloor.

ISCHRAY

Wilderland: the Woods

Class: Prime

These Beasts can only be found on foggy mornings, wandering spookily through the mist and trees. They eat sound by transforming it to wisps, and their age can be determined by the length of their antlers.

KAFERSAFT

Wilderland: the Woods

Class: Trite

Sprouting from Kafersaft trees, these leaflike Beasts are some of the most common in the Woods. Their stems are actually small mouths, which suck the tree's antioxidant-rich sap through its branches.

LOCHMORDRA

Wilderland: the Sea

Class: Legendary

Lochmordra dwells in an unknown place deep within the Sea, rising to terrorize sailors or devastate coastal villages. His mouth is so large, it can swallow ships whole.

LUFTHUND

Wilderland: the Woods

Class: Mythic

Tricky to find and trickier to tame, as they are fiercely independent. Resembling large black wolves, they can grow as large as six feet long and four feet tall. They can turn entirely into wind, like a rush of smoke billowing past, and their Lore can conjure storms and wind gusts. Absolutely magnificent! Also highly dangerous.

MISKREAT

Wilderland: the Woods

Class: Familiar

Pesky little pests! Living in colonies at the edge of the Woods, these wrinkly creatures steal into nearby towns and smash any fields of pumpkin, squash, and—occasionally—turnips.

MURROW

Wilderland: all

Class: Trite

These field mice have spikes protruding from their backs which whistle loudly when the wind blows through them, warning away predators.

NATHERMARA

Wilderland: the Sea

Class: Mythic

A giant lamprey, capable of both water and electric Lore, that can only be found in the Sea's darkest depths. One also happens to be my most cherished friend.

NITNEY

Wilderland: the Mountains, the Woods

Class: Prime

Though blind, this Beast's powerful sight Lore can deceive your eyes. Excellent Beasts for traveling circuses and carnivals, though they can be very shy.

OYSTIX

Wilderland: the Sea

Class: Trite

Producers of beautiful pearls or perilous explosives? One may never know until opening its shell to discover what lies inside.

PTERODRAGYN

Wilderland: the Mountains

Class: Mythic

This "dragon" is entirely made of stone but uses a powerful magnetism Lore to propel itself from the ground. As it does not lay eggs but carves its young out of rock, it is not technically a dragon, however it may resemble one.

RATTLE

Wilderland: all

Class: Familiar

These ratlike Beasts were wrongfully blamed for the spread of the Kankerous Plague seven centuries ago and have since had a poor reputation. But they are very clever, and their plant Lore can stop food from spoiling.

SILBERWAL

Wilderland: the Sea

Class: Mythic

Though nicknamed a "whale dragon," these Beasts are also not dragons, as they do not have wings and cannot fly. But similar to dragons, they love anything shiny, and their underwater caves are often full of sunken treasure.

STINGUR

Wilderland: all

Class: Trite

These beelike Beasts glow in the dark, but do not mistake them for simple fireflies, as their stings are quite painful.

STOOLIP

Wilderland: the Woods

Class: Trite

These Beasts live in clusters and resemble mushrooms, but their caps can induce drowsiness and sleep when suctioned to the skin. Removing the caps does not cause the Beasts any harm.

STYERWURM

Wilderland: the Woods

Class: Prime

These giant worms resemble trees, but don't be fooled! These Beasts are highly dangerous and not picky eaters—at least, not once they shake their food to death! Personally, I've always found them rather cute.

TADPIKE

Wilderland: the Woods

Class: Trite

Found in sources of freshwater, these baby Tadhops are magical filters—it is safe to consume water from any ponds, lakes, or streams in which they reside.

TURTLETOT

Wilderland: the Sea

Class: Familiar

These turtlelike Beasts have large shells made of coral, and because coral makes a delightful, colorful home for all sorts of tiny creatures, at their adult size, Turtletots become miniature Beast and animal hotels. Buggy guests beware, though—your room service just might eat you!

VAMPIRWING

Wilderland: the Mountains, the Jungle, the Woods

Class: Familiar

Watch out for these! Fond of dark, damp places like caves or hollowed-out trees, their combination of sound Lore and dark Lore makes their screeches so powerful at nighttime that they can knock you unconscious for a whole day. Your sleep will be quite restful, though.

ZIGGOPATCH

Wilderland: the Woods, the Mountains

Class: Familiar

These molelike Beasts have handy tracking Lore due to their excellent sense of smell. They can sniff out a source of fire or water over four miles away.

ACKNOWLEDGMENTS

Like Barclay, this story swept me on an unexpected adventure, and I would not have made it to the end without the support of many people who ventured into the Woods with me.

To my agent, Whitney Ross, who immediately understood the heart of this book and made it shine: thank you for believing in me at a time when my self-confidence was deeply shaken. I am lucky to have you as a champion.

To my editor, Kate Prosswimmer: thank you for the cheers, the phone calls, the brainstorming sessions, the spreadsheets, the incredible feedback, and the overwhelming amount of enthusiasm and guidance. I could not have found a savvier or more amazing partner for this tale, and I very much look forward to the next adventure.

To the rest of the team at McElderry, including Nicole Fiorica, Justin Chanda, Karen Wojtyla, and Bridget Madsen: thank you for giving Barclay a fantastic home. And thank you to Chrissy Noh, Lisa Moraleda, and Shivani Annirood for helping this series find its way into the hands of readers.

Thank you to Petur Antonnson, who illustrated an absolutely breathtaking cover. And to Sonia Chaghatzbanian and Karyn Lee for designing this book to be as fun and beastly as its contents. (I am still not over the mushrooms!!!)

To Christine Lynn Herman, the first person I confided in when I decided to attempt a middle grade novel: thank you for being my best friend.

Thank you to my early readers, including Axie Oh, Sarah Glenn Marsh, Tara Sim, and Amanda Haas—without your enthusiasm, I wouldn't have had the confidence to keep going. Thank you to the Philadelphia Low Groggery collective, including Katherine Locke for the mushroom knowledge and Alex London for reminding me that I needed to just write the book I wanted to write. Thank you to Akshaya Raman, the savviest of world-builders, and to the rest of my critique group, including Meg Kohlmann, Melody Simpson, Katy Rose Pool, Janella Angeles, Erin Bay, Kat Cho, Claribel Ortega, Mara Fitzgerald, Alex Castellanos, Maddy Colis, and Ashley Burdin—there is no one else I would rather be in a cult with. And thank you to Rory Power, for the group chats and writer retreats, to Allison Dillon, for cheering me on, and to Zoe Sivak, Viola's honorary big sister.

To Lauren Magaziner: thank you for welcoming me to the world of middle grade, as well as for being a fantastic friend.

To my fiancé: thank you for being my hooman.

To Jelly Bean: thank you for inspiring Mitzi's wild antics.

To my brothers: thank you Ryan, fellow Pokémon Master, and thank you Connor, for my very first and favorite Wilderlore fan art.

To my YA readers who followed me to these books: your support truly makes me feel like the luckiest of writers. You are all part of the wilds now.